A PROMISE TO KEEP

by
MELONY TEAGUE

D1319194

A PROMISE TO KEEP by MELONY TEAGUE

ANAIAH ROMANCE
An imprint of ANAIAH PRESS, LLC.
7780 49th ST N. #129
Pinellas Park, FL 33781

First Anaiah Romance print edition January 2020

Edited by Candee Fick
Book Design by Laura Heritage
Cover Design by Laura Heritage

Anaiah
+Press
Books that Inspire

For my daughter, Kristi
Thank you for believing in my dream and helping it come true.
Watching you grow in your faith walk is a treasure to me. I love you.
Let's always do Starbucks together.

ACKNOWLEDGEMENTS

First, thank you, reader, for giving this debut author a chance. My wish is to provide a few hours of respite from this crazy world and a laugh along the way. It truly takes a tribe to write a book and this one was no exception. Thank you to my writer's group, Glenda Dekkema-Burkholder, Marguerite Cummings, Carol Ford, and Claudia Loopstra, who have been my writing sisters for years. My debut novel would not have happened without you. Thank you to my ACFW critique partners, Kristin Dowd, Alynda Long, and Jeanie Nance, who encouraged me to dig deeper. Thank you to the other critiquers on the ACFW loop who helped and cheered me on. Thank you to the many authors who have encouraged me along the way, you know who you are, and the list is long. I need to mention Carla Laureano and Brandy Vallance, who have been so inspiring and gave me the best advice in the early days of my writing career. To my travel partner, Susan Anne Mason, thank you, and thank you for being in my cheering section. Special thanks to Kate Breslin for the long chats and for imparting such wisdom. I want to be like you gals when I grow up. To my dear friend, Carrie Schmidt, who has talked me off so many ledges. She could have a degree in counselling just from the experience she gained. Thank you, and you know I love ya.

Thank you to my street team who have been waiting patiently for this story. You are so special. I love you all. My Beta readers are a wonderful group of individuals who cared about this story, thank you to Andrea, Alynda, Christina, Jeanie, Carrie, and Kristi.

Thank you to Rachel McMillian for your sage advice. To Jen Turano, your honesty and guidance has been invaluable, and I'll never forget our meeting in person in Cincinnati. You know I'm a huge fan of your work. To Jill Lynn Buyten, who has been fantastic in answering my gazillion-and-two questions, thank you! To Pepper Basham. You know why.

I had so much fun doing research for this book. I thank Dr. William Etzkorn, who helped me out with medical research, and John Catoul, a professional firefighter who helped me out with the rescue scenarios. To Tara Ross for helping me out with the climbing terms, thank you. All errors are my own.

I can't express how wonderful it is to be working with a dream editor like Candee Fick. Thank you, Candee, for making Savannah and Michael's story shine. Thank you to Anaiah Press for getting excited about this story of my heart. Last, I can't express how much I appreciate and cherish the support of my husband, Rory, and my children. Thank you for taking up the slack and cooking while I was on deadline. Kristi, thank you for catching all my typos. I love you all.

Most important, thank you to my Jesus who has been close to me through it all. You know and have my whole heart.

PRAISE FOR A PROMISE TO KEEP

"A delightful romance sure to please anyone looking for a story about second chances, grace and hope. This one has all the right ingredients!"
　　　—**Catherine West**, award-winning author of *Where Hope Begins*

"With beautiful tenderness, Melony Teague has given us a window into the joy, sorrow, humor, and soaring love of characters that come alive. Be ready to have your heart stolen in this must-read fiction debut."
　　　—**Mikal Dawn**, author of the EMERALD CITY ROMANCE series

"A Promise to Keep by Melony Teague is a welcome addition to the contemporary romance genre. Layers of laughter, chemistry, and unexpected intensity make Michael and Savannah's story a wonderful surprise! A Promise to Keep *shows the skill of a talented author who can sensitively tackle subjects like cancer and grief while still producing a laugh-out-loud story! I can't wait to read whatever Melony Teague writes next!*
　　　—**V. Joy Palmer,** Author of *Love, Lace, and Minor Alterations* and *Weddings, Willows, and Revised Expectations*

"With charm, wit, and romance, Teague's debut novel takes readers on a journey of second chances, grace… and a trusty fern. Hope and humor blend throughout the story, balancing deep emotions with lighter moments and a sweet romance besides. A bright new voice in Christian fiction!"
　　　—**Carrie Schmidt**, ReadingIsMySuperPower.org

AUTHOR'S NOTE

In creating this story, I set the dreaded high school reunion in the town of Point, New York. If you search for it on a map, you won't find it. It is a fictional town where my characters came of age, and from there, they ventured out to find their futures. When I came to writing the theater scene, my inspiration was *Cyrano de Bergerac* because I've long loved this hauntingly powerful and clever story that was written by Edmond Rostand in 1897. The original version was in French and has since been translated into English, most famously by poet Brian Hooker in 1923. What I found most interesting about the long-nosed swordsman's plight was that his struggles are as relevant today as they were in the nineteenth century. The struggle against prejudice, falsehood, and compromise is as real today as it was then, if not more.

CHAPTER 1

ONLY A PROMISE TO A DYING man would make her attend her twenty-year high school reunion.

Savannah Sanderson glanced at the large clock in the empty corridor of Point High. She had twenty-seven hours, forty-six minutes, and some seconds before the party—just enough time to work herself into a panic before the reunion dinner and dance. She'd arrived a day early to ease herself into the whole experience, but being alone with her thoughts wasn't helping.

Savannah ran her fingers over the combination lock that secured what used to be her locker, feeling a peculiar connection to it since she'd stowed so much deep within her heart. The cold gray metal cabinet once held tokens of her dreams. School was out for the day and would soon be out for the summer, but she imagined the locker was filled with somebody else's things, someone with wild

1

and idealistic dreams of his or her own. She prayed the occupant's future wouldn't shatter like hers had.

The kitten sticker on the top corner had survived two decades of students. The matching backpack she'd toted from class to class, faded and worn, was still stashed in her closet at home. She couldn't bear to part with that symbol of her survival of the awkwardness of high school. The magnet of her favorite rock band, which had held her schedule, had probably been replaced by a pouting pink-haired diva magnet. Times had changed, and she had, too.

At thirty-seven, she didn't consider herself old—but maybe a little old fashioned. If she updated her locker now, she'd add magnets with the faces of love-song-singing crooners with velvet voices and perhaps that new actor in the latest happily-ever-after romance movie whose name she couldn't recall. As a librarian, she saw people come in daily wishing to escape into a fictitious world with handsome heroes and feisty heroines and their happily-ever-afters. She was almost ready to think about where her story was going beyond the covers of her favorite novels. It was one thing to daydream, in love with the idea of happiness. It was quite another to find it.

She leaned her forehead against the cool enameled door, steeling herself for the days ahead. Tomorrow night, the building would flood with noise and laughter of her former classmates. For now, she must face the abandoned hallways with a heart just as empty. Only wispy recollections of her teenage years remained. It was strange how the happier memories brought her the most pain. Still, she was ready to let those memories back in. To heal.

In five months, it would be a year since Nick had left her to face her future alone. She'd done her best to prepare herself for the inevitable, but nothing had primed her for the phone call from the hospital that October night. She'd rushed to Nick's side, counting each minute with him a gift.

Between labored breaths, he begged her, "Promise me you'll go to the reunion."

"I can't go without you. I can't face…"

"You won't be alone, Savannah. I want to go, but as things are right now…" Even with tubes and monitors keeping him alive, Nick didn't come right out and say what they were both thinking.

"I need you to go. For me."

"But why? Why would you say that?"

"Can you trust me this one last time?"

Despite trying to be brave for him, a tear trickled down her cheek. He reached up to wipe it away. Nick wasn't playing fair, and he had to know it. How could she say no? Savannah gripped his emaciated hand as if she could pull him back from heaven's threshold.

In that sterile room in the palliative-care ward, she made the promise one hour and twenty-three minutes before the monitors announced his arrival at the gates of heaven.

At the funeral, they said Nick's unwavering faith was an inspiration to all. If Savannah heard "Everything happens for a reason, dear" one more time, she'd lose it. All well-meant but not helpful. Savannah let the platitudes and the sentiments wash over her, but she remained tight lipped, her anger simmering below the surface.

Things were not supposed to end with her sitting dry eyed in the front row of their church, having cried all her tears in the months before Nick left this earth. She wasn't supposed to be saying goodbye to the man who'd swept her off her feet in high school. They were supposed to grow old together. They'd promised to share a lifetime. God hadn't been listening to that promise, had He? It was as if God weren't listening to her at all.

Her prayers since then had been scattered, unfocused and reluctant at best, and she didn't know what to do about it. She'd successfully hidden from her church family and society at large, burying herself in her work and her books. She'd found valid excuses why she couldn't make it out to church—except on bake sale Sundays, of course.

Even so, she'd kept her promise. Now, standing in front of her locker, she lifted her chin and gazed toward heaven. "Okay, I'm here, Nick," she whispered. "Now what?"

"Savannah?"

She screeched, the sound rattling the windows of the aging school building. With one hand over her beating heart, she swiveled to find the source of the deep voice over her right shoulder. Standing in front of her was a six-foot, broad-shouldered, chestnut-haired stranger. She wondered whether she'd lost her mind and conjured a hallucination of one of her bookish heroes. He shoved a hand through his cow-licked mane and stepped closer.

When he didn't vaporize, she blinked and waited. Maybe her new contact lenses were malfunctioning.

He cleared his throat. "I'm sorry I scared you."

"The janitor said no one was here. Classes are over for the day, so I thought I was alone."

"You're not alone." He winked. The man actually winked at her.

Savannah stepped backward and collided with the lockers, the clattering of the impact reverberating in the silent hallway. Nothing much had changed there. After all, there was a reason they printed *Accident Waiting for a Place to Happen* below her photo in the yearbook.

Was he a current faculty member? No. If so, he wouldn't know her name. "Are you here for the reunion? It starts tomorrow. I'm a day early." One look at the man, and he'd set her off babbling like a jittery teenager. With her back against the lockers, she inched sideways toward the exit.

"Yes, I am. Me, too."

She stopped her sidestepping to make sense of his words. "You, too?"

He backed up, his hands raised like she was a crazy lady about to lunge at him. "Yes, I'm also a day early."

If he was here for the reunion, that meant he had been in her class. There was a familiar sparkle in his blue eyes. Could it be—

"You don't recognize me?"

Embarrassed, she tried to picture what he would have looked like twenty years ago. By the tone of his voice, she should know who he was. Maybe her trusty locker would open and swallow her, saving her from her impending humiliation.

Nick would have known. He knew everybody.

* * * *

Michael McCann had promised himself he'd never set foot in Point, New York, again, let alone the high school. But May was typically a slow month for him and his team, so he'd made the trip. However, the dread churning in his stomach was worse than when he executed a complex rescue extraction. And not just because Claire had sweet-talked him into helping the setup committee secure all the balloons to the makeshift dropped ceiling in the gym. Once he finished with the decor, he planned to escape for a walk around town.

But now, while roaming the halls in search of the custodian and his ladder, he'd found Savannah outside his senior classroom. He hadn't meant to startle her, but when he'd called her name, she'd jumped and twirled to face him. Her eyes were as wide as a mama deer caught in the jeep's headlights. The familiar spike of adrenaline surged in his veins, and he waited for her to recognize him. She was more beautiful than ever.

The sight of her in flight mode sent him into damage control with his hands extended to calm her.

She ran her hands down the side of her dark blue jeans as if to smooth the nonexistent wrinkles, then shoved a hand in his direction. "Savannah Sanderson."

"I know." He winced at the use of her married name. She'd always be Du Toit to him.

Her eyes widened. "You know?"

She had lost the purple-rimmed glasses somewhere along the way but not her Americanized South African accent. He'd always loved that about her. Yes, loved. Nope, he wasn't letting his feelings loose again but rather would keep them firmly in the past, where they belonged. Except his accelerated heartbeat did not comply. She bit her lower lip; he tried not to focus on what it was doing to his insides. He concentrated instead on the telltale crease on her forehead peeking out from behind the bangs of her butterscotch-colored, shoulder-length hair.

She shifted from one foot to the other.

He raised an eyebrow. "We were in the same grade, same chemistry class. Literature class, too." He wouldn't make it easy for her. Something about being forgotten did that to him.

She inclined her head. "Mr. Slater's class?" He pinpointed the moment she connected the dots as her eyes widened and her jaw went slack. "Michael? No, it can't be..."

"It's me." He cringed inside, thinking of how he'd been a late bloomer, shedding his extra pounds once he left Point. He'd pushed the limits at the gym to prove to himself he wasn't that awkward, chubby, pizza eating loser anymore.

"But Michael was..."

He sighed. Best to get it out of the way so they could talk about the real stuff—their time apart. "Fat?"

"I wouldn't say that, but certainly not, well..."

She made an up-and-down sweeping motion with her hand and inspected him from head to toe. It reminded him of science class, except this time he was the unfortunate specimen under the microscope.

He flexed a bicep. "Ripped?" He was proud of the hours pushing weights and of his fitness training. The effort he'd put in had transformed him from a lazy, doughnut-eating young man into someone he hardly recognized himself. It was no wonder Savannah hadn't at first. And she had never looked at him *that* way before. It felt more awkward than he'd imagined.

Judging by the pink hue creeping up her neck, she was embarrassed that he'd caught her appreciating his physique. As kids, she'd always swatted him when he read her mind, so he kept out of reach just in case. His half-hearted attempt to keep a straight face failed when she gasped and covered her mouth. She shoved past him and hotfooted it down the hallway.

It took about three seconds for him to realize she was running away—from him. How ironic. He should let her go. He should get on a plane and never look back, but then, history would repeat itself. He didn't want that. The time had come to pursue her, even if it was just down the corridor through his old stomping grounds.

Michael followed the squeak of her sneakers as they echoed down the hallway.

"Oof!" There were sounds of a struggle.

What in the world?

He rounded the corner to find the janitor on the ground with his mop and pail, trying to untangle himself from Savannah. Frothy soapsuds slid down her face, proof the mop had won this round. The janitor in his blue coveralls, showing a row of white teeth, enjoyed the attention a bit too much. Michael couldn't stop the guffaw that escaped his lips or the chuckle that followed—until she straightened, her fiery eyes narrowed and her arms folded over her chest. "It's not funny, Michael McCann."

Uh-oh. He swallowed. Before he could think of what to say, she lunged for the fire-safety exit and set off the emergency alarm. That was Savannah for you. She still had a knack for the dramatic, and he loved her for it. Michael shook his head. A flight out of town was looking more and more appealing. His feet begged to flee to his rented four-by-four.

Save for the promise he'd sworn to keep, he'd be on the outskirts of Point already, heading for the Canadian border. His high school years were a mixed bag of experiences, some good and some bad enough for him to bury deep and cover with a layer of selective amnesia for good measure. Especially when it came to Savannah Du Toit and Nick Sanderson.

Where was Nick anyway? He would have to face him sooner or later, so he might as well get it over with. He lunged past the janitor, ducked out the exit, and left the redbrick building behind him. "Savannah, wait!"

Michael dashed through the courtyard, but there was no sign of her. He heard the river gurgling and rushing in the distance, its banks likely swollen with the spring rains. He turned away from the sound toward where he had parked his jeep in the visitor parking lot under a blossoming tree. He spotted her approaching the parking lot, beneath two apple trees. The pink blossoms stood no chance against the rising gusts surrounding him. Dark clouds gathered on the horizon, and then, the wind kicked up a notch, swirling sand into his eyes. The scent of the approaching rain washed over him. By the time he caught up to Savannah, she was out of breath.

She mumbled a string of words through clenched teeth. What was she spitting mad about?

"I shouldn't have laughed." He hated to see her upset. Not that it was the first time they'd been in fits of laughter over her knack of tripping over things. Nick had given her a hard time about it, too. And she'd laughed with them. But still, he knew what it felt like to be maliciously laughed at in those same halls, always feeling like he never quite fit in. "Listen. I'm sorry."

Savannah spun on her heel and jammed a finger in his face. "You're sorry? Where were you when we needed you, Michael? When Nick needed you?"

"I…" What was she talking about? Nick had never really needed him. More like he'd needed Nick's friendship.

"Do you know where he is? Do you?" She threw her arms up in the air.

On instinct, Michael grabbed her hands, mostly to keep them from slapping him but also to still their trembling. He bent and pulled her in, eye to eye, and bit back the growl building in his belly. He should be the angry one here after all—things between them hadn't gone according to his plan, and now wasn't shaping up to be any different.

"Calm down. It's been almost twenty years, and the first thing you want to do is fight?"

Her eyes darted all over the almost-vacant parking lot, looking for an escape. Michael held on. If he let her go, she would run. Running away never solved anything. Not really. He knew that firsthand. She'd chosen Nick, stayed with him. Speaking of which, where was Nick now?

Savannah looked down.

"Look at me. Where is he?"

She turned to him, her dark gray-blue eyes mirroring the approaching storm. Her chin trembled, and the misery in her eyes hit him like a sucker punch in the gut. A sound, much like a whimpering puppy, spilled from her. Then, she turned her face away.

What was she keeping from him? "Where is Nick?"

He almost didn't hear her strangled voice over the crack of thunder. "He's gone."

"Where? Will he be back soon?" A deep-seated feeling of dread weighed like an anvil in the pit of his stomach.

"No, Michael. He's gone."

Tears coursed down her face—not good. He was going to give Nick a piece of his mind. "He divorced you?"

"No, no. He…" Her shoulders slumped as if the fight had gone out of her. He could feel her wedding rings on her finger, so divorce wasn't the reason for Nick's absence. Michael stilled, trying to make his mind work. The tattered American flag whipped back and forth on the flagpole, adding to the noise. Savannah's hair blew across her face, sticking to her tear-soaked cheeks.

He couldn't make sense of what she said. He and Nick may have had their differences, but he'd never expected things between Savannah and Nick to go wrong. If Nick wasn't here and they weren't divorced, then it could only mean…

Almost imperceptibly, Savannah shifted from pulling against him to leaning into him. He released her hands, and her arms circled his waist, clinging to him like she belonged there. Only, she'd never belonged to him and never would. He tucked her head under his chin and held her close. The storm of emotion inside him intensified the churning in his belly.

It wasn't a stretch to figure he wasn't going to like the answer to his question, but he needed to know. His mouth close to her ear, he yelled over the howling wind, "What happened?"

"Cancer stole him away from me," she said. "It wasn't supposed to end this way." Her body shuddered in his arms, her voice bordering on hysteria. "He's dead!"

Not Nick. Not his childhood best friend who had always been so full of life. The truth hit him hard enough to buckle his knees, and he took her down with him until they knelt on the pavement in the darkening parking lot, wrapped in grief and sorrow as heavy drops of rain stung. "I'm so sorry. For everything." He hadn't been there to protect her from heartbreak. He pulled her closer as regret flooded through him. Any opportunity to reconcile with Nick drained away in the deluge of grief. Her keening, almost lost in the wailing wind, seared his heart and burned through to his very core.

One thing was certain—he would not be flying out on that plane. At least, not today.

CHAPTER 2

MICHAEL WILLED HIS FEET, CLAD IN the leather loafers he reserved for press conferences, to move the remaining three feet toward the doorway. *I'd welcome a callout to a high-altitude mountain rescue right at this moment, risk of landslide included.* Anything to avoid the bullies from his past—and the painful memories of searching for love. He took a deep breath and stepped into the decorated gym, but the stubborn phone in his pocket remained silent. As much as he wanted to see Savannah, he'd have to take care to steer clear of Clingy Claire.

The reunion was in full swing. The nostalgic nineties bass line thumped in time to his pounding headache. Already twenty minutes late, he needed to get in there and make sure Savannah was all right. The knotted muscles in his shoulders added to the pain at the base of his skull. *Coward. How bad can it be?* If Savannah hadn't recognized him at first, maybe nobody else would, either.

He didn't want to be seen as the old Michael. He was a new man, both on the inside and in his appearance. Armed with that rationale, he tugged at his leather jacket sleeves and pushed through the heavy door to face the Point High alumni class of '99.

Michael took it all in. The gymnasium, transformed into a nineties dance club with tables arranged around the room, was filled with people from his past. Their "Look how she let herself go" judgments and their snooty "Look who turned out to be a loser when voted most likely to succeed" whispers permeated the room. He was grateful to have survived this long. Some days, the truth of how it could have all been so different crushed him.

Each table, covered with a blue tablecloth, had a votive candle in the center next to a vase of white and blue flowers with a large gold *20* sticking straight up above them. Well-supplied food tables lined the wall on his left. Low-flamed gas burners kept large lidded trays of food warm, and on the other side, cakes and pastries were set out in buffet style. Michael caught the scent of spicy chili and crispy fried chicken, tempting him to delay his search for Savannah. He'd get some grub later, once he found her, made sure she was all right, and settled his nerves. She'd accused him of not being there for her and Nick, and he wasn't going to make that mistake again. First, he needed to find a dark corner, where he could scope out the scene and perform a search and rescue from there if necessary.

He spotted the perfect place. The large fern perched on a pedestal next to the stage would conceal him nicely. He took a step forward, but Claire pounced from where she'd no doubt been lying in wait to ambush him. Wearing a red dress, high heels, and a thick layer of charm, she snagged his arm and snuggled up to him.

"Michael McCann, just the man I've been waiting for. I've been telling everyone how much help you've been." She erupted in high-pitched giggles while batting her eyelashes, ones he was sure couldn't be real. That charm focused on him with sniper precision, like a laser sight right between the eyes, niggled at him. His seventeen-year-old self would have lapped up the attention, but back then, she wouldn't have noticed if she'd tripped over him. But now… with a few battle scars on his heart, he steered clear of women like her. He'd left that life behind, for good.

"That's quite a welcome. I don't know what to say." *Isn't that the truth?*

"Don't say a word. Right this way." Claire marched him toward the dance floor as if he held the keys to the proverbial castle, like she was dead set on showing him off. To make matters worse, the singer on the music track challenged the crowd to entertain the notion of a life after love, cutting too close to his reality.

The dance floor was full of adults reliving the joys of their teenage years. Claire clung to his arm like a limpet mine, and no amount of shrugging got her loose. "You did a wonderful job." She pointed to the silver and gold balloons. "You were so brave climbing that ladder." She waved her hand. "There isn't one balloon out of place." Michael inched away, but Claire clamped her hand back onto his arm.

Flattery wouldn't get her anywhere. She'd picked the wrong man. It may have worked twenty years ago, but not anymore. Still, Claire tugged on his arm like a Chihuahua hanging on to a Saint Bernard, and he couldn't exactly make a scene by growling at her and flinging her off. He had to get free. Hiding his panic, he planted his feet and concentrated on breathing at a normal rate. Years of training in crisis control paid off, big time.

Someone delivered a hefty slap to Michael's shoulder, dislodging Claire. *Phew! Free at last.* Michael swiveled to face his savior. The man before him sported a wide smile and twinkling green eyes. They could belong to only one guy. "George McDougal?"

"Hey! Michael McCann?"

"It's so good to see you, man!" He'd bet a million bucks George had no clue how true his words were.

Claire reached for him. "But...but, Michael, we have so much to talk about. But..."

Michael dodged out of her grasp. "Excuse me, Claire. I really need to talk to George." He threw his arm around the beaming George's shoulder and turned him toward the punch table, then picked up the pace to get to safety.

"Michael, I almost didn't..."

"Yeah, I know." Michael dropped his arm as they got closer to the food tables and faced his rescuer. "You didn't recognize me." He leaned in. "Unfortunately, Claire did."

"Ah, got it." George rubbed his receding hairline, which seemed to be a new addition along with his bulky frame. "Say no more." George picked up two tumblers and ladled in some punch.

Michael's shoulders relaxed, and he shook his arms, hastening the effect. "I owe you."

"You always had my back at school. Just returning the favor." George handed him one of the red plastic tumblers. "It's fruit punch. Straight up."

Michael gave the purple liquid a sniff, just to be sure. "I guess they have rules now."

George wiggled an eyebrow. "After *someone* spiked the punch at our prom, I'm not surprised." They exchanged a knowing look.

Michael had consumed a few too many cups while watching Nick and Savannah slow dance. George had helped by handing freshly spiked cups to him one after the other, resulting in an epic hangover the next morning. It'd been over a decade since he left that habit behind. He knew better now.

"How have you been?" George launched into the obligatory small talk, but small talk was more welcome than having to deal with Claire.

"Good, thanks. I'm looking for Savannah. Have you seen her?" Michael scanned the room. She was late. Very late. Would she show up at all after yesterday's meltdown? Both his and hers.

George frowned. "Savannah Du Toit? Haven't seen her. Wasn't she your pal Nick's girlfriend?"

"Yes, that Savannah." He wasn't going to discuss Savannah's situation with George. It was her story to tell. He struggled to keep the conversation going. "So, do you still live in town?"

"No, I live in Boston now, and I'm married, if you can believe it, to a New York City girl. We—"

A booming laugh interrupted George. He pointed to where big-mouth Neville's fan club gathered, swallowing each of his words like popcorn in a movie theater. "He's been at it for half an hour. Telling everyone who'll listen about his latest sales award." George shook his head. "It's sad, man. It's like a eulogy to himself." He turned toward the far side of the room and leaned in closer. "And Hanna over there, she's married to him. Poor woman. Can you believe it?"

He spotted the women in question, standing off to one side. Hanna wore a tight-fitting black dress and about six ounces of makeup. No self-respecting women should wear that much Lycra at their high school reunion. Despite the fact her ensemble was paired with a face-lift, she was a shadow of her cheerleading days, without the dazzling smile. By the looks of things, she didn't want to be here, either. In addition to her scowl, she was clutching her cup, as if it were a lifeline. He'd give the couple a wide berth.

How'd they end up together? "They hated each other in school."

"Yeah, I know, and I think they still do. They have five kids, and he sends them off to some fancy boarding school. From what my sister tells me, you can bet Hanna's not drinking straight punch."

Oh man, was everyone looking at him through a then-and-now lens, too? He felt sick to his stomach. How had he fallen into that trap? Probing past Hanna's veneer, he now saw a worn-down woman in need of compassion. Not wanting to propagate gossip—or what was amounting to a local soap opera—Michael rummaged in his addled brain for a change of subject. "You still got that red sports car?"

His face radiant, George clapped him on the back. "For sure. Drove her to Boston myself. Parts are hard to get these days but not impossible. She's still as beautiful as the day my dad handed me the keys."

Michael downed the sickly sweet punch, coughed, and wiped his mouth with the back of his hand. That punch could kill a man. It wasn't doing anything for his headache, either. He needed water. Then, he'd take cover behind that fern until he spotted Savannah.

First, he had to get rid of the foul taste of that punch. "They got any water around here, George?"

George sniffed and waved toward the double doors at the side of the gym. "There's the fountain in the hallway."

"Ah! Good idea." Taking extra care to stay out of Claire's line of sight, Michael made his way through the dimly lit gym, dodging through the throng on the dance floor under flashing lights, and aimed for the exit.

* * * *

It crossed Savannah's mind that hiding behind a fern topped pedestal was stooping to a new low, even for her. However, it was a step up from hiding under one of the tables with their ample tablecloths, since she couldn't keep a lookout from under there. Michael had appeared at the door, looking handsome in his leather jacket. He'd scanned the room, and Savannah's breath caught in her throat. Had he been looking for her? No. He'd gone straight to Claire. Savannah felt queasy as Claire clung to him like a vine in her dress that looked like it had been painted on her hourglass figure. It wasn't any of her business if Claire draped herself all over Michael, but it had bothered her, which was weird. She'd put it down to being protective of her longtime friend, but that wasn't the whole truth. She ducked farther behind the foliage and watched Michael exchange a few words with George. Then, he'd marched toward the exit and escaped the teeming gym.

Good. She'd have a few moments to relax. She scanned the room for anyone else who would recognize her if she plucked up the courage to ease herself out of her hiding spot. Ugh! Why had Nick insisted she come? Nobody remembered her, she assumed, since she'd arrived in Point as an immigrant midway through grade seven and she didn't have the advantage of growing up with everyone else since daycare. All the way through graduation, despite Nick's and Michael's attempts to make it otherwise, she'd been the outsider.

Nick and Michael had broken her out of her shell and pulled her into their circle. She would let them get away with teasing her when she said something South African, like "Ja. I'll be there now now." Or that time when she'd called the only traffic light in Point a robot and the trunk of Nick's car, the boot. Nick and Michael had rolled around laughing. Her lips curled upward at the memory. From then on, they'd appointed themselves her translators.

She spotted the unmistakable George and ducked farther into her hiding spot amid the foliage. She'd spoken to him all of twice in her eleventh grade year, only because he'd hung out with Michael sometimes. He'd been skinny with an unruly mop of brown hair in those days. George now sported a bald spot, a paunch, and his recognizable wide grin despite his red nose and sweaty face.

She'd changed, too. Even with the ten-pound weight loss over the last two years, she couldn't fit into the jeans she once wore. She'd have to lose another ten pounds to get back to what she weighed at seventeen. That wouldn't happen unless she chopped off a limb.

Savannah popped her head out from behind the luscious fronds. George was talking to Mr. Slater on the other side of the room. She expelled a breath and eyed the punch table. Perhaps some punch would settle her stomach. She darted out from behind her cover and sauntered over to the drinks table like she had all the confidence in the world. The punch was cold, sweet, and—disgusting.

"What on earth is in this punch?" Nobody paid any attention. It was her talent for remaining invisible in a crowd, even without the help of a large fern. A person could be in a room full of people and still be alone.

Savannah was thirsty enough to brave another cup of punch. She grabbed a napkin, and the plastic cup buckled under her grip as she slunk back to her hiding place. If she'd packed a novel in her purse, it would have passed the time while she waited for the night to end. She had fulfilled her promise to attend after all. Maybe she could catch Michael before he left and say goodbye properly. Hopefully, a proper farewell would leave a better impression. What was it about him that made her fall apart? Michael must think her a pathetic mess after her humiliating breakdown yesterday.

Something about him had broken through to her buried emotions. After all, she hadn't cried since the funeral. After Nick died, she'd picked up the pieces of their lives and moved back to Ithaca and worked at the various libraries to make ends meet and pay off the medical bills. She'd kept her chin up. In fact, she facilitated the bookmark workshop at the library and was the first to raise her hand whenever they needed extra help with community programs. Anything to keep her mind off the fact that she had no one to go home to.

No one needed her anymore, except maybe old Mrs. Delaney, who could never find the book she was looking for in the mystery-and-suspense section. Her lips curved. Mrs. Delaney, she suspected, used that as an excuse only to prolong their chats in the library and was quite capable of finding her own missing books.

Mrs. Delaney's visits to the library were always a highlight of her day after Nick died. The experience of losing their life partners and their love of fiction had created a bond between them.

Safely behind her new verdant friend, she spied a fruit fly doing laps in her cup. "Ew!" If she wasn't so thirsty, she wouldn't care. Nor would she give up her fern to get a fresh cup of punch, because that would mean she'd have to again fight her way out from behind the fern, where she was comfortably hidden. She chased the fly around with her index finger. The little bug had a particular talent for evading her. Finally, she scooped him up with her finger and flicked him out of the cup.

Right into Michael's face.

CHAPTER 3

THE SYRUPY LIQUID TRICKLED DOWN HIS forehead. Being sprayed with punch was almost as big a shock as finding Savannah already occupying his chosen hiding spot.

Savannah's mouth hung open, her eyes wide.

"Well, now that I've found you, I guess I don't need that fern anymore."

She blinked. "What?"

"I was going to hide behind it and—"

"Looks like I beat you to it." Savannah's eyes sparkled in the disco lights, a whiff of her honeysuckle perfume awakening his senses.

"Why were you hiding?"

Savannah raised an eyebrow. "I could ask you the same question, McCann."

"Long story."

"Uh-huh." She turned her face away, a smile still playing on her lips. "I'm not proud of it, but I was trying to avoid…"

"Me?"

"Er… yes."

Ouch. That hurt, but if there was anything Savannah had always been, it was honest with him. Always. Even if his fragile ego was at stake.

There it was. In the dimmed lights, the blush crept up her neck and into her cheeks. As much as he might not like the reasons for her evasive movements, he wanted the truth. Did she want nothing to do with him, or was there some other reason for hiding from him? She maneuvered closer to the feathery foliage until the flowerless plant obscured most of her face. A well-positioned leaf fell over her left eye, much like a pirate's eye patch.

Here goes, the search for truth. "Why hide from me?"

Savannah studied the floor like it was a treasure map. "I made such a fool of myself yesterday."

"You mean when you tripped over the janitor?"

She tilted her head. "I was referring to the parking lot meltdown."

Ah yes, he'd never forget the feel of her in his arms. He was the fool. Time to divert attention from his crazy yearning heart. He cleared his throat. "If it makes you feel better, I've forgiven you for not recognizing me."

Her pink lips widened. "That's true. I didn't recognize you with all the rippling muscles."

His ego approved of those words a bit too much for his liking. "Are you staying behind that plant all night?"

"Maybe. I'm not good with people." She sneaked a peek through the leaves at their classmates, who were oblivious to her fears.

"Some things never change." Michael extended his hand. "Come on. Let's get out of here."

"Really?" Savannah pressed her fingers to her smiling lips and seemed to let the tension seep out of her slender shoulders.

Maybe she was as eager as he to leave the reunion behind them. Maybe she'd agree to take a walk in the moonlight. Maybe she'd—no, he was letting his imagination run wild. He cleared his throat. "I'm always ready to rescue anyone in distress. It's what I do for a living."

Savannah handed him a napkin. "Sorry about the punch." While she downed the rest of her punch, he wiped his forehead.

He folded it and handed it back in case she needed to wipe her sticky fingers.

She tucked it into the now empty cup and shoved both of them into the pocket of her knee-length emerald dress, almost the same shade as the fern. He held back a smile at her nervous gesture. He wasn't making her feel uncomfortable, was he?

Her eyes narrowed. "Wait. Aren't you here with Claire?"

Throwing his head back, he fought the urge to roll his eyes like an adolescent. He hated that he'd been ignored at school for not being one of the sporty, popular boys, and now that he'd sprouted those rippling muscles Savannah referred to, suddenly women like Claire took notice. He wasn't a hunk of meat. However, if Savannah assumed that he and Claire were together, then there'd be others thinking the same thing. They'd be the talk of the town by morning. He didn't like people jumping to conclusions, especially the wrong ones.

Michael rubbed the back of his neck and looked down, causing a curtain of hair to fall into his eyes. He shoved the renegade locks away and took a breath. "Savannah, I need you to do me a favor."

A frown appeared. "What?"

"Dance with me."

"Now? Just a second ago, we were preparing to make a dash for it."

She shrank even farther into her secure spot, her arms wrapped around herself like a shield, as if the plant wasn't enough. Getting her out of there was going to be a bigger challenge than he'd thought. He shrugged out of his jacket and draped it over the nearest chair before he leaned toward where she stood behind the plant. "I'll explain later," he whispered.

He plunged his hand into the greenery, grabbed a slender wrist, and tugged. Savannah emerged with a leaf on her shoulder, and he brushed it off before steering her into the hopping throng with his hand at the small of her back. Through the speakers, another popular artist sang a perky song about how she shouldn't have let some dude go—oh, and her loneliness was killing her. Ha! He could tell her about loneliness. Still, he wasn't lonely enough to want to be on the dance floor with Claire.

Settling into a lazy side-to-side shuffle in front of Savannah, Michael hoped it would pass for dancing, and he plastered a smile on his face. *Fake it till you make it.*

He stepped toward Savannah and put a hand on her waist. Her body was as stiff as a spinal board. He bent until her ear was in line with his mouth. "Can you at least pretend to enjoy dancing with me?" He straightened and continued with his dance moves.

Savannah's face was pale in the strobe lights, her movements spasmodic. "I can't."

"Why?" There it was again, the familiar pang of rejection. He masked his feelings with a dazzling smile. A last-ditch attempt to win her over.

She stood with one hand on his shoulder, on her tiptoes to reach his ear. "It's complicated."

He spotted Claire elbowing her way toward them. He'd wonder about Savannah's cryptic answer later. He had to do something now, and Savannah's whisper in his ear had given him an idea.

With one arm around Savannah's waist and the other behind her neck, he tipped her into a classic ballroom dip. Her eyes widened. She clutched at his shirt—right before he pressed his lips to hers amid whoops, hollers, and enthusiastic applause. Their lips were jammed together in a wedding-photo pose, unmoving. Then, her lips quivered—and not in a good way.

He swung her back upright and saw her twitchy right foot aim for his shin. He took advantage of her forward momentum by pulling her into his arms, hearing a peculiar crunch. Pressing her face into his chest, he stifled any potential choice words escaping her lips. He lowered his lips to her ear. "Don't say a word. Please."

The crowd parted before them as he strode to the exit and down the yellow halls of Point High, Savannah trying to pull her hand from his. How was he going to get out of this tight situation? Maneuvering an injured hiker down a rock face in a stretcher—that he could do. But get himself out of trouble with Savannah—that was another thing. And it was something he hadn't needed to do in twenty years, making him out of practice.

They got as far as the doors in front of the principal's office. "Can I talk now?" Savannah said. "Do you realize what this looks like?"

He ignored her. A few more steps, and they were out in the fresh air.

"I'll explain everything when we get to the car." The words didn't have the effect he was hoping for. He was sure Savannah's bloodcurdling screech could be heard clear across the river. The unladylike protest certainly wasn't helping his already-throbbing head. He should never have come back here. He should have...

"Help! Somebody, he's kidnapping me."

At least, the wry tone in her voice was better than that infernal squawking. "Oh, come on, Savannah. Trust me." He stopped and put his arms around her again. "Just play along for one more minute. I'll explain everything."

"Play along?" She wriggled in his arms. "What on this good earth is going on?"

"Just pretend you're happy to be carried away into the sunset." Her squirming wasn't helping his blood cool from having her so close.

"It's pitch dark."

And that made it worse. Holding a hot-blooded woman under twinkling stars in the dark was one thing, but this woman, Savannah, his high school crush—it was all too much. "Not literally. More in a they-lived-happily-ever-after kind of way."

"Oh, I know all about those fictional happy endings, Michael, and this isn't one. Have you lost your mind? Bullying me into compliance is not producing happy feelings right now. Let. Go. Of. Me."

Without ceremony, he opened the back door of the jeep, tossed her in, and slammed the door. His keys jangled as he dug them out of his pocket, hopped in the front seat, and started the engine. On Monday, he'd come back to retrieve his jacket from the lost and found before he flew home, but the immediate priority was getting away from Claire and her tribe of gossipers. Backing out of the parking spot, he continued to ignore Savannah's numerous questions. He had a few of his own, but they'd keep for now.

Michael turned out of the lot, rammed his foot on the gas pedal, and sped north out of town. He slammed on the brake at the stop sign, then tapped his fingers on the steering wheel and waited for the driver in front of him, who seemed intent on breaking the record for the slowest car to turn onto the road that led toward Niagara.

"Come on. Come on," Michael said.

As soon as the road cleared, he motored through the intersection and down the road, watching the needle on the speedometer climb. The faster he found a place where they could talk and straighten out this whole mess, the better.

Two miles out of town, Savannah popped her head between the two front seats. "You realize, because of your Oscar-winning performance back there, everyone thinks we are a... a thing."

A genuine smile spread across his face. He'd foiled Claire's attempts at clinging, and at least, in the eyes of his classmates, he'd got the girl of his dreams? "From the cheers we got, I'd say we have their approval. I had to make them believe we were a thing. Otherwise, Claire would be planning a wedding by Sunday."

"But it's a lie. We are not a thing, and now, everyone thinks I'm... cheating on Nick with you."

"What are you not telling me, Du Toit?" He ignored her married name. It only added salt to his already-stinging wounds. His pretense, dip and kiss included, may have got him out of the clutches of Claire, but at what cost? Savannah's trust? *Double fool*. He should have just told Claire to back off. He winced. That wasn't his style, had never been.

"Nobody knows about Nick except you!" Her words were half plea, half cry.

Those words snapped something inside him. Would she have told him about Nick if he hadn't followed her into that parking lot and begged for the truth? A truth that bonded them in a way, but now, he was way over his head. This reunion was supposed to be executed with precision and zero risk. His heart wasn't going to get out of this untouched—that was sure. He'd have to man up and sort out this mess. For Savannah's sake. He pounded the steering wheel. "Nothing but trouble. I knew I'd find trouble here, but did I listen to my gut? No. Three nights in Point. What could possibly go wrong? I'm sorry. I really messed up."

The wail of a siren behind him led to a quick check in his rearview mirror as flashing blue lights reflected through the jeep. In his line of work, he saw police and emergency responders' lights all the time without flinching. This time, his stomach sank.

"For the love of chicken pie. Really?"

CHAPTER 4

SAVANNAH SWIVELED TO GLANCE OUT THE back window and clamped her hand over her mouth to stifle her giggles. Hearing her amusement might push Michael over the edge, and even though that thought brought on more laughter, she tried to conjure up a measure of pity for the man, who was clearly having a bad day.

Michael pulled over to the side of the road and rolled his window down as the officer sidled up to the car. "Good evening, Officer." Michael sounded like he was actually having a good one. Maybe he should have gone into acting.

The officer's uniform was impeccable, his buttons glistening in the beams of his cruiser's headlights. "You were going fifteen miles over the speed limit, sir." He leaned into the car, his gaze sweeping the interior and landing on her. "Do you always ride in the back seat, ma'am?"

Savannah's mouth went dry. "Er, no. I'm usually the one doing the driving, Officer." *Stupid, stupid. Maybe someone overheard my kidnapping speech and called the cops. Why did I say that?* Of course, she'd been the one to drive since Nick's illness, so it was an automatic response, but did her words sound suspicious to someone who knew nothing of her past?

The officer scratched his chin. "Why don't you hop into the front passenger seat, then, while I talk to Mr...."

"Michael McCann." By his dry tone, Savannah figured Michael was still not amused.

The officer glanced up the road. "I knew a guy by that name. Hightailed out of town so fast he didn't even kick up any dust. Driver's license and insurance, please."

She studied the uniformed man from his hat, mustache, and slim build to his gun belt. What was his name? Had he been in their class? Old man Jenkins's son?

Michael's head fell forward onto the steering wheel, and he groaned.

The officer peered in through the window. "Are you all right, sir?"

"Yeah, just fine." His voice was at odds with his words.

"Name's Officer Jenkins. Have either of you two been drinking?"

At least, they could honestly say no to this question this time. Twenty years ago, not so much. They'd all reeked of spiked punch.

Michael's tone was all business. "No, sir, and this is a rental car."

Officer Jenkins nodded and pulled a little book and pencil from his belt. "Driver's license, please."

"I don't have it with me. It's in my jacket pocket at Point High."

The officer sniffed and adjusted his hat. "You mean at the reunion? I'd be there if I was off shift."

So, he was a classmate. Savannah patted her pockets. Empty except for a sticky napkin and a crushed tumbler. How did that get there? It dawned on her that her purse was stashed behind the fern, where she'd apparently also left her senses.

"You're not missing much," Michael mumbled.

Savannah grinned, thinking about that horrible punch and her earlier view of the festivities through the fern's fronds.

Officer Jenkins rubbed his temples with his left hand and held his pencil between the fingers of his right. "I'm sorry, sir, but you need to turn right back and get your license. Looks like I'll be appearing at that reunion after all." She bet he'd be pleased to be showing up in front of his classmates in uniform on a Saturday night. After all, he'd been voted most likely to join the force. He puffed out his chest. "Thought I'd miss the whole thing since my shift ends at midnight. I'll be following close behind, so don't try anything stupid."

Too late. Stupid was their middle names tonight. Between Michael's escapades while evading Claire and her own part in pretending they were together and then enjoying being in his strong arms way too much... Michael's concern for her felt so good. She wasn't used to being taken care of. Hmph. It wasn't like she needed a man anymore. Right?

Officer Jenkins gestured toward the empty passenger seat. "Come on now, little lady. Get up front."

Savannah scrambled over the console between the front seats, accidently stepping on Michael's elbow in her hurry, and planted herself in the passenger seat, choosing to ignore the "little lady" remark for now. Michael rubbed his elbow and glared at her. Served him right for getting them into this mess. The smell of his cologne wafted her way, something earthy and spicy, reminding her of being dangerously close to his beating heart as he held her. With shaky hands, she reached for the seat belt, clipped it, and then tugged her dress over her knees.

Michael turned the jeep back the way they'd come.

Savannah turned away, tamping down another surge of giggles. A police escort back to the reunion. How nice. What would Claire and her entourage think of that? "Well, what do we do now?"

"We get my jacket, and hopefully, the good officer will be kind enough to just give us a ticket—and not toss us in jail for the night—and he'll let us get out of town for real this time."

"I meant about, er...us." She picked at a loose thread at the hem of her skirt.

He shot a pleading glance her way. "You're not going to throw me to the wolves, are you?"

She took pity on him. The poor man had endured enough for one night. "You mean Claire? No."

He relaxed, then reached over and squeezed her hand. "Thank you."

As they drove toward Point High, Savannah's hope of staying under the radar crumbled. There was no way around it—she'd have to face the music. Or at least, the people dancing to the music. Walking back into the gym with Michael would need some explaining, especially given the curious presence of the good officer. They would have to come clean about Nick and their pretend kiss—there was just no way around it—but that didn't make the butterflies in her stomach any more cooperative. With fingers splayed across her abdomen, she tried to still their panicked fluttering or at least cause the imaginary insects to fly in some sort of ordered formation. *How did things get complicated so fast?*

"I have to tell them about Nick."

"You don't owe them anything. If they draw the wrong conclusions..."

As flattered as she felt, he was hanging on to that "we are a thing" idea a little too eagerly for her liking. "Michael McCann, your grandmother taught you better." She turned her best librarian frown his way. "For shame."

"I guess you're right. I'm sorry. I shouldn't have put you in this situation. It's just that Claire..." He shuddered—just like she had after her first sip of that horrid punch.

"I know, but as impressive as your act was and as hard as this will be, I'd rather people know about Nick than assume I'm cheating on him. He doesn't deserve that."

"I get that. But do we have to tell them there is no *us*?"

The little boy, hidden inside the bulky hunk of a man, couldn't pretend for the rest of the night that he wasn't a single man without a date to the reunion. "Of course."

"Come on, Savannah."

"You up and kidnapped me. Besides, I don't think 'Let's get out of here' constitutes asking a girl out on a date."

Michael nodded, keeping his eyes on the road as the cruiser followed close behind. The streetlights threw intermittent shafts of light into the jeep. "Savannah, will you go out with me?"

She put her hand over her heart and the other wrist to her forehead in a mock swoon. "Oh, Michael, you are so romantic. How could I resist?"

"There. I asked." He glanced at her and winked. "If you say yes, then we are not lying if we tell them we're a thing. A small beginning of a thing but a thing nonetheless."

Savannah shifted to study his expression. "Are you serious?" She'd craved hearing these words from him when she was sixteen until Nick swooped in and stole her heart.

Michael turned into the Point High lot and parked. Turning to her, he cleared his throat. "I am. I've got it all worked out. We can hang out tomorrow. Visit our old haunts in town. There's a waffle at your favorite place with your name on it." A shadow obscured Michael's face, but the plea in his voice was there, deep and clear.

"I don't know what to say." After all this time, he was asking her out? But it was just for appearance's sake. Not exactly how she'd imagined things.

"For old times' sake."

Blindsided by his request, Savannah sat still and stared into the night. She couldn't turn back time. Not that she regretted her relationship with Nick, but that life seemed so far removed from the present. To face another day, she'd put her heart safely away, buried with him.

"Tell you what"—Michael reached for the door handle and paused—"you only have to come out with me once. After that, you'll be free to leave. We'll say our goodbyes, and I'll fly back home on Monday, and that will be that. The end."

The end. Inexplicable pain stabbed her already-scarred heart. Was that what she wanted? The end? For once, her fear of the unknown was dwarfed by an overwhelming sense of loss, of saying goodbye again. Goodbye to Michael, to their friendship, to what might have been, and to what may be.

Savannah's clenched hands rested in her lap. "There can't be an end without a beginning."

"Then, let's make it official." He held out his hand to shake on it, like they'd done as kids, only without the spit. "No obligation."

In the nearby field, crickets sang. As if their song were enough to convince her, they cheered her on, coaxing her and asking what she had to lose.

Good point. She had already lost so much. What harm could one day with Michael bring? In the sleepy town of Point? Not much risk there.

She sighed. "Okay, but I get extra whip on my waffle."

Michael grinned. "Whatever the lady wants, the lady gets." They shook on it. "Shall we?"

Not waiting for her response, he hopped out and walked around to open her door. That was Michael—ever the gentleman. Even in his rebellious teenage years, he'd always been kind and considerate to her.

She took his offered hand—so warm and reassuring, his steadiness supporting her as she scrambled out of the car to stand before him.

The ominous click of the car lock echoed into the night as if to signal a turning point. She took a deep breath and glanced at the officer waiting on the sidewalk. "Let's get this over with before Officer Jenkins gets ideas of throwing us in lockup."

Side by side, they made their way to the school entrance. By the sound of the thumping bass and the raised voices, everyone at the reunion was still partying amid the dancing lights like it was 1999. Maybe she could still duck behind the fern. Despite her earlier decision to face this head on, the temptation to grab the jacket and run taunted her and challenged her deepest motives. As Officer Jenkins held the door open for them, she felt the comforting touch of Michael's hand at the small of her back, giving her courage.

The music came to an abrupt halt when Officer Jenkins entered the gymnasium behind them. All eyes were on the trio.

The officer joined them and lifted a hand in greeting. "It's all right, folks. Mr. McCann left his jacket and needs to retrieve it. No need for alarm. Carry on."

As the mumbling and whispering behind fingers ensued, Michael raised both hands, as if to make sure everyone knew they weren't cuffed, and quieted the crowd. "Your attention just for a moment. We have some news to share with you all."

The murmurs got louder. "You remember Savannah Du Toit?" Michael glanced at her. "She married Nick Sanderson after graduation, and—"

Savannah put an unsteady hand on his arm. "Thanks, Michael, but I need to do this."

He nodded. "Over to you, Savannah."

Officer Jenkins stepped up to stand on her right. "Are you okay, ma'am?" he asked, his voice quiet. "What is this about?"

"I need to make an announcement."

"Now?" he whispered in her ear.

Savannah nodded, her eyes blurring with unshed tears.

Jenkins straightened and turned to the crowd. "Quiet down, everyone. The little lady has something to say." He employed his best official tone, then directed his steely no-nonsense-on-my-beat gaze at Neville Cartwright and his entourage, who were blurred by her unshed tears. She'd heard his vile snickering above the din.

Savannah swallowed to clear the lump rising in her throat and glanced at Michael. He nodded his support. She felt his hand at her back, warm and comforting.

"I'm sure most of you remember my husband, Nick. I know you're wondering why he's not here tonight with me. Nick dearly wanted to be here. He told me so just before..." Her voice cracked, and a tear slid down her cheek. She swiped it away with the back of her hand. Officer Jenkins also stepped closer to her, offering his silent support. Bradley! That was his name. Her heart warmed a little at his gesture.

"The truth is, he battled cancer for most of our married life." She determined to push through the collective gasp, including one from Michael, who couldn't have known the whole truth. She blinked back more tears. She could do this. For Nick. "Just as we thought we were in the clear, it would show up somewhere else, and the rounds of treatments, doctors' appointments, and the crippling fear began again. Each one eating away at Nick. In the end, he was a whisper of the fun-loving guy you all knew. But he never lost heart. He never gave up hope. He never ever took one day for granted."

She could sense Nick's quiet presence almost tangibly in the air, fortifying her thumping heart. "He never lost faith that, after his last breath, he'd be stepping into a new body, a new and perfect place with no more sickness."

Her voice wobbled, and a few nodding heads spurred her past the trembling fear that had seeped right into her core. "But he wanted me to come back here. To the place we met."

Stillness descended on the gym that not even Neville dared disturb. Even Mavis in the front row, who had been working away on some gum like a llama chewing its cud, stopped midchew to listen. "If Nick were here, he'd be thanking you all for being part of our lives. Part of our history. And I think he'd ask you to take the time you have left on this earth to live life big. Or, at least, live it well." She glanced at Michael, seeing more in his eyes than glistening tears. "And you know he'd finish off by cracking a joke."

Chuckles and smiles tumbled through the crowd like dominoes, encouraging her to finish what she needed to say. The words she'd resisted for so long. Saying them aloud would make them true. She'd have to embrace the truth in the days ahead, and she'd have to find a new future—without him.

To finally face the fact he wasn't coming back.

Blinking back the tears that threatened to undo her, she cleared her throat and took a deep breath. "For me, I'm here to…to remember Nick and to start over."

CHAPTER 5

MICHAEL MOVED TO STAND BESIDE SAVANNAH, on her left, his hand at the small of her back. A show of support, or so he told himself. It wasn't because he was bursting with pride for the way she held her chin up in front of everyone. It wasn't the way she honored Nick or said the words she needed to say. It also most definitely wasn't the sudden rush of emotion moving his feet closer to her because he had to, because she drew him, because she stood alone—facing life head on with more courage than he ever had.

The urge to rest his hands on her shoulders pulled Michael off balance. Instead, he moved his hands to his sides and focused on keeping his breathing even. Somehow, instinct told him she needed to do this on her own. For Nick. For herself. For her future.

Maybe even for his.

Tension rolled off her, and her voice faltered, but she pressed on. "Life with Nick wasn't easy. He was a great guy, but the ups and downs of his diagnosis gave new meaning to our 'in sickness and in health' promises. I never imagined 'till death do us part' would be our reality so soon."

Sensing she had something more to say, Michael remained beside her, close enough to let her know he was there.

"I..." She glanced at him, then linked her fingers with his. Her eyes shimmered. "Michael and I wanted to remember and honor him. Thank you for listening."

A wave of relief swept through him as one person, then another applauded, until everyone was paying tribute to Nick. He'd been one of those guys everyone knew and loved. Michael tugged her against his side, gathering her close to him, like a mother hen with her chicks. His arms encircled her, pulling her against his chest. His eyes watered. Must be the dry air in here.

With her public hand-holding gesture and by linking their names, Savannah had kept her word. Claire wouldn't bother him anymore. Tomorrow, they'd spend the day together. Then, he'd have to let her go. Again. Like he'd promised he would. He shoved the struggling hope that they might have a future deep down, where it would not grow into something more.

As much as they wanted to fool Claire, he was in danger of fooling himself. He'd have to keep his wits about him so he didn't make that same mistake twice, no matter how proud he was of Savannah at this moment. He was sure that part of her visceral reaction yesterday, when she told him about Nick, was because it was the first time she'd admitted the truth—to herself, out loud. He knew from personal experience that denial could be a place of comfort, but one couldn't stay there for long.

The crowd turned back into their huddles, chattering as the DJ repositioned his headphones and punched a few buttons in preparation for restarting his retro-music set. Savannah's breathing slowed, and she gazed up at him, and Michael relished the feel of her in his arms. His pulse raced. How was he going to survive a whole day together and avoid embarrassing himself? When she was nearby, his mind got muddled by his heart.

Officer Jenkins cleared his throat. By the twinkle in his eyes, Michael knew he was jumping to all sorts of conclusions. "If you can retrieve your driver's license now, we can get this sorted out, and I'll be on my way."

"Right." Savannah untangled herself from his arms, dashed behind the fern, and emerged with her purse slung over her shoulder. "I'll just..." She blushed and then escaped in the direction of the ladies' room.

Officer Jenkins followed Michael to his jacket, still draped over the chair where he had abandoned it. Away from Savannah, his brain kicked back into gear. "I'm so sorry about all this, Officer."

"So, you are the same guy I knew, huh?" Officer Jenkins frowned. "Didn't recognize you, McCann. Call me Bradley."

"Bradley? Bradley Jenkins?"

He flashed his badge as proof. "Yes, it's me."

Jenkins had grown up to be nothing like his father, even though they shared the same profession. Bradley was fair and compassionate, unlike his father, who'd ruled the town with an iron fist.

Once the formalities were done and Bradley had given a moderate fine and a sternish warning, the officer looked as if he wanted to say something else. The slight shake of his head indicated a change of mind. Instead, he met Michael eye to eye. "Don't give me a reason to hand you another ticket, McCann." He tipped his hat. "Good night."

He turned on his heel and stalked through the bopping crowd, which parted like the Red Sea. Michael exhaled as the gym door swung shut.

"In trouble with the law already, McCann?" George could never resist a tease. "In town for just over twenty-four hours and already making trouble, huh?"

Michael winced. "It's not like that. Those days are long gone. I've changed."

"That ticket you're waving isn't helping your argument much."

"Okay, you got me there. But I'm not a kid anymore, George."

"Sure, Michael. Sure." George accompanied his words with a hefty shoulder slap. "So, you and Savannah, huh?"

"Yeah, it's all very new." At least, outwardly. He'd secretly held on to the dream of him and Savannah for years.

"Quite a shocker about Nick. Always liked him."

The space between them filled with the awkwardness that always came when guys avoided getting emotional.

Nick had always been the one who inspired Michael to be better, do better. He'd also been the one who got the girl, ultimately driving a wedge between them. But George didn't need to know that, and Michael wasn't ready to confess, least of all to him.

George raised his eyebrows, awaiting a reply.

"Yeah." What else was he supposed to say?

Another awkward moment passed, and George cocked his head toward the food tables. "Let me get you more punch."

"No, thanks. That stuff is…"

"Awful. Yeah, I know." George rocked on his heels, mischief in his eyes. "I think I might have improved it."

"Like I said, no, thanks."

"Suit yourself. I'll just go get some myself. Nice seeing you, McCann."

Michael was tempted to head back to the fern, but that seemed silly after everything that had happened. He stuffed the speeding ticket in his pocket. Maybe it was time to face up to things, too. If Savannah could take a step forward, then so could he. His classmates knew him as a troublemaker, but he'd left that part of his life behind. Trouble was, George had trouble seeing that. Maybe Savannah would, too?

One night back in Point, and he'd already run into all sorts of uncomfortable situations. So unlike his career, where he oversaw three rescue teams and had earned the nickname Double-Check Mike. With every rescue situation he tackled, he weighed the risks and laid out contingency plans. Yes, he double- and triple-checked all the equipment and ran drills all the time, but his caution always paid off.

Unlike his plan to spend tomorrow with Savannah—without contingency plans or backup strategies. But it was only one day. What harm could there be? He'd stowed his heart behind a stone barricade and double-checked the lock. One day wouldn't damage those safeguards.

However, he sensed a hairline crack in his resolve the moment Savannah walked back into the gym, her gaze searching for him. Her smile dazzled him. He followed her every move, the swish of her emerald dress, every step she took in the heels that accentuated the curve of her calves. Every bit a woman. Maybe he did need more punch to strengthen his resolve.

* * * *

Main Street, where the walls had eyes and everyone knew everyone, might not have been the best place to meet on a Sunday morning, but it was too late to change plans. Savannah had agreed to spend the day with Michael, and there was no turning back. A glance at her phone confirmed it was almost nine. He'd turn up at any moment. The morning breeze blew her loose hair around her face, bringing with it the scent of roasted coffee beans and bacon from the breakfast place across the street mingled with the apple blossoms from the adjacent park. The blend of fragrances brought a sense of anticipation.

Earlier that morning, deciding whether to wear her favorite ankle-length skirt or her new blue jeans had been trickier than she'd expected. She'd spent too much time deliberating. In the end, she'd gone with the comfortable, practical jeans and a blue capped-sleeve blouse. She'd ditched the contact lenses and wore her new tortoiseshell-rimmed glasses.

Wiggling her toes in her favorite sandals, she regretted not getting one of those special-offer pedicures advertised on the sandwich board in front of the salon and spa.

She inhaled the morning air, held her breath, and exhaled, releasing the pent-up tension contracting her shoulder and neck muscles. She could do this. Nick would want her to live life to the fullest in his honor, but a twinge of guilt still niggled, like a pebble in her shoe.

Her life would never be the same, and she might as well embrace it one step at a time. Breakfast with Michael was another step in the right direction. Dear Mrs. Delaney at the library would be proud of her. How many times had she endured the same old well-meaning pep talk? Savannah's lips curved at the memory. *"You can't hide in the library, with your books, entrenched in your comfort zone, dear. If I can join the bridge club and learn to swim at my age, then you can try some new things, too."*

"What are you smiling about?" Michael's husky morning voice jolted her back to the present.

Why did the man sound so good? Freshly shaven and showered, with slightly damp hair and a sandalwood scent, he looked and smelled as wonderful as he sounded—no use denying it.

"I..." Without a coherent thought in her head, her mouth opened like a fish going for bait.

Michael watched her with a boyish grin, like he was used to women turning to chowderheaded mutes in his presence. "You ready for that waffle?"

"Extra whip, remember?"

Michael opened the door of the waffle café and waved her in with a bow. She trotted past him, ducking her head as her cheeks warmed. She needed coffee before she could find his exaggerated chivalry amusing. The obligatory gumball machine stood just inside the door, and she wondered whether she'd still get a couple of extra gumballs if she hit it just right.

"Table for two?" A chirpy teenager in a black apron smiled at them with menus clasped to her chest. They followed her swaying ponytail into the dining area. All the attendees visiting for the reunion had clearly settled on the same place to have breakfast before heading home or attending the 10:30 a.m. church service. Every table and booth was jammed with chatting, chewing out-of-towners and Point residents enjoying their waffles...except for one small round table in the middle of the restaurant.

Savannah felt all eyes on them as they sat across from each other. She felt worse than she had during the kiss in front of everyone on the dance floor. Even the larger-than-life airbrushed blonde bombshell and the rock and roll king on the wall seemed to be watching. She hung her purse over the back of the chair as Miss Ponytail handed them two menus and scuttled off to fetch the coffeepot.

"Nice private table, huh?" His low chuckle got her hackles up, and she hid behind the menu. Not letting it go, he leaned in. "I take it you're not a morning person?" he asked in a stage whisper.

Savannah winced. "Could you wait until I've had at least one cup of coffee before harassing me?"

"I already ran three miles this morning."

Savannah held her hand up. "Stop. Just stop."

Michael's eyes took on an impish twinkle. "You should probably wave at Mrs. Murphy's bingo club over there."

She was in no mood for his teasing—at least, he'd better be teasing. Savannah swiveled to confirm four gray heads close together, their watery eyes following her every move. Nothing like that fishbowl feeling before breakfast. She put down her menu and sat up straighter. She wasn't going to allow herself to be a shrinking violet. She'd stand—or sit—her ground. Nothing to see here. She was having a perfectly innocent breakfast with a handsome friend. There. That was all.

The coffee arrived, and the fragrance of the dark roast excited her taste buds. The first sip was hot and heavenly. Her eyes slid closed in response. "Mmmmm…good."

Michael shoveled two teaspoons of sugar into his black coffee and stirred. "I was thinking we could go visit some of Nick's favorite spots in town."

"Like the gorge and the water tower?" Those were the guys' favorite spots. Not hers. She should probably clarify what they'd do before agreeing to tag along.

Michael nodded.

Dread filled her. "Will I be required to climb the water tower?" Back in the day, she hadn't thought twice about scampering up to join the boys, but with age had come a crippling fear of heights. One she'd have to admit to the fearless Michael McCann.

"Look. Part of my job is keeping people safe. I think I can handle a water tower."

"What do you mean?"

"I've been a technical rescuer for a long time."

"You have?" Savannah sat back and studied him. "I pegged you for a car salesman."

He clutched his chest like she'd shot him at point-blank range. "Ouch. That was low, even for you."

She could muster only a small smile, given the way her stomach was churning. "What if I fall?"

"I promise you won't fall. I mean, that place is full of memories of happier times." Michael's eyebrows arched. "You don't want to get home and regret you didn't do it."

"We'll see." She sipped her coffee and eyed him over the rim of her cup. This grown man was familiar, just like the friend she'd always known, yet so different. The rebel boy, always getting up to mischief, had turned into a man with a respectable job. A job that had Savannah breaking out in hives, just thinking about the dangers he must face on a regular basis.

Michael set his cup down and glanced over her shoulder. "How hungry are you?"

"Reasonably. Why?"

"Nothing. Except I just spotted Neville in the corner over there, and guess who's with him?"

Savannah examined his face for clues. Was he pranking her? She kept her face neutral. "No."

"Yes."

"Claire?" Savannah's head began to throb.

"Right. Looks like they've joined forces." He craned his neck, a frown puckering his brow. "Don't know where his wife is. What do you say we get out of here? We can come back for your waffle tomorrow." She could feel the prickle of speculative gazes on her back. Maybe she'd take him up on his escape route willingly this time.

Savannah put on her best Officer Jenkins voice. "Are you hightailing it out of town again?"

"Sure. I mean, I'd rather have bacon, to be honest. Waffles are *your* thing."

After his run, he must be hungry, yet he'd sat with her in the middle of the fishbowl, about to order a waffle, because he was kind. Now, he was offering to help her escape public scrutiny, which was also considerate of him. All under the guise of an "I'd rather have bacon" line. But he wasn't fooling her—he'd offered to take her somewhere less obtrusive. Somewhere safe.

She drained her cup. "Okay, Mr. Wise Guy. Let's go find you some bacon."

CHAPTER 6

MICHAEL MOPPED UP THE LAST OF his egg yolk with a chunk of toast and popped it in his mouth. Savannah's poached eggs sat untouched next to the empty fruit bowl.

"Are you gonna eat those?" He pointed his fork at them.

"Three eggs and a plate of bacon not enough for you?"

"I'm a grown man."

A smile tugged at her lips as Savannah shoved her plate his way. Gone was the awkward teen he'd once known, transformed into a stunning woman but very much the same friend he'd always loved. Perhaps just a bit improved. She hadn't seen him get into one of his famous brooding moods since they'd been reunited, because he wasn't the guy he used to be. He'd also changed, and only time would tell whether she still thought he was the impulsive, crazy guy she once knew.

Michael stabbed each yolk of Savannah's abandoned eggs with his fork and dipped long strips of toast into the gooeyness as it oozed out onto the plate. He usually ate alone, so having an audience was new. Granted, they had fewer observers than if they'd stayed at the waffle café. The all-day breakfast place would have been their second choice, but they agreed to avoid Main Street. They'd driven out of town toward Letchworth Gorge and found a quaint family-owned place along Portage Street. The aroma of the quality coffee emanating from the open window had sealed the deal.

Now, the midmorning light shone through the window onto their table, illuminating the dancing dust in the air. Outside, on the patio, the chickadees sang their distinctive song while hopping between the table legs to find dropped morsels.

The cowbell over the door jangled as a young couple maneuvered a stroller through the doorway. The toddler, tucked into a fleece blanket, slept while the waitress led the young parents to the table in the corner. Michael watched with a pang of longing in his chest. He'd long given up the dream he'd have a family of his own. Not many women had stuck with him past the casual first or second dates.

Michael wiped his mouth with his napkin. His chair creaked as he leaned back to let his food settle. Savannah sat straight and still, her eyes on the family in the corner. She twisted her wedding rings. What was going on behind those glasses of hers? Sometimes, he could read exactly what she was thinking; other times, like now, he sat clueless.

Savannah turned from the family and caught him watching her. Her eyebrows peeped over the frames of her glasses. "What?"

"Are you okay?"

"I'm fine." She took off her glasses and polished the lenses with the bottom of her shirt. She held them up to the light streaming through the window. Cleaning spotless glasses was definitely another one of her stalling tactics.

"Do you usually chase your fruit around your bowl and pick at your toast when you're fine? Those chickadees ate more breakfast than you did."

"No."

"Is it me?" He held his breath, steeling himself for her answer.

"No, you've done everything to make this trip less of a nightmare."

Tension drained from him, replaced by a frown. "I don't understand. You don't like being in Point?" Not that he could blame her. He wasn't exactly thrilled, either.

"I do, and I don't." She shifted in her seat. "As nostalgic as it all is, it's hard to remember when Nick isn't here."

"We don't have to go to the gorge if you don't want to. We can—"

"No, I have to do this. Remembering the good times will remind me we had a good life together, even if it was shorter than I would have liked." Her lashes batted back the moisture in her eyes, and his heart ached for her. "It's just that seeing families with young ones…"

He shifted in his chair while Savannah rummaged in her purse.

"I'm sorry. I just got something in my eye."

He wasn't convinced, but he let it go.

She extracted a handkerchief from her purse and dabbed her eyes behind her newly polished glasses. "I'm here for a week, and I want to explore all our old haunts. Well, except for the orthodontist's office. I've done my time there." She grinned, her perfectly aligned teeth backing up her claim.

Had she been denied a family of her own, too, or had it been a choice? He wasn't ready to broach that subject quite yet, but he wanted to wipe away her misery—to make her laugh.

"Maybe you need some new memories."

She looked at him as though she could see into his soul. "Maybe I do." Her voice was soft and strained.

They paid for breakfast and joined the birds on the patio. Beyond the railing, the grass and shrubs were coming back, having endured winter's worst. The combination of new shoots and old shrubs created a beautiful wilderness among the jagged rocks and garden ornaments. Between the paving stones at his feet, a tiny pansy with yellow-and-black petals resembling a cheerful face stood about three inches tall. Careful not to crush it with his heel, he stepped over the resilient little flower and followed Savannah. Their footfalls crunched on the loose gravel as they ambled toward the jeep.

Michael broke the comfortable silence between them. "Where to first?"

"I'm not sure. So, how long are you in town for?"

"That depends. I'm on call, so unless someone gets themselves into trouble, I've got time." He raked his hand through his hair, hoping he didn't sound too eager. He didn't want her to think he expected anything from her or to know that he'd planned on staying only a couple of nights. He'd already extended his hotel booking, just in case.

"I was thinking maybe we can leave the town stuff until Monday."

"Town stuff?"

"I want to go see the old library where I got my first job and the cobblestone church."

"And the water tower?"

Savannah slowed her steps.

"Y-yes, that, too. If I can pluck up the courage to climb up there. I'm not as brave nor as agile as I once was."

"Really? It's not that high, and I promise I'll be right there with you."

"McCann, if I fall to my death, I'm holding you responsible."

She'd called him McCann, which usually made him cringe at the association it held with his former lifestyle, but coming from her lips, he could come to like it again. "Fair enough, but I rescue people, so don't go getting ideas of getting into a mishap just to test my skills."

Savannah batted her eyelashes. "I wouldn't dream of it." She put a finger to her cheek and tapped. "Can we take a ride past my parents' old house?"

"Old house?"

"They moved to Florida after a few too many New York winters. It was soon after you'd left town actually."

Michael flinched at the reminder. Savannah went on, oblivious to his discomfort.

"A year after Nick and I married—we'd taken a gap year after graduation while we decided what courses to take—my parents sold the place and moved. About the same time, Nick and I moved to Ithaca to go to college."

Michael mentally kicked himself for not staying in touch. He really shouldn't have cut all ties with the past. What else had he missed out on because of his self-preservation?

"I had no idea they'd left town. Do you still live in Ithaca?" Maybe he could visit her there during one of his training sessions.

"We were there for about six years before we found out Nick was sick. We'd graduated and had been working at our first jobs for two years before we got the diagnosis. In the end, we moved closer to Nick's oncologist and his treatment centers, and for a while, we rented out our apartment in Ithaca. So, it was an easy transition back to the apartment after Nick died. It's familiar. I'm glad to be back there."

If his math was correct, Nick had battled that despicable disease for over a decade. A pang of guilt stabbed his heart. While he was living it up with his pals, his best friend had been fighting for his life. But wishing he could turn back the clock wouldn't help things. He could look only ahead, one day at a time. "Near Cayuga

Lake? We've had a few water search and rescues on that lake."

"Yes. The Ithaca College Library isn't far from the south end of the lake. I interned there, then after college worked as an assistant librarian until after Nick died, when I moved over to the Adelson Library at the local center for birds and biodiversity. Now, I also do the occasional shifts at the Uris Library and the law school library. Don't let it be said I don't like variety."

Savannah shoved a stray lock of her golden hair out of her face. "I spend most of my time at Adelson, though. The bird-watching crowd is rather passionate about their feathered friends." She winked, a smile playing at her lips. "They'd be bored with chickadees and be scampering into the bushes in search of the elusive pink-footed goose."

They stopped under the shade of an old oak tree next to the jeep and turned to face each other. Time to lighten up the conversation. "I've never seen a pink-footed goose."

She rocked back on her heels and stuck out her chin. "Exactly."

Michael narrowed his eyes. "You made that name up."

"I didn't. Look it up if you want." Her grin made him all the more suspicious.

"If we save the amazing and wonderful Point attractions until last, that leaves the gorge, but I'd rather get there earlier in the day." If they didn't linger over those promised waffles, they could be at the gorge before ten.

"Good point. Any special places you want to include in our epic tour down memory lane?"

She had him there. He'd thought the reunion would be a quick in-and-out thing—no lingering and minimal remembering. Boy, had things turned out different from plan A. Though plan B—escorting Savannah around the area—wasn't the worst way to spend his time. Even if it was a pathetic attempt to make up for not being there when she'd needed him. "I hadn't thought about it much."

She tilted her head. "Wait. Were you..." She poked his arm and then wagged her finger. "You really were going to hightail it out of town right after the reunion, weren't you?" Savannah hopped into the jeep.

"Maybe."

She reached for the seat belt and clipped herself in. "So, what made you stay?"

He shut her door and strolled around to his side of the jeep. Maybe she'd have forgotten her question by the time he got in. He wasn't ready to answer that question—at least, not out loud. He clambered into the jeep, turned the key, and turned up the air-circulating fan. "I thought I'd spend some time looking for the red-necked grebe."

"Very funny, Michael. There's no such thing."

He shifted into reverse and turned to Savannah. "As real as your pink-footed goose. Let's go exploring. Maybe we can find a few rare fowl of our own."

CHAPTER 7

I T WASN'T LIKE SHE WAS MAKING a life-changing decision. All she had to do was decide whether they should turn left or right. Left would take them back to Point, while right would take them up the hill toward Portageville and the gorge. Sometimes, making the simplest decisions overwhelmed her. She released a slow, audible breath as Michael waited for her to tell him which way to go.

"Left. No. Right."

"Are you sure?"

"Sorry. Right."

Michael drove up the single-lane road. The silent power lines stood sentry as if supervising their journey. Tall trees flanked the road, sporting freshly sprouted greenery. They passed a green-roofed barn on their right and a plowed field on their left before whizzing by scattered houses with bulky pickup trucks parked in the driveways and an obligatory evergreen in the front yard. Some people had parked utility trailers off to the side.

Savannah willed herself to relax. She was supposed to be having fun, but her stomach churned thinking about the unfairness of it all. It should have been Nick driving her along these roads. After passing the Letchworth parade grounds on their right, they drove under the rusty underpass with the graffiti only on the top half—as if the artists could spray "I love Rosie" only as far as their arms could reach while dangling over the side of the bridge. Did Rosie get *her* happily ever after?

They rounded the bend and continued down the hill to where the train line briefly ran parallel to the road, its silvery rails glistening in the midmorning sun, before going its own way. They crossed the bridge that marked the end of Livingston County as the river rippled over the flat rocks beneath it. They headed toward the double verandas of the Victorian inn on the corner of Main and Hamilton, about half a mile from Letchworth State Park. The restored redbrick inn, with its freshly painted white pillars and railings, attracted tourists and locals alike. She gritted her teeth, thinking of that time when she'd strolled this way with Nick. He should have been the man beside her still.

Michael pulled off the road into the inn's dusty parking lot. "Let's walk. It's a beautiful day." He walked around to the back of the jeep while she scrambled out, being careful not to catch any small pebbles in her sandals. The Genesee River encircled the town like an embrace. If they wanted to see the falls, they'd have to go to the Letchworth State Upper Falls. But they couldn't tackle those when she was wearing sandals.

At the back of the jeep, she found Michael with his well-used backpack already slung over his shoulder and his other hand resting on the hatchback door, giving her a pleasing view of his muscular arm beneath his T-shirt.

"I came prepared." His proud little-boy declaration warmed her heart.

"I didn't." She patted one of the bulges on the backpack. "What have you got in there?"

"Two bottles of chilled water and some snacks." A knowing grin brought out a dimple in his cheek. Good call on the provisions. "Always thinking of your stomach." Her grin hid her suspicion that he was watching out for her. Being cared for like this would take some getting used to. She'd had to be the one doing the caring for so long. She relished the feeling.

His footwear was more suited to walking than her sandals, but carpe diem. No more time to waste. She tossed her purse into the back of the jeep, and Michael shoved the door closed and locked it.

"My parents drove through here many times on their Sunday afternoon outings. I thought you might find the neighborhood interesting." She pointed up Main Street. "Let's walk up this way and see how far we get."

Main Street in Portageville was nothing like Point's Main Street. In fact, Point seemed like a metropolis compared with Portageville. Savannah strolled next to Michael, and they turned onto Church Street.

Savannah and Nick had always laughed at the fact that Church Street was devoid of churches. Both the

Baptist church and the chapel were on Pike Street. Although to be fair, only one was an actual church.

They meandered until they came to Pike Street, and Savannah heard someone playing the organ as they drew nearer to a Greek Revival style building. She pointed at the grayish-blue building with its clear Gothic windows. "Did you know, the chapel is actually a rehearsal space for professional organists who come from all over to tickle the ivories and stomp the pedals? Not your average Sunday service organ playing, to be sure." She pictured nimble fingers dancing across the keys and producing the intricate and beautiful notes and trills they could hear. The sign outside simply read, "Thanksgiving Service, 10 a.m." Nick had died a month before Thanksgiving last year. She shoved aside the memories of the last Thanksgiving she'd celebrated or, rather, not celebrated—her first as a widow.

Michael's brows drew together. "A bit early for Thanksgiving, wouldn't you say?"

"The chapel only has one service a year. The rest of the year, they rent the space out."

"What for?"

"Professional players need somewhere to practice, with good acoustics and plenty of time to hone their skills. It's neat, huh?" The richness of the tones called to her soul as they washed over her.

"Yeah, if you like that sort of music."

"Have you heard Bach's famous music played on the organ and most known by its use in movie soundtracks?"

His blank look prompted her to mimic the opening notes. "Dah-da-dah, da-da-da-da dah-daaaaaa…"

His eyebrows inched upward. "Oh yeah, you mean the creepy music."

She nudged him. "It's not creepy at all. Just dramatic."

"If you say so."

"Nick and I attended some of the classical concerts when we were first married." That was before things had changed and pushed music to the bottom of their list while daily survival became the priority.

Michael scrunched up his nose. "I'm more of a boy-band kind of guy myself."

Savannah lost it in a fit of giggles, trying hard not to snort-laugh. "Boy band? Seriously?"

Michael's unrepentant expression just made her laugh more. They walked a little farther until she could no longer hear the bass notes of the organ reverberating through the air. They stopped to let a delivery man in gray coveralls unload a van full of fresh floral arrangements. He carried two large vases across the sidewalk in front of them, up the stairs, and through the sunflower-yellow double doors of a building that looked like it should also be a church, complete with a bell tower and arched stained-glass windows. A sign on the side of the off-white exterior confirmed it wasn't a church but instead had been turned into an events venue and adjoining bed-and-breakfast. They were likely preparing for a wedding.

Savannah admired the remaining arrangements in their crystal cases. The scent of cream lilies and pink roses, delicate and sweet, tickled her nose, causing her to sneeze, twice, three times. She was going for a fourth when Michael tugged on her arm and moved her past the van and the offending flora.

"Allergies?"

Her eyes stayed half-closed in preparation for another sneeze. "I don't know. I've never had this reaction before."

She gasped and held up a finger. "Wait." Another sneeze. Her glasses, now lopsided, had slipped to the end of her nose, probably making her look like a stereotypical librarian. She slid them back into place. "Aha! Maybe *that's* why I couldn't stop sneezing at Nick's memorial service."

"White lilies?"

"Yes! It was... Achoo! It was horrible. I was so embarrassed."

Michael's lopsided smile meant he was probably picturing the whole scene. She made a mental note never to buy lilies for the library foyer, and she scurried out of range of their scent. Side by side, they continued down the street.

Between the gray-roofed white houses with their noticeable lack of picket fences, the occasional red barn lent color to the landscape. One mowed lawn led to another with lines of trees separating them.

Savannah chuckled. "This reminds me of my parents. Mom would say, 'I just don't know how people can live like that. No fences. Unlocked doors. I can't get used to it.' Nick would just shake his head and tease about throwing away her keys. Mom thought not having fences and bars on the windows was asking for trouble." Her mom could be dramatic at times. Another reason she was glad they lived in Florida—in their gated community—to make Mom happy. "And the small-town idea of not locking your car or front doors made her anxious."

"She'd like my place." Michael nudged her and chuckled. "I have two deadbolts on my door, a peephole, and an intercom. It's like a prison."

"Wow! Ithaca is a little more...chill." Memories of South Africa, her birth country, were fuzzy, but she did remember the locks and bars as well as the fragrant smell of meat and boerewors cooking over charcoal fires, part of life most weekends—even in the winter. People loved to gather and socialize, and there was none of the North American hibernating. And she wasn't referring to animals.

Michael slowed his pace. "Do you ever wish you'd gone back to visit South Africa? Did you ever think of going back there to live?"

She shook her head. "No. It's not the same as it once was—things have changed." There and here. Portageville wasn't the same without Nick. She pushed her glasses back to the bridge of her nose and gazed into the blue sky. A few clouds had gathered, but the sun shone bright, as if unaware of her swirling emotions. "My mom used to say you could never go back to the way things were. People moved on. She'd say, 'Nothing stays the same, and you never find what was.'" Memories of being blissfully happy, walking these streets as newlyweds, somehow gave her mother's words more impact. Would the dull ache in her heart ever leave?

"Do you miss them since they've moved away?"

"Yes and no. Sometimes, I miss them and wish they were closer. Other times, I'm glad their distance shielded them from what we were going through. I didn't want them to worry too much. Having to be strong for their once-a-week phone call was about as much as I could handle."

Michael nodded, which warmed her heart. The man's empathy was a rare gift. Could he be willing to try to understand what it was like in her darkest days? Others had pitied her—she'd hated that. And then, there were those with their platitudes, one for every kind of tragedy or messy situation.

Michael rubbed his chin. "And now?"

"After Nick died, they helped me move back to the apartment and came to stay for a few weeks. I needed that."

"I'm sorry, Savannah." His steps faltered and he came to a halt. He turned blue eyes to study her face. "I wish I could say something to..." His voice was thick with emotion, which brought her own far too close to the surface.

She reached out and touched his arm for a moment. "I know. Thank you." She plastered a smile on her face. "Okay, your turn. You left town after Nick and I got engaged. Then what?"

Michael rubbed the back of his neck. "I did a whole lot of things I probably shouldn't tell you about."

"Why not?"

"College became one big party. I did okay, but I lived for weekends. Some of the crazy things I did would make your hair stand on end. Like whitewater rafting, bungee jumping, and extreme hiking. I thought I was invincible. I was young…"

Memories of a few of the stunts he'd pulled in high school flooded back. Like that time he'd toilet papered Neville's car. "And stupid…"

"Can't argue with that one. But I soon learned I wasn't invincible. It's only because of another first responder that I survived."

Savannah drew in a breath, and her feet faltered.

He ran a hand through his air-dried hair, which looked way too good. "So, I volunteered for a while, then worked myself up and became a professional rescuer. Now, I train rescuers. But that's a story for another day."

She turned to face him. "Michael—"

"Let me finish."

She met his earnest gaze. There were no teasing crinkles around his eyes, no hint of a smile on his lips.

"I should have died. I realized I'd been given a second chance. So, I wanted to pay it forward. I worked hard to become a skilled rescuer. I've been overseeing three different teams for the last three years. And when we're not doing national rescues, we keep ourselves active by being on call with the local fire department."

He'd almost died and she hadn't known. He wasn't the only one who'd failed to stay in contact. A whisper of unease wound up her spine. All this time, she hadn't given him enough credit. Here, she'd thought his new look was because of superficial reasons, but in fact, he'd transformed his body for a nobler purpose. She'd pegged him as reckless and foolish. Were his motives beyond reproach? He was highly trained and responsible for others. She still didn't love the fact that when a call came in, he answered and risked his life. Not once, but all the time. Meaning, he might have to run off at any time. His lifestyle was as far from predictable as hers was from adventurous.

Emotions swirled within her as the breeze rustled the new leaves overhead. The sun slid behind the gathering rain clouds. The branches on the trees swayed in response. Still, could she risk getting close to a man who lived a life of instability only to lose him? She would have to tread carefully if she wanted her heart to heal and then remain intact. She'd loved Nick wholeheartedly, and here she was, savoring Michael's company. There was something to be said about hanging on to a familiar, comfortable friendship like theirs.

Michael rubbed his flat stomach. "Come on. Looks like rain. Let's get something to eat back at the inn while the thunderstorm blows over. My treat."

Savannah followed him up Main Street toward the inn, but she knew the storm brewing inside her heart wouldn't blow over anytime soon.

* * * *

Michael sat across from Savannah early on Monday morning in a decidedly less crowded waffle café. She seemed to relish every bite of her promised banana-and-pecan-topped waffle. Whipped cream slid down her fingers, and she caught a dollop of cream with her tongue before it hit the plate, much like a cat. She took a bite, and a cloud of powdered sugar settled on the rims of her glasses and her eyelashes.

Savannah dabbed the corners of her mouth with her napkin. "I believe in eating waffles the same way I eat my hamburgers."

"With lettuce and ketchup?"

He'd bet if she didn't have her mouth full, she'd have stuck her tongue out at him.

"Cute. No utensils needed." She took another bite and closed her eyes. "Mmm... This was worth the wait."

Michael took a swig of his lukewarm coffee, hiding his smile. He'd finished his bowl of oatmeal, which reminded him of the porridge his grandmother used to make. Except, being Scottish, she had stirred in blobs of butter that melted, blending with the brown sugar and hot milk. When she'd passed away, he had no reason to return to Point, until now. He was free to watch Savannah enjoy her waffle—without the rest of the town watching them.

Yesterday, when he'd left Savannah at the Point Roadside Motel, she had lost some of her initial vibrance. He couldn't tell whether it was something he'd said or whether she was worn out from spending the whole day traipsing around Portageville with him. Because of the rain, they hadn't gotten around to the gorge. However, she was more relaxed this morning, with her hair piled on top of her head in one of those messy buns. In her case, it fell into the classification of messier messy bun with tendrils of escaped hair framing her face. He couldn't take his eyes off her.

"I'm afraid I might freeze up." Her face drained of color. "I guess I've lost that youthful wild abandon." She looked at him, her eyes filled with fear. "Define *overly cautious*, and that's me."

"You don't have to—"

"I'm going to be brave. I can do it if you promise to catch me." She grabbed the ladder and hoisted herself onto the bottom rung.

"I promise." He chuckled, edging closer to the ladder. "At worst, I'll be a soft landing." He'd promise to keep her safe for the rest of her life, if she would let him.

One rung at a time, she made slow progress, stopping after each to breathe and testing each step before putting her full weight on it.

For someone who climbed far more dangerous places for a living, he should be able to do this in his sleep. He kept an eye out in case Savannah faltered and stayed close all the way up the ladder.

Savannah peered over the top rung. "I did it."

"Granny McCann could have climbed up here quicker. What took you so long?" His grin was lost to her while she scrambled onto the ledge. He'd teased Savannah for years as a way to break the tension when they were teens, and old habits were hard to shake. Michael pulled himself up and stepped onto the platform.

"Now that I'm up here, it doesn't seem as bad, but I'm not looking down." She scooted away from the railing and leaned her back against the tank, keeping her gaze on the horizon. Savannah's eyes shimmered, and her cheeks were rosy from the climb. "You know, I was the luckiest girl alive to have you and Nick as friends back in high school."

"Yeah, it really was a special time, although I wouldn't relive it." He settled in beside her, taking in the view of the buildings and trees surrounding them.

"No? We were carefree and young and…you know." She shrugged. "Carefree…"

"Speak for yourself. Though I choose to remember the best of that time, there was so much going on inside me. I guess that's why I left." He was thankful they looked out over the town and not at each other. He didn't want to go into the reasons he'd left. Not yet. "Do you remember when Nick dropped that bottle of cola?"

"It exploded all over the sidewalk—made it sticky for days. What a mess." She peeked down and then jerked her gaze back up, reaching for his hand.

"The ants loved it." He gave her hand a comforting squeeze before stepping to the edge of the platform.

"And the yellow jackets. Did you get stung, too?"

Savannah tugged her hand out of his grasp. "Yes, and Nick thought it was hilarious."

Michael gripped the railing and surveyed the town below. "It's weird to be up here, looking down on Point, thinking about all the things we did as youngsters. Granny McCann would turn in her grave at what they've done with the new grocery store." He pictured the new big-box store he'd passed on his drive into town. "Granny believed in supporting small family-owned businesses."

"I'm sorry." The compassion in her voice was that of someone who was acquainted with grief. "How long has she been gone?"

"I'd just turned thirty when she passed. She was a special lady."

"She was a saint raising a hooligan like you." Savannah nudged his arm.

He nodded. "The older I get, the more I realize how hard it must have been for her. I wish I'd visited her after I left town, but she understood. She visited me at my apartment in Detroit."

"Why did you settle on Detroit?"

"It's central and close to the airport and the helicopter pad. It's really home base—well, a base, not so much home. I'm not there much during the summer, and in the winter, the rescues are more like long-line rescues. That's when we're called out for avalanches or recoveries, like when people have slipped through thin ice in places where helicopters can't land."

Savannah nodded in slow motion and rested her hand on his forearm. "Aren't you afraid sometimes?"

"Not really." He looked out over the rooftops of Point. "We train and prepare for those scenarios. Sure, there are risks, but we weigh them carefully. If the risk to my team is too high, then we call it off. It's as simple as that. Emotions are dangerous, and there's no place for them on a rescue mission. It sounds harsh, but it's the truth." The warmth of her hand distracted him more than he cared to admit. "So, Miss Tour Guide, what's next on the itinerary?"

"Will you come with me to the chapel?"

"What—another church?" He faked a frown. "Cobblestone church this afternoon is not good enough for you?"

"Have you ever been to the almost smallest chapel in the whole world?"

"What are you talking about?"

"The smallest chapel in the world, according to the record books, seats six people and is near Niagara-on-the-Lake on the Canadian side." Her eyebrows peeked over the rims of her glasses. "There's also a tiny church just outside of Point. It was built in an attempt to break the world record. They didn't quite manage it—they were off by a couple feet. I need to see it one more time."

The pleading look in her eyes and the wistful tone of her voice undid him. He'd do anything to make her happy. Even traipse off to see a mini church. "Let's go."

He led the way, helping her find the next foothold before stepping down, murmuring encouraging words all the way, just like he'd done numerous times when helping someone during a rescue. It was rather different doing the same for someone you cared for. It took them far longer to climb down the ladder than it had to climb up. By the time their feet hit solid ground, Savannah was trembling.

"You did great." He pulled her into a sideways hug. "No more climbing for the rest of the week, okay?"

She nodded and peered up at him, a weak smile curling her lips. "McCann, I hope you are ready to see an almost-record-breaking chapel, no ladders and no stairs."

"You bet. Lead the way."

Savannah led the way to his jeep, and they drove out of town, Savannah giving him directions all the way. About fifteen minutes later, she pointed to a gravel driveway. "Pull over here."

Michael parked under a maple tree. They followed a shaded path that meandered through a gate into a grassy area. He scratched his head. "Why did you want to come here?"

Savannah turned to him, her eyes widened. "Of course. You don't know."

"What?" He stopped in his tracks.

She grabbed his hand and tugged him along behind her. "This is where Nick and I got married."

Her tortured words caused a sudden and irrational surge of adrenaline in him. He'd avoided their wedding all those years ago and definitely didn't want to revisit the memory of it now. They rounded the corner to find a clearing where two manicured boxwoods flanked the tiny chapel in a well-tended garden. Pansies and foxgloves and purple irises bloomed between the shrubs, far too cheery for his current mood. The tranquil scene mocked his bewildered thoughts. The knots in his stomach wound tighter with every step toward the little chapel, but he stood his ground beside her, offering his support, as he had done at the water tower.

Savannah pointed at the painted blue door. "This is the 'something blue' part. Cute, huh?"

Michael clenched his jaw to hide a grimace while Savannah stepped through the doorway. It was like he'd been sucked into a kid's movie where the white rabbit handed him too much of the growing potion. He ducked his head and joined Savannah inside. The sun streamed through a stained-glass window at the front of the church. There would be enough room for a bride and groom, a minister, and two or three family members at most.

Savannah pointed to the beams of sunlight that threw patches of light onto the rug. "Nick and I stood here. He looked so handsome in his tuxedo." Her face shone with little-girl fairy-tale wonder.

Did she have any idea what she was doing to his heart?

"My parents sat over there in the teensy pew. When we stood to say the prayers, Dad stayed hunched over. You know how tall he is." She stepped to the right and pointed to the floor. "And this is where the best man should have been." She imprisoned him with her gaze, paralyzing him.

Pain in his jaw intensified. He forced himself to relax despite the hurt deep in his soul. "I know. I should have been there. I just…"

He deserved the agony that seared his heart. He'd run away before, and now, he faced the resulting list of what-ifs and regrets. What if he'd told Savannah how he felt about her when he had the chance? What if he'd taken a chance at loving her, really loving her—like Nick had gotten to do—and put their friendships in jeopardy?

"But you are here now." She stepped toward him, her hand outstretched, inviting him to share her bittersweet memories.

Heaviness settled in his chest. There was no use thinking about the what-ifs. He couldn't change history. The walls closed in on him. "I'll wait outside."

He broke out into the fresh air—paced in front of the very place he never wanted to see. Why was his heart pounding out of his chest?

Savannah dashed out of the tiny chapel and found him. She placed her hand on his shoulder, her sympathetic touch torture to his whole being. "What's wrong?" The concern in her eyes caused him to wince.

"I…" There were no adequate words to articulate the emotions inside him. He wasn't sure whether he understood them himself. As he stared at his feet, shame washed over him. He didn't want her searching eyes to find him weak and foolish.

"Claustrophobia?"

"Something like that." He grimaced at the half truth. "I'm sorry. I'm not claustrophobic, but that place…"

"Do you want to leave?"

"No. Just give me a minute." He'd thought that hanging out at their old haunts was triggering her emotions, making her grief worse, but instead, here he was the one unable to cope.

His knee-jerk reaction was to say goodbye here and now and leave Savannah to her memories of her life with Nick. Regrets about how he'd handled falling in love with his best friend's girl still haunted him.

His time of running had to end. And it had to end now.

CHAPTER 8

SAVANNAH FELT LIKE A TRUCK HAD slammed into her. "I'm sorry. Could you please repeat that?"

"Let's hop over the border together."

Her breath caught in her throat. Where had all the air gone? "But why?"

"As much as it's good to remember, let's make some memories of our own—new ones, ones that don't...hurt." He waved toward the chapel, and the bittersweet emotions from her moments inside flooded back.

He had a point. Could she give herself permission to live a little? "You mean, live in the moment? You know, throw caution to the wind and just be." Sarcasm dripped from every word as she waved her hands in the air.

"You don't sound convinced." He stepped closer and rested a hand on her shoulder.

"It's all very reckless, Michael. You know I'm not the impulsive type."

"Look. If we don't take this opportunity, we'll always wish we had." He nudged her chin up until their gazes met. "I dare you."

That was low. He knew she couldn't let a dare go, even as her nerves zinged in warning. Everything seemed to pause to hear her reply—the bees stopped their buzzing, and even the red squirrels halfway up the maple tree trunk halted their game of tag.

"I'm scared." She blinked back hot tears. She was tired of being such an emotional wreck.

"I'm not asking you to dangle from the side of a mountain, Savannah."

That would be safer than risking more time with Michael. Alone.

He cupped her face, and she leaned into him, her eyes sliding shut. She couldn't deny that his tenderness sparked a longing in her. In the midst of chemotherapy and nausea, she'd been the comforter instead of the comforted, though Nick had done his best. It had been too long since she'd allowed herself to be cared for this way. His gentle hands lingered on her skin. He'd always treated her with such kindness. And, he'd gotten better with age.

"Savannah, I'm not asking you to commit to anything more than a fun trip to Canada. Just for the rest of the week. That's all. No expectations, no strings, no life-changing decisions."

Could she go with him? Should she? She'd belonged to Nick for so long she didn't know how to be otherwise. To be her own person, free to do as she pleased. And being alone wasn't the end of the world. She valued their rekindled friendship. It was a rare opportunity to hang out with someone who knew her so well. Maybe making new memories wasn't such a bad thing, like the old days when Nick and Michael had been the best of friends.

"Please, I'll arrange everything." Michael leaned his forehead against hers. "All you have to do is come along and enjoy. I'll take over tour guide duty and…"

She stepped back, raising her hands. "Whoa…okay, I get it."

Everything sounded wild and tempting. For years, she'd cared for Nick—right to the end. Then, she'd retreated into her shell and quite liked it there. This trip to Point for the reunion had been a stretch for her. Her goal had been to heal and try to face life without Nick. Now, Michael was freaking her out with his weird anti-tiny-chapel behavior and the promise of what she dared not hope for.

She couldn't think with him standing so close to her. She met his gaze. Oops. Wrong move. His pleading eyes hinted that maybe he needed this more than she did, and they threatened to undo the last of her resolve.

This was a far cry from having to decide whether to turn left or right. This was admitting maybe she wanted to discover what awaited them on the other side of the border besides maple syrup and butter tarts. This was admitting that Michael McCann had gotten under her skin, in a good way.

Guilt slid through her. How could she feel this way when she'd loved Nick for most of her life? Nick had been fun-loving and easygoing. Michael was intense, passionate, and—scary. Yes, there was his magnetic

* * * *

At precisely eight in the morning, she cracked open her door to find Michael in khaki shorts and a white T-shirt. She'd overslept, but he was up and ready to hit the road. At his feet were his backpack, an overnight bag, and a large pillow—a clue he'd never grown out of the attachment to his favorite pillow. An image rose in her mind of her and Michael on their way home from their eighth grade trip, sharing his pillow in the back of the bus.

His fresh scent of sandalwood and soap mingled with the aroma of the coffee in his hand. She opened the door farther and peered into the motel parking lot. Seeing no one, she stepped out and yawned. The birds in the trees lining the road that ran along the front of the motel made far too much noise for a Tuesday morning. Didn't they get the memo—chirping wasn't allowed until after nine?

"Got your passport?"

Savannah ignored him. She didn't want to hear questions before she was properly caffeinated. She pointed at the cup in his hand. "Is that for me?"

Michael nodded and handed it over.

"Thanks." She sipped the dark liquid, and it gave her the kick she needed. She hadn't slept much. Try as she might, she hadn't managed to hide the evidence of her restless night. It was apparent from her slippers right up to her unruly hairstyle. Getting her contacts in had been about as much as she could accomplish before he knocked on her door.

She'd been having second thoughts—okay, make that second, third, and fourth thoughts. All night, she'd flipped between going on this crazy tour with Michael and turning tail and running back home. She'd finally come to a decision, and now was the time to confess. Well, maybe not right now. Her sluggish brain needed more caffeine. She'd have a few more chugs of the hot brew before she told him. No need to rush the bad news.

"No need to rush." He leaned against the railing, waiting for the caffeine to hit her bloodstream.

Another sip fortified her resolve. Just a bit more, and then, she'd spill the truth.

"Ready to go?" He quirked an eyebrow, his lazy smile making what she needed to say even harder.

She placed her hand on his chest, clutched the coffee in the other, and dredged up the courage to look him in the eye—without squinting in the bright morning light.

She drew in a breath, but the words lodged in her dry, scratchy throat.

He narrowed his eyes and shook his head slowly. "You've changed your mind, haven't you?" The disappointment in his voice was thick and heavy.

"Look. I'm sorry." She infused calm into her voice. "I've been trying to figure this all out. You have been so kind to me, and I'm afraid—"

"You're afraid of living?" The coldness in his voice was like a slap in the face. She recoiled and retreated back into the doorway as if he had done just that. "I know you're grieving for Nick. I can see it in everything you say and do." A muscle ticked in his jaw, his eyes hard as granite. "He's not coming back."

"Don't you think I know?" She spat the words. "Don't you think I get that message loud and clear every time I wake up next to an empty space in our bed? That irreversible reality screams at me every time I unlock the front door after a long day at work. *He is not here.* I hear it in the silence—every time."

She wouldn't cry. She was done with tears—with the fortitude of fragile glass. Would she ever get over the emotional ambushes grief sprang on her at the least provocation—at a sound, a smell? They told her the first year was the hardest. She had survived the first six months, thinking the next three would be better. They weren't. Not yet.

Michael covered his face with his hands and shoved them up into his hairline. His shoulders heaved as the air around them crackled.

She hadn't intended to hurt him, yet she had. A dull ache settled in her belly. Was she making a mistake? "Are you angry with me?"

He dropped his hands and looked at the sky as if he juggled words in his mind, sorting them and deciding which ones to use. When he finally looked at her, she hated herself for causing the pain in his eyes. "No, I'm just disappointed."

She sighed. And that was before she told him what she was truly afraid of. He opened his mouth to say something more, but she silenced him with her fingertips on his mouth. "Wait. Let me finish."

CHAPTER 9

MICHAEL FELT LIKE HOT COALS SEARED his lips. It took every ounce of his willpower not to move under Savannah's featherlight touch. Yet if she was backing out of the trip, he didn't stand a chance. What was that she'd said the night of the reunion? "Can't have an end without a beginning"? She mustn't know what an effect she had on him, or she'd run. It would all be over before it began.

She removed her fingertips and dropped her gaze. "What I was going to say, before you jumped to conclusions, was that I was afraid that almost a week with me would ruin our friendship."

He wanted to ruin their friendship so much it moved into new territory. But he wasn't about to reveal that quite yet, so he put on his best poker face and tried to slow his pulse.

"I'm not spontaneous. I like to have things planned. I'll ask you a gazillion questions. You'll have to make sure

fine. Her hair, now brushed and gathered into a neat ponytail at the nape of her neck, shone like spun sugar in the clear morning light.

She hitched her large leather purse higher up her arm and peered at him from beneath long eyelashes that weren't hidden behind her glasses for once. "It is if you only got about three hours' sleep."

He clamped his lips together. He'd managed around four hours' sleep, but he guessed for different reasons. Aside from planning their route and tailoring it to include things she'd enjoy doing, he couldn't forget her cheek resting on his chest. One moment, she was there, trusting him; the next, she was backpedaling faster than he could change gears.

And then, there was the way she'd sat beside him in the cobblestone church. Gone was the exuberant faith he'd made fun of in youth group, replaced by a subdued—hurting even—expression of worship. He sent up a silent prayer for the patience he'd need to gain her trust.

Michael slung his luggage over his shoulder and followed Savannah. The scent of vanilla and coconut wafted his way as she walked toward the parking lot, dragging her traveling case on wheels behind her. He was grateful she hadn't teased him about his pillow tucked under his arm. A frequent traveler like himself needed something familiar and predictable, and for him, it was his pillow.

Savannah led him to a shiny black convertible. His pulse picked up. He'd never driven a high-end convertible before, sports model or not. How'd she afford this baby on a librarian's salary?

"I'm impressed." He pictured a drive with the roof down, in the sunshine, with the wind in their faces. How much space would they have for luggage?

Savannah frowned and waved her hand in dismissal before she dug in the purse hanging over her shoulder. She pulled out a pair of sunglasses, unfolded them, and perched them on top of her head. It would take extra self-control to keep a light foot on the gas pedal to avoid Officer Jenkins on their way out of town in this beauty.

"Well, what are you waiting for?" Savannah's voice pulled him out of his daydream.

He pressed the fob to unlock the trunk. The lights on the car right beside his dream car flashed, and the doors responded with a sickening click. He peered around the side of the sports car to find a tiny Smart car tucked in next to it—painted bright orange, the color of fruity candy. Another reason to get out of town before anyone, especially George, saw him driving this car. What was it about this woman and her tiny churches and tiny cars?

"You have got to be kidding."

It was her turn to smile. "Oh, did you think we were driving the—" She threw her head back. From deep inside, laughter bubbled up. Tears streamed down her face while he stood ramrod straight and unimpressed. An unladylike snort accompanied her laughter before she bent over to catch her breath.

"Are you quite finished?" He shook his head. The sound of her laughter did funny things to his insides.

He'd make it a goal over their remaining time to hear it as often as possible, even if it came at his expense.

"I'm sorry, but you should have seen your face."

"If you want to get to Canada before the end of the millennium, we'd better go." Time was moving on, and he didn't want to waste a moment with Savannah, even if he wouldn't be speeding along with the top down like he'd thought.

She stood up and saluted. "Yes, sir."

They squeezed their baggage and his pillow into the trunk. After spending five minutes adjusting the seat and the mirrors so he could drive the small-scale car, they set off toward Niagara Falls. He was more than ready to leave Point—and the memories associated with it—far behind.

* * * *

Savannah hadn't laughed so hard in years. Every time she pictured Michael's stunned face when he realized they'd be driving in her tiny car, she cracked up. The more he scowled, the funnier it got. The more she laughed, the louder he turned up the music. By the time they were waiting behind a string of cars crossing the border into Canada, her heart felt significantly lighter than it had in a long time.

The Niagara River churned below as they drove over the Rainbow Bridge. They edged forward as the van in front of them moved past the Canadian customs. After a fleeting glance at their passports, the lady at the booth waved them through with a cheery "Welcome to Canada."

Michael took them onto Hiram Street, then turned up a small ramp into a parking lot. Large bird-shaped cutouts hung from the three-story cream-colored building.

"Our first stop. Welcome to this bird aviary I know you'll love."

"Oh, Michael, I had no idea this place was here. How did you find it?" Her heart swelled at the thought that Michael would go out of his way to pander to her love of birds, even if he wasn't a fan himself. As long as she didn't end up with bird poop on her shoulder, she was excited to explore the bird sanctuary—she donned the baseball cap she'd stashed in her bag just in case.

Michael led the way to the entrance, where a sign on the side of the building claimed they'd arrived at the world's largest free-flying indoor aviary. Large urns overflowing with colorful annuals sat in front of the lime-green pillars painted with peacock-feather designs, giving the place a cheery feel. Michael pushed through the double glass doors and headed straight for the ticket counter. She dug in her purse and handed him her credit card.

"Not this time, sunshine. Can't a guy spoil a girl?" He winked at her and handed his card to the lady in the ticket booth with a satisfied grin.

She sighed. "Fine. But you can't spoil me the whole time." She returned her card to her purse and then rubbed her hands together, hardly able to wait long enough for him to pay. Tickets and a colorful brochure in hand, he turned to her and chuckled.

"What?"

"Nothing. I mean, I knew you'd be interested in birds, but I didn't anticipate you getting this excited."

She shrugged. "Hey, when you hang around bird people, you get like this. Not often you get to see live tropical species, either."

The lady behind the counter handed them two small containers of seeds. "Those are for the lorikeets. Just open the containers when you get to Lorikeet Landing, and they will fly down and sit on your hands."

Michael stashed the seeds in one of the large pockets of his khaki shorts.

She tugged at his sleeve. "Come on. Hurry."

"What happened to the no-rushing rule? We've got plenty of time."

She rolled her eyes at his endearing smile. *Now*, he wanted to stick to the rules. "I love birds."

They checked out the map in the brochure, and the times for meeting the birds with a handler were listed below it. She glanced at her watch. It was almost time for the first session. "Let's go to Animal Encounters first."

"I thought we'd leave that till last."

"Not a chance, McCann. Are you a little nervous to meet the big birds?"

"Maybe more than a little, but I'll man up and be brave." He puffed out his chest in fake bravado, causing her to giggle. He should have gone into acting.

At the enclosed area designated for close encounters with birds, a mother helped her young son, about the age of seven, hand an umbrella cockatoo back to the young man who worked there. Michael and Savannah got into line behind two teenage girls wearing matching shorts, T-shirts, and bright pink sparkly sneakers. The girl in the pink hoodie bounced from foot to foot while her friend attempted to hang on to her moving arm, face drained of blood. Despite the bird handler's calm assurances, the less-than-enthusiastic teen squeezed her eyes shut every time the bird flapped its wings.

Savannah nudged Michael until he bent, his ear inches from her lips. "She's terrified."

"She looks like I did when I met your bird, Henry, for the first time. Remember?" he whispered.

Savannah nodded in the girl's direction. "Oh yes. But you didn't whimper like that."

"No, but I wanted to. I pretended to like Henry. I had to be cool to impress you."

"You were trying to impress me?" She raised an inquiring eyebrow at him.

Michael's face remained passive, not giving her a clue to his thoughts. She, on the other hand, was acutely aware of how close he was. If he just turned his head...his lips...

Savannah caught a flash of cobalt-blue feathers over his shoulder as a lady walked into view behind him. "Oh, Michael, look." Her heart raced. A macaw with magnificent silky blue feathers and yellow rings around his eyes called to them with his gravelly squawk—he sounded more like an excited goose than an exotic South American bird. He blinked at them from his perch on the lady's arm as if he assessed whether they could be trusted.

Savannah approached the new arrival. She clasped her hands to keep herself from reaching out and startling the bird. "Can I hold him?"

A line of people was quickly forming behind them. The bird handler, in her twenties, with black hair tucked under a cap, smiled at Savannah and Michael, who were first in line. "His name is Nippy. He is a hyacinth macaw. Have you held a bird before?"

"I had a white cockatoo when I was in high school." Savannah held out her hand, and Nippy stepped over and grasped her with his large gray claws. The bird was heavier than she imagined; her arm sagged under the weight.

Michael reached out to support her elbow, and she glanced over to find a lopsided grin on his face. "Henry got cranky as he got older. He bit me a few times."

"If you think he was cranky then, you should have seen him after I left home and he moved to Florida with my parents." She scratched Nippy's head, and he leaned in, guttural sounds of pleasure coming from his throat. Savannah smiled. "Now, my dad and Henry compete to see who can be more cantankerous."

Michael laughed, and Nippy squawked even louder, as if to join in on the joke.

Savannah beamed at Michael. "It's all for show. Henry is about twenty-five now. Dad adores him. When they moved, Mom decided he needed a girlfriend."

Michael's eyes widened, and his jaw went slack. "Your mom got your dad a girlfriend?"

"For Henry. Not my dad!" She giggled, and the macaw bopped up and down on her hand.

The bird blinked at her as if to say, "Tell me more." Savannah clicked her tongue at him. "Catching up on all the bird gossip, are we?" He pecked at her baseball cap. "Michael, pass me some seeds." He dug in his pocket and produced the container, removed the lid, and handed it to her. Savannah distracted Nippy with the sunflower seeds. He squawked, ducked his head, and picked through the bowl. Then, he cracked the seed with his sharp beak, and the shells fell to the ground.

Michael's closeness sparked fluttery feelings in her stomach. Ones she'd ignore for now and focus on the bird in hand. "Henry and Nikita are just like a typical married couple. Spats and makeups and a few eggs along the way." She and Nick had been the same but without the eggs. Nippy cocked his head.

Michael seemed to have lost his nervousness and stroked the downy feathers under the bird's beak. "It's like he's listening to you."

Savannah nodded. "Of course, he is. Right, Nippy? Such a beautiful creature." Michael put his arm around her, causing her heart to skip a beat. She turned to him. "Did you know this was on my bucket list? I've always wanted to be this close to a hyacinth macaw."

The tender sparkle in Michael's eyes gave him away. "You may have mentioned it a few times in high school."

He'd remembered. A lump rose in her throat. He'd done this for her. Even though he tolerated birds, he didn't love them the way she did. "Thank you."

After Nippy cracked and ate all his seeds, between renewed attempts at dislodging Savannah's cap, their time was up, and they handed the gorgeous bird back to the lady.

Savannah bounded all the way to the main aviary, where Michael followed close behind her, pointing to rare species who hid among the lush tropical foliage. Savannah looked up their names on the board posted along the walkway. A gathering of burnt-orange scarlet ibis quenched their thirst as they drank from the waterfall with their long beaks. The male golden pheasants with their stunning red and gold feathers strutted and scrounged for seeds and berries. Could this day get any more perfect?

Michael stood beside her, taking it all in. He'd really done this for her. Maybe she could come up with something that he'd love to do—as long as it didn't involve anything too crazy.

"What do you say we—" Savannah turned to Michael, but he wasn't there. He'd rushed over and crooked his arm to help an elderly woman up the ramp toward the exit. Based on the woman's wide smile, clearly he was turning on the charm while doing it, too. It was more than his need to be a hero; it was the tenderhearted man under the tough veneer that touched Savannah's heart and took her breath away. Savannah offered up a silent prayer of thanks as she tucked new memories into her heart.

Having seen the old lady safely out, Michael trotted back to her with a grin. The conservatory-style glass roof allowed natural light to reach the lush tropical foliage on all three levels of the aviary.

"Can we stay here all day?" Savannah lifted her face to the sunlight and breathed in the balmy air.

They strolled to the designated landing for feeding the birds and opened the remaining container of seeds. By the time they'd been covered by lorikeets as promised by the ticket lady, a nearby commotion drew her attention to a scarlet ibis nest. A pair of bright orange long-beaked birds swooped down amid the dark gray fledgling's whistle-like squeaks. "Oh, look! How sweet. The parents are feeding their little baby!"

Michael's stomach rumbled. Maybe that signaled an opportunity to take care of Michael in return. It wasn't like she was trying to find a way to his heart through his stomach, as the old adage claimed. She was just taking care of him, even if he'd claimed to be a grown man. All morning, she'd been aware of Michael watching her, making her laugh, putting her needs first, and it was time she did the same for him.

She glanced at her phone. It was way past lunchtime. "I guess it's time to find you something to eat, too, or you'll get as cranky as Henry." Savannah poked his ribs.

"Thank you." He patted his flat stomach. "My stomach agrees. I know just the place."

CHAPTER 10

IT WASN'T STRIDING ALONG A MOUNTAIN trail, but the look on Savannah's face when she had held Nippy made it all worth it. If Michael had his way, they'd be miles away from the crowds with the mountain birds as their only companions and not driving through one of the most well-known tourist attractions in Canada. Time with Savannah had changed his mind about sightseeing this way. He'd endure the crowds all week if it meant having her by his side.

Maybe in time, he'd break down Savannah's mental barriers against adventure in the great outdoors. Perhaps he'd one day scale the emotional barriers, too. Still, the glow of happiness on her face all the way through lunch had caused answering warmth inside his chest that he couldn't blame on the pizza they'd just eaten.

They were driving along River Road toward the heart of the Niagara Falls tourist area. On his own, he'd avoid the commercialized attractions. Tall casinos and hotels towered above them as they made their way down the well-tended parkway. Thankfully, the Tuesday crowds were subdued compared with those keen to view the famous waterfall on the weekend.

"Ready for the boat tour?"

Savannah tore her gaze away from the river. "Excuse me?"

"There are two options. We take the boat tour from this side today, or we wait and go on the other one when we head back over the border."

"No, no. Let's do it today while we're here."

That decided, he steered toward the parking lot. Baskets hung from the lampposts and overflowed with red and white flowers, adding to the manicured feel of the place. Elaborate floral displays also graced the median, in contrast to the rustic locations he preferred. The stone wall and wrought-iron decorative railing along the edge of the gorge kept the camera-toting tourists safe.

"Ever been on a boat?"

"I haven't, and it's about time I did. Even though I'm afraid I'll suffer from seasickness, I've got to give it a go."

He admired her willingness to take a tiny step toward risk, glad he was the one adding one more memory to their list. He raised an eyebrow and gave her a sideways look. "You mean, before you get old and decrepit."

"You are much older than I am, McCann."

"Ouch. That hurt." He grabbed his chest like he'd been shot in the heart. "I'm only eight months older. So, go easy."

They drove past the Queen Victoria Place teeming with people who sought nourishment at the restaurant and shelter from the blazing sun. Savannah eyed the gift shop, which likely had keepsake mugs and trinkets. He groaned at the thought of swimming upstream against the tourists unloading from those red double-decker sightseeing buses and the monstrous ones with their fancy air-conditioning. But he'd battle the crowds if it made Savannah smile the way she had at the bird aviary.

As they pulled into the lineup for paid parking, Savannah rummaged in her purse and produced her credit card.

He held up his hand. "I got it, thanks."

"Oh, no, you don't. You still have to dig your wallet out of your shorts. You've done so much already. I'm paying for parking."

"Fine, but dinner tonight is on me. I'm particularly looking forward to dessert."

"There you go, thinking of your stomach again. We've just had lunch."

"I'm a grown—"

"Man. You keep saying so." Savannah leaned across him and handed the attendant her card. A whiff of her perfume surrounded him, quelling his argument, while the attendant swiped the card and handed it back to Savannah.

The boom lifted, and Michael was grateful for the size of the car as he maneuvered between two badly parked SUVs.

Maybe driving a tiny car wouldn't be so bad after all. He easily parked Savannah's car between the bulky cars.

Michael struggled out of the tiny car seat and closed the door. As he stretched his arms above his head, his spine cracked and clicked into place. He glanced at his watch. There was just enough time to see the falls from the walkway before getting on the boat. Where was Savannah? He bent and peered through the window. Savannah sat stiffly in the passenger seat, frowning like she was trying to solve the problems of the world. She didn't move.

He trotted around to her side of the car, opened the door, and peeked in. "Are you okay?" Had he upset her?

"Yes. Let's go see the epic Horseshoe Falls." Savanah hopped out and strutted toward the crossing. She reminded him of one of those pheasants they'd just seen at the bird place. He couldn't keep the grin off his face.

He followed her across the parkway toward the mist rising above roaring water. He picked up his pace, hoping for a glimpse of her face in the moment she caught sight of the iconic Niagara Falls. Would Savannah be in awe of the sheer volume of the cascading water the way he'd been the first time he saw it?

They dodged families with strollers and couples walking hand in hand. Michael found the perfect spot to admire the view. Savannah said nothing as the water roared past them, her expression unreadable.

The wind blew fine spray their way, a welcome reprieve from the heat rising from the concrete walkway in the full sunshine.

"So? What do you think?"

"I'm thinking how crazy anyone would be to go over there in a barrel. Look at that volume of water."

"Didn't I tell you? We've got tickets for a barrel ride after the boat ride."

Savannah's eyes widened, and her face drained of color.

His stomach sank at the look of sheer terror on her face. "I'm kidding." He grabbed her hand to steady her. "I'm sorry."

She yanked her hand away and mock punched his arm, but there was no smile to ease his regret. "Don't scare me like that."

"I didn't mean to upset you."

"You should know there are a few things I'm afraid of. Danger like that is one of them. And spiders."

"Well, now, I'm with you on the spider thing." He shuddered.

He tilted her chin so their eyes met. The breeze tousled her hair around her face, and he tucked a stray golden lock behind her ear. The vulnerability he found in her eyes brought out his protective instincts. "I promise, I will never ever put you in danger. I mean it."

"No barrels and no dangling off mountains."

"No barrels."

"And..." She waved her hand in a circle, coaxing words from him.

"No rock-face climbing." He'd allow her that. Until she experienced a soothing sunrise or a magnificent sunset by his side from a mountain, she'd never really know how the majesty of God's creation affected him. Calmed him. He held her gaze, willing her to put aside her fears and hear him out. "All you have to do is trust me."

She opened her mouth and then clamped her lips in a tight line. Had he given her enough reason to trust him?

"You can trust me." And she could trust God. Was she ready to hear that?

She stared deep into his eyes, searching for a promise. "Can I?"

"When have I ever let you down?" *When I wasn't brave enough to tell you how I felt about you?* He shoved that thought way down, where it belonged. No use rehashing the past. Not now when she was inches away from him, her eyes flickering with emotion like a black-and-white silent movie with no subtitles. He could only guess what it all meant.

Savannah looked down and seemed to be studying her toes. "What happens after dinner tonight?"

What was her point? She wasn't kidding when she said she wasn't spontaneous. Was she one of those types who insisted their whole itinerary be preapproved? "I don't know. We'll have to see if they turn the lights on during the week this time of the year. If they do, then you have to see the falls at night, too. They're quite something."

She glanced away. "Have you, um… Where are we staying tonight?"

Ah, so that was it. She was worried about sharing a room with him. "I've booked two rooms at a B & B. Okay?"

When would his high school reputation stop coming back to haunt him? She'd noticed his improved physique, but had she figured out his change of heart? Did she really think he would take advantage of a grieving widow? His actions would have to speak louder than his words this time.

Savannah nodded, and the held breath whooshed from her lips. "Wonderful. Thanks for making this easier for me. I don't know how to explain what it's like to overthink every decision. I'm always on hyperalert." Her voice wobbled and she reached for his hand. "It's like when Nick died, the rug was yanked from under my feet and I'm still crawling around on the floor, trying to find my glasses."

He pulled her to him and wrapped her in his arms. His heart ached for her pain. He'd do whatever it took to see Savannah happy again for more than just one day.

Forever.

Even if it meant giving up mountain climbing.

* * * *

Savannah had never seen anything so amazing or felt such a surge of power. Her squeal earned her some pointed looks from the sea of red-poncho-wearing passengers on the lower deck of their vessel, as if they could hear her over the squawking seagulls flying above them. Spray from the cascading water hung in the air. The misty colors reminded her of God's promise after the Flood.

She turned to Michael, cupping her hand around her mouth. "Look at the rainbow!" The shuddering roar of the engine working against the surge of emerald water almost drowned out her voice.

Michael nodded. He pulled his poncho hood back over his head, then tucked the wild strands of his hair into it. She was beginning to like the longer hair on him—as long as he didn't put it into a man bun. Drops of water slid down the few uncovered strands and dripped onto her face. She blinked; then Michael swiped the drops away with his fingertips, smoothed back a lock of hair that had stuck to her face, and tucked it into her hood. His body heat warmed her, and his presence steadied her in a way she couldn't explain. That she didn't want to explain.

"How much closer do we get?"

His face was inches from her ear. "As close as you like." The look on his face earned him a swat. Was he flirting?

"I meant, how close do we get to the falls?" All this yelling made her throat hoarse.

"I don't know. I've never been on this boat before."

"What?"

"I said, I've never been on this—"

Savannah held up her hand. "I heard you, but I'm surprised."

Michael leaned in. Their slick ponchos stuck together. "I thought you'd like it, so…here we are."

She grinned up at him like a kid with a chocolate-dipped ice-cream cone—with sprinkles. He was entirely too good to her. She really was going to have to think of a way to repay his kindness.

"Do you think we can get to the railing?" Any more yelling, and she was going to lose her voice for sure. She craned her neck to see around the stocky man holding a toddler in front of her.

"Give me your hand." She put her hand in his and relished the feel of his warmth and strength.

Michael slid past and pulled her behind him. His bulk cleared the way like a snowplow in January. He politely weaseled their way to the perfect spot on the pointed bow of the boat because she'd asked him to. He knew just how to make her feel treasured.

The air currents whipped at their faces as the boat strained to get closer to the raging cascade. Her cold fingers curled around the slippery railing, and she held on. Frigid waves of spray lashed the river ferry and took her breath away. The rolling waters beneath them pushed the boat around like a cork bobbing under the stream of a faucet in a bathtub. Except the steadying presence of Michael beside her allowed her to enjoy the moment and not be automatically on high alert. Maybe if she trusted God in the same way, she'd begin to live unafraid once again.

An average tourist on the deck above them may consider this merely a thrilling ride, but to her, it was a victory. She'd done something brave. She'd put aside her fear of the boat sinking—except for that little thought concerning how many people could get to the life jackets in time if this thing sank. She'd left her overanalyzing neurotic thoughts on the bank with the onlookers. And she'd taken a risk and made a memory. One small step for her, one giant step for her self-confidence.

Michael's reassuring hand in hers didn't hurt things, either, nor the way he'd tucked her dripping hair behind her ear with such tenderness earlier. The vibrations from the mechanical bowels of the boat sent tremors of excitement and anxiety through her. She was coming to life again.

The sound of the boat's engine changed as they drifted away from the falls and back toward the dock. Something had shifted deep inside her. An odd feeling of coming home when she was miles from her home—and from Point, her high school hometown. The whole way back to the riverbank, Michael's hand in hers warmed her right to the core. She lifted a silent prayer of thanks for this man who'd donned a red plastic poncho just to bring her a few moments of happiness. Was her heavenly Father using Michael to win her back?

They followed the stream of people off the boat, removed their ponchos, and deposited them in the bin. Savannah wiped her hands on her jeans. "We should have taken a photo on deck."

"What? And keep evidence of our drowned-rat look?"

"Are you saying I look like a drowned rodent?"

"Not at all. I was speaking for myself." A pair of dimples appeared along with his innocent smile. "Everyone else looked like drowned rats." His grin supported his argument. "You looked like a…a…"

"Come on. Think fast, McCann."

"A sea nymph."

"Impressive. That's some fast thinking. And where have you seen a sea nymph?"

"In movies." She almost cracked up at the smug look on his face.

"Not a book person?"

"Yeah, if they have pictures."

"As a librarian, I insist you read a proper book." She poked him. Keeping her serious face on was getting harder.

"As an adventurer, I insist that you live some of those experiences in your books." His voice held a measure of teasing, but his face, inches away, had lost its smile and gained a raised eyebrow.

"You don't get wet reading about sea nymphs." She held his gaze. She would not back down. The adventures she'd embarked on via the pages of hundreds of books took her to places she wouldn't have dared go in real life.

"You also don't feel as alive as you did just now."

"True." Their gazes held, an unspoken understanding passing between them. What adventures lay in store for them for the rest of the week? This boat trip cost her a measure of courage—all the bravery she was likely to muster—but Michael could have other ideas. Maybe he'd be happy with the wax museum and a wine tour? As long as it posed no risk to her person, she was game. Maybe by the end of the week, she'd have him reading. What sort of book would he—

"What are you cooking up in that smart brain of yours?"

"Why, nothing at all, McCann. Nothing at all." Nose in the air, she stalked past him, squeezing the water from her damp ponytail. After humming all the way along the walkway back to the elevator, she broke into a tone-deaf version of a song from a musical about washing men out of one's hair when Michael caught up with her.

After the second time around, she laughed at his dejected look. "I'm kidding!"

"Don't scare me like that, little sea nymph. Now, let's get some dinner."

She shook her head. "Do you ever think about anything else?"

"I'm not answering that. And since I'm buying, let's go fancy."

Changing the subject, was he? "How fancy?"

"Did you pack a dress?"

A million butterflies had invaded her stomach. "A girl *always* packs a dress." Aside from the reunion, she hadn't dressed up in a long time. "Maybe I'll even add lipstick to the mix."

Michael's eyebrows danced. His eyes sparkled with mischief, the laugh lines around his eyes more pronounced. "You're really living it up, huh?"

"Wait and see. Now, come on. It's a long walk to the car." A girl had to keep some surprises up her sleeve.

She hoped that wherever Michael had chosen for them to stay had a large tub in which she could soak before dinner. They were only halfway back to the car by the time they went by the copper-roofed buildings they'd passed earlier and her feet hurt. The roofs were once shiny copper, now tarnished to a greenish gray—they reminded her of her life. Once happy, now tarnished with sadness. Yet Michael walked by her side, at the ready to help her buff it up once again.

Gratitude filled her wounded heart. The first day of their escapade to Canada had already exceeded her expectations, but maybe the best was yet to come?

CHAPTER 11

THE ELEVATOR ROSE TO THE TOP floor of the upscale hotel, and Savannah's stomach sank. When Michael had said fancy, he'd meant *fan-cy*. The luxurious touches were everywhere, from the plush carpet under her feet in the foyer to the lavish floral arrangements on the shiny tabletops. She was surprised they hadn't managed to squeeze one into the elevator. The piped music intended to soothe nerves wasn't working for her.

At the B & B, she'd put on her red lipstick. It was too much, so she'd grabbed a wad of tissues and rubbed it off. By the time Michael had knocked on her door, her lips were dry and swollen and she'd been forced to reapply the lipstick in haste to hide the red stain. She'd mistakenly bought that twenty-four-hour stuff, and it didn't come off easily. She must look like a clown with extra collagen.

Why had she gotten into knots about lipstick anyway? *What was I thinking when I said I'd add lipstick to the mix?* It's not like she was flirting. *This isn't a date, is it?* The flutters in her stomach intensified. She couldn't be on a date—with Michael. *It's just dinner. A fancy dinner with a kind, albeit handsome, man. Friend. Man friend.*

"Hope you're hungry. I checked the menu online and it's a three-course meal."

Michael's chatter pulled her back to the present. Her belly was in knots. So no, not hungry. Time to divert attention from herself. "You clean up well, McCann."

And he had. Michael looked dashing in his jacket-and-jeans ensemble. Thankfully, there was no man bun; instead, he'd tied his hair back in a neat ponytail at the base of his neck just above his collar. A look she rather liked. He'd even gone as far as wearing a tie.

"Why, thank you. You don't look so bad yourself."

She'd only packed two dresses for her trip. The green dress she'd worn to the reunion had punch stains on it. So the only option she'd had was to wear the black dress, and she'd smartened it up with a string of pearls and some earrings. Time to set the record straight. "Just so you're clear, this isn't a date."

"I hope not." He stuffed his hands in his pockets. "Matter of fact, I don't date."

Wow. Not what she'd expected. Relief flooded her. This wasn't a date.

He doesn't date? Interesting. The elevator dinged and the doors opened. Michael's hand on the small of her back only intensified the quivering in her already-disoriented stomach.

"The restaurant is this way." Michael nudged her forward.

"Can you lead the way? I don't like walking first when I don't know where we're going."

"Uh, sure." Whatever his thoughts about her unorthodox request, he kept them to himself. With a deep breath, she followed him along the mirrored hallway. She kept her eyes ahead to avoid seeing her swollen lips or pale face. Or her disastrous hairstyle. Michael might get away with a ponytail at dinner, but she couldn't. Not even the how-to-do-an-updo video tutorial she'd watched on her phone had saved the day. If only they'd gone for hamburgers at a drive-through.

The carpet gave way to a shiny navy floor. Above the entrance was an archway fashioned like a wave, as if a surge had made it into the restaurant and solidified into painted white plaster over the doorway. She half expected Neptune himself to welcome them in, trident and all, except it was a stylish hostess who took their names and led them through the foyer into the restaurant.

"Wait until you see the view," Michael said over his shoulder above the clippety-clop of her heels.

The hostess led the way through the restaurant with soothing white decor accented with vivid blue, dotted with groups of people laughing and chatting, lending a festive ambience. The modern, clean feel of the restaurant promised a night to remember. Okay, maybe this was better than a drive-through. The hostess stopped at a row of azure tufted velvet booths that overlooked the iconic waterfall through massive windows that stretched from floor to ceiling.

Savannah caught sight of the view beyond and gawked at the majesty of it all, forgetting her nerves. "Breathtaking."

"I knew you'd love it."

She tore her gaze from the scenery. Michael stood beside the booth, waiting for her to scoot in first. She settled across from him on the plush bench. After handing them a pair of menus, the hostess listed the specials of the day and left them alone.

The bottle of sparkling water arrived. Michael poured it into the cobalt-blue wine glasses on top of the crisp white linen tablecloth. He raised his glass. "To adventures."

She couldn't say a thing around the lump in her throat and opted to clink her glass against his, blinking back happy tears.

"I know. I'm rather overwhelming, aren't I?" Michael winked at her and reached for her hand.

"You are so good to me." A fleeting thought about why this gorgeous and caring man didn't date flitted through her mind. Any woman who would turn down a man like him would have to be crazy, deluded—and blind.

"Hey, all part of the experience." His fingers curled around her hand, gently belying his words. "We've got plenty of time to enjoy our dinner before the fireworks begin at ten."

"How are we going to top that? We still have the rest of the week. I think we've already hit the jackpot."

"I think we can come up with something." His gaze swept over her face and not the view outside.

What did that mean? Before she could ask, the fresh-faced waiter appeared and Michael withdrew his hand. The entrées listed on the menu stimulated her appetite. She ordered the Caesar salad starter and herb-crusted chicken, then handed back the menu.

"Would you like to order your dessert now or later, ma'am?" The waiter, pencil poised, leaned in her direction.

"Later, I think. Thank you." At that, he stood up straight with a disapproving frown and turned to Michael.

"And for you, sir."

"I'll have the crab salad to start, followed by the Angus steak. And I'm going to order my dessert now." Michael's eyes shone with mischief. "I'll have the doughnuts with the hazelnut filling."

The waiter bowed and then sashayed toward the kitchen.

Michael leaned closer to her. "He obviously takes his job seriously."

"I thought he was going to give me a lecture for not ordering dessert there for a moment," she whispered.

"No dessert? That's not like you."

"What do you mean, McCann?" She raised an eyebrow before gazing at the view. "I can't make up my mind between the carrot cake and the peanut butter pâté. That's all."

"So, get both."

She snapped her gaze back. "Not in this dress."

"We'll walk it off tomorrow." He leaned back, and his eyes lingered on her for a moment longer than she was comfortable with.

What was he thinking? On second thought, maybe she didn't want to know. She could feel her face heating, probably close to the same shade as her smudged lipstick. "Is that your solution for everything? Walking it off?"

He took a sip of the bubbly water. "To be honest, it is. Walking clears my head. With each step into a hike, my troubles seem to shrink."

"What kinds of troubles do you have in particular?" There was something different about him that she couldn't quite figure out. "You seem to have it all together."

"Thank you. It's all a ruse. I'm not perfect, for starters."

"I know." She tried to suppress her smile. "You are horribly flawed." And suitably wonderful, but no need to tell him that.

"Thanks for noticing." His grin faltered. He dropped his gaze to the napkin beside his plate and fiddled with a folded corner. "Here's the thing. My work isn't just mundane clerical work." He lifted his hand. "No offense."

"None taken. It must be quite something to fly off at a moment's notice because someone's gotten themselves in a tight spot."

"And usually, a tight spot is the best-case scenario. It isn't always that easy." His mirthless voice brought home the reality that although she'd once faced Nick's death by his side, Michael faced the frailty of life every time he was called out—alone. Which also meant that if she opened her heart a crack, she ran the risk of losing him the same way she'd lost Nick. Still, Michael took his job seriously, and his Good Samaritan ways endeared him to her. It was like a tug-of-war with her heart.

"I'm sorry. I didn't mean to joke about it." Did he have someone he could talk to and process the things he saw on the job? How many times had his heart been wounded by the trauma? She reached for his hand. "How do you deal with casualties?"

"It's tough. We're trained to deal with it. They require us to debrief and see a therapist after any incident that doesn't end well. But still, sometimes I wrestle with guilt, wondering if I could have done just a little more to affect the outcome. After years of doing this, I realize no matter how many times I revisit each instance, there's only so much I can do. The rest is out of my hands. And in God's..."

Her heart ached for him and his bravery. She squeezed his hand to provide what little moral support she could. "Does your work have anything to do with why you don't date?"

"Yes and no." His lopsided grin made an appearance. She tore her gaze away. She was pushing it, but she wanted to understand why a handsome man like him was still single.

"Yes, because..."

"Yes, because most women aren't able to separate who I am from what I do."

Her gaze lingered on their joined hands resting on the table. She barely managed to hold back a wince. So, she wasn't the first woman to think so. She'd have to chew on that concept later when she had time. "And the 'no' part?"

"Maybe I'll tell you one day."

She extracted her hand from his, and folding her arms, she sat back. "Keeping secrets, huh?"

"It's not really a secret, my little blue bird." A mysterious smile appeared on his face, almost like he was daring her to guess. "At least, I don't think it will be one for long."

"You're right. I intend to weasel it out of you."

* * * *

The fireworks over Niagara Falls might have been scheduled for ten, but sitting across from Savannah in her finery caused all sorts of fireworks within him. Just the way she said things in her own way, observing the world with her unique brand of humor and intelligence, made her irresistible. She'd stunned him speechless in that black dress. And her hair pinned in some sort of twisted knot on top of her head, tendrils framing her face with kissable red lips, wasn't helping, either. The ensemble was only adding to her appeal and making his pulse race. He'd have to play it cool, like he did in the midst of a high-stakes rescue.

Michael stabbed his fork into her moist, dense cake. "Are you sure you don't want some doughnuts since I'm tasting your carrot cake?"

"I don't like doughnuts."

"Really?" He pointed his cake-laden fork in her direction. "Not even freshly fried ones with chocolate-hazelnut sauce inside?"

Savannah shook her head. "No, thanks. Go ahead and taste the carrot cake. Best I've tasted."

He gave the morsel a sniff. The scent of cinnamon masked any smell of cooked carrot. It didn't smell bad, but he wrinkled his nose anyway. "Vegetables shouldn't be in cake."

"Don't tell me you've never had carrot cake with cream cheese frosting?"

"Nope. This is a first. And I usually have my cream cheese on bagels." He eyed the cake. Savannah's laugh set off another explosion inside him. He hadn't experienced sparks of emotion like this since they'd hung out in high school. The more time he spent with Savannah and the more she let down her guard, the more his heart threatened to burst with those old feelings he'd had for her as a teenager.

Only this time, they were stronger. Reignited. More than just a crush. It was like the reunion lit the fuse and now he was in danger of displaying his feelings across the sky. He feared letting her see just how hard he was falling for her — again. She wasn't ready.

She'd told him earlier that this wasn't a date. And it wasn't. It was more.

He noticed the sparkle of candlelight off her rings. Nick's rings. No, he'd rather focus on listening to her laugh, seeing her come back to life. This was him watching Savannah unfurl like the rosebuds in the vase between them on the table. Even if it meant he had to eat carrot cake.

"Are you laughing at me, sea nymph?"

"You bet. You're looking at the cake as if it's a battered cockroach."

After one last look at it, he popped the cake in his mouth and his taste buds didn't protest. "Not bad."

"See. If you hadn't tried it, you'd be missing out."

"All right. So, does that mean you'll try something new, too?"

She raised her eyebrows. "Like what? I already went on the boat, and that was scary enough at first."

"I don't know. I saw on the website they have a dinner where you eat blindfolded in the dark from a specially prepared menu."

"Oh no, Michael. My mind would concoct all sorts of worst-case scenarios. The joys of an overactive imagination."

"Relax. They had it in March. We missed out. But my point is—this week is all about no regrets. No what-ifs." Was he willing to take a risk and tell her all his secrets? No, she wasn't ready to hear them yet.

"Agreed. You haven't told me what your regrets in life were. Care to share?" She sipped her coffee without leaving a trace of red lipstick on the rim of the cup.

His biggest regret was letting Nick be the only one to ask her out. "The things in my life that bring regret are not so much things I did. More like things I didn't do. Words I should have said. Moments I should have cherished. It's funny, but in hindsight, I see them all clearly. It's harder to recognize an opportunity you're missing while you're in it."

Outside, the light had begun to fade to subdued hues. The candles in the restaurant cast a warm glow. The waiter stopped at their table with the coffeepot and topped off their cups, then left them to their desserts.

Michael snagged another forkful of cake, waved it around, and changed the subject before he ruined their evening by airing his feelings. It was too soon. But in the meantime, he had the chance to delve into more of what made this incredible woman tick. "What would you still like to accomplish in life?"

"I know it sounds odd, but I want to learn to give myself permission to live again. For years, Nick's condition meant our priorities were treatments, surgeries, recovery, and surviving. If there were things I wanted to do, I'd look at them in light of whether they mattered more than being with Nick. When compared to that, everything else seemed frivolous and unimportant. I hardly dared to plan too far ahead." Her eyes shimmered in the candlelight. "There were many hours of waiting in doctors' rooms, a few trips to the ER, and, of course, those daylong chemo sessions. The only thing that really kept me from climbing the walls was having a book tucked into my purse at all times."

"I wish I'd known." So much for no regrets. Here, he felt the pain of losing contact with his friend by running off to be a hero to strangers, meanwhile becoming a stranger to those who'd mattered most—like his grandmother and the Sandersons.

"I do, too. The more Nick needed me, the less appealing everyday activities seemed. Even a trip to the local coffee shop on my own seemed self-indulgent, unnecessary."

"And now, do you still have your nose in a book most of the time?" Did she have one tucked in her purse just in case their evening went south?

"I know you think I hide behind my job and my literature, but I also do research."

"Uh-huh." Popping the cake into his mouth, he raised an eyebrow.

"Well, I did some research for the bird-watchers in Ithaca. I also help those who delve into their family history dig up archived materials. The historical society is closely linked with the library archives. Not everything can be found online."

He aimed his fork at her plate again, but Savannah pulled it out of reach and pointed her fork right back.

"Back off, McCann. For someone who didn't think vegetables belonged in cake, I'm in danger of losing most of it. You're not having another bite." Her face didn't convey the sting her words suggested, and as she nibbled the cake, her eyes twinkled.

"Research, huh?" Michael couldn't resist teasing her. "I thought you sat around all day, reading those sappy romances."

"What do you mean?" A crease formed between her brows.

"You know, those books where all the guys can't keep their shirts on and miraculously have six-pack abs while the ladies are all red lipped and swooning."

Savannah covered her red lips with her fingers.

He'd noticed her lips and spent most of the evening trying to forget their appeal. "Not that there's anything wrong with red lips. Yours look just fine." More than fine.

"My tastes are more in line with the classics and contemporary romance."

Time to poke the bear. "So, you don't read the books in the discount department store with half-naked men clutching their women?" He raised an eyebrow, leaning forward to better see the emotions that were bound to flit across her face. "Aren't those considered contemporary romance?"

"Usually, they're historical." Her cheeks turned an adorable pink. "You'll find the man is a duke or something. The ones with modern titles are usually millionaires. But those aren't the only romance books out there. The ones I read are different. They're heartwarming, and I like happy endings."

"Who doesn't?"

"You'd be surprised. Some authors love to kill off their most beloved character."

"Okay, I bet the fans love that. What about reading biographies or nonfiction?"

"I do. Especially when doing research." She set her fork down and steepled her fingers. "Look at it this way— when you're working, you have to hike and climb and rescue people. You do what you have to do for your job. It's probably not the same as when you go on a hike for leisure. Right?"

"Right. Worlds apart, almost." He picked up his fork and aimed to snag some more cake. She pulled the plate away again and shoveled the last bite into her mouth. He could almost see her lining up her case against his misconceptions. He sat back, ready for her comeback.

"So, it's like this. When I read for pleasure, it's to relax—to escape, almost. Life is messy enough as it is. Fiction is safer, and I know I'll get my happy ending. Every. Time."

The irony of their conversation wasn't lost on him. He'd spent his lifetime checking out emotionally to avoid pain. From the time his parents died to when he'd left Point to run from his feelings for Savannah, through his subsequent relationships when they didn't measure up to her, until now.

He kept his feelings for her a secret, as he'd always done. Except the more time he spent with her, the more the dread of losing her trumped his fear of getting his heart broken. However, until the balance tipped, he'd keep his lips sealed. Especially since he still hadn't reconciled himself to the fact that she'd been Nick's wife and that she'd always compare them. Maybe not intentionally, but how could she not?

Until he was sure she could love him back, he'd have to be content to test the waters. But if the waters were calm and welcoming, assuring him she was ready, there would be no holding him back. If she would have him— she'd have all of him, heart and soul. The clinking of silverware faded as he held her gaze. Time to dip his toe in the water.

"Savannah, you can still have your happy ending." His heart thumped in his chest. He was taking a chance by bringing this up so early in their time together. But he couldn't keep his thoughts inside any longer.

She stared out into the dark, where the lights shone on the falls. "Maybe, if it's worth the risk."

"The risk of heartbreak?" He understood. To gain a happy ending meant risking rejection, being vulnerable and putting your heart out there. He could run headlong into a dangerous mountain rescue with his emotions trained and buttoned down, but he wasn't sure he'd fare as well when it came time to baring his soul to Savannah. At least, not yet.

He put his fork down, no longer interested in his dessert. Or hers. "Do you ever wish you could turn back time and make a different choice?"

"Sometimes." An impish grin emerged. "I wish I'd bought an extra pair of jeans on sale last week." She sipped her coffee and looked at him with intent. "Are you asking whether I'd still have married Nick, knowing how it would end? Probably. I mean, nothing I could've done would've saved Nick. Not even my prayers."

Sounded like her faith had been shaken. Understandably so, but his heart still ached for her.

Savannah gazed into the darkness as the lights twinkled below. "I'm sorry. I didn't want to dampen the mood. It's just that sometimes I miss him so much it is a physical ache."

"Would you like to leave?"

She sat back, her eyes misty, and shook her head. "What about the fireworks?"

His heart skipped a beat. "You want to stay?"

She nodded, blinked back her tears, and reached for his hand. "No regrets, remember?"

"No regrets." He clung to the hope that, by the end of the week, they'd still hold to their pact.

CHAPTER 12

SAVANNAH HAD LOVED THE MASSIVE FIREPLACES and bookshelves in the various rooms of the century home B & B during the tour after they checked in, but now, the mysterious creaks and groans from the structure after midnight—not so much. She couldn't blame it on her overactive imagination. There was a distinctive creak on the stairs. Not once but three times—closer with each skulking footfall.

She peeled the covers off and wound her fingers around the corner of her pillow. Not the best weapon, but it was all she had. Lowering one foot to the floor, she edged off the bed. Her other foot touched the cool wooden floor, and she eased herself upright, careful not to stand on a noisy floorboard.

Her lamp was on, but she craved more light. Light meant security—or at least, the illusion of it. The footsteps in the hallway stalled outside her door, and she froze. Her heart thumped so loud that whoever was out there must have been able to hear it. She fought to quiet her breathing.

From her position next to the bed, she spotted a shadow through the space under the door. Clutching her pillow, she eyed the distance to the adjoining bathroom. If the doorknob turned, she'd lunge for it and lock herself in. Seconds dragged, feeling like hours.

At last, the sinister steps receded back down the stairs. She stood there for quite a while, not knowing what had just happened. By the time she climbed back into bed, her feet were like ice blocks. She wished Nick were there to warm them. He used to ask whether she was trying to give him frostbite, but she'd just snuggle closer and tell him to stop being a baby.

Her heartbeat returned to its predictable rhythm. Memories of Nick and their life together ushered her into dreamland.

Early the next morning, Savannah cornered the owner of the B & B before breakfast in the dining room. "Are Michael and I the only guests in the house?"

"Yes. Just you two." Beverly set a basket of croissants on the sideboard. Her smile while serving them an early breakfast was the same as last night when she was locking up after a long day.

Savannah pulled out her chair and sat down, marveling at Beverly's exuberance. The slender woman must be in her late sixties, although she carried her age well. She wore black culottes and a sophisticated white blouse accented with a string of pearls. Her salt-and-pepper hair was slicked back in a bun at the nape of her neck, and her coral-colored lipstick accentuated her warm smile. How did she do it? Savannah wasn't comfortable with the company of others for too long, let alone strangers. She was trying hard to stifle a yawn, while the older women bustled around.

Beverly paused beside Savannah's chair. "However, we're expecting another guest tonight." Beverly put a plate of rye toast on the table and turned to Savannah. "Why do you ask?"

"Oh, it's nothing. I thought I heard some strange noises last night."

"Really?" Their hostess ducked back into the kitchen through a pair of squeaky swinging doors while Savannah eyed the jar of strawberry jam in front of her. She spread the linen napkin on her lap to catch any wayward dollops of the jam she intended to slather on those delicious-looking croissants. Hopefully, Beverly had gone to fetch the coffee.

The aroma of freshly brewed coffee wafted through the doors and taunted Savannah's senses as Beverly walked back in with a pitcher of orange juice. She moved around the table and set the jug down in front of the vacant table setting, where presumably Michael would sit. "You saw us lock up after you and Michael got in, but Bruno and I have a cat. Perhaps you heard her? Her name is Skittle."

It would have to be a very large cat to make the noises she'd heard. Was she paranoid? She shook it off. Her suspicions faded with the arrival of a new day.

She didn't believe in ghosts, so who could have lurked outside her door? If it happened again tonight, she'd ask Michael whether he'd heard anything from his room on the first floor. His room was next to the staircase on the level below hers, so if anyone was snooping around, he'd know.

Savannah glanced around to make sure they were still alone. "Do you have anything local to satisfy the more adventurous among us?" She was referring to Michael, but she'd keep that snippet of information to herself for now.

She needed to do something to thank him for his above-and-beyond duties as her tour guide and companion. After last night's fancy dinner, it was her turn to pay for something extravagant. But what did one get a man who didn't value material things? He was more into experiences.

A dark-haired man wearing a chef's hat and apron and an impressive mustache popped through the swinging doors and deposited plates of mouthwatering buttermilk and blueberry pancakes on the sideboard. "Good morning." He nodded and disappeared back into the kitchen.

"That's Bruno. Have you met?"

Savannah giggled. "I think we just did."

Beverly scooted the vase of daisies over to make room for a basket of condiments. "Did you try the zip-lining along the river?"

Savannah fought a sudden rush of dizziness. "No, and please, don't mention that in front of Michael. I'm looking for something less petrifying."

Beverly tapped her finger against her lips. "Let me ask Bruno. He might know." She ducked back into her kitchen, presumably to speak to her husband.

As the newlywed couple who'd been on their way out had shared yesterday afternoon while Michael was taking care of their check-in, Beverly and Bruno had run their B & B from their Victorian-style century home together for years. Between lingering looks at each other, which had Savannah blushing, they'd told her that Serendipity B & B's doors were open to visitors all year round except in December and January. That's when the owners flew off to join the rest of the snowbirds in Florida.

Soon, Beverly returned, a plate of bacon in hand. "Bruno says there's an ultimate couple's escape and spa package at the Fallsview Spa." She winked at Savannah as she set the bacon down next to the croissants.

"Anything suitable for *non-couple* friends?" Savannah hoped Beverly would get her meaning. The way Beverly eyed her, she wasn't hopeful.

"In that case, you might want to check out the antique bookstore and the orchard next door. There are also various carriage rides in Niagara-on-the-Lake for all kinds of *friends* to enjoy." Savannah liked the idea of an activity that would save her feet. Beverly glanced at Savannah's wedding rings and raised her eyebrows. She wasn't hiding her skepticism.

Savannah raised her chin. "I've known him almost all my life. We are just friends." A picture of his twinkling eyes as he stole mouthfuls of her cake caused her to hold her breath.

"Of course, dear. We hear it often enough. Then, they come back a year later on their honeymoon." Beverly had the gall to wink. Again.

Savannah's cheeks burned. She scooted her chair back. She paced to the sideboard as if in search of those croissants, waving her napkin as she went. Perhaps Beverly wouldn't notice her embarrassment. She wasn't naive about romance, but she had a hard time putting Michael into that picture. At least, with her. Although he might make a wonderful husband, she didn't think he'd settle for a sedate life. Michael was intense, passionate about his profession, and altogether too good for her. She wouldn't hold him back, nor could she ever ask him to give anything up just because of her fears. So, yes, good old friends. It could never be more. Besides, there was the question of whether they shared the same faith, as shaky as hers was. She grabbed the basket of croissants and turned back to the table.

"Michael's one of my oldest and dearest friends. He was also my husband's best friend."

"Was?" Beverly busied herself readjusting the already-perfect flowers.

When was the woman going to bring out the coffee? "No, no, it's not what you think." Savannah's jaw ached from the polite smile pasted on her face.

"You don't have to explain anything to me." Beverly opened the jar of homemade jam and set it back on the table. "It's none of my business, dear."

Michael's approaching footfalls cut their conversation short. She was caught between wanting to explain and digging in her heels, in protest against

Beverly's foregone conclusions. Savannah set the basket of croissants on the table as Michael bustled in.

"Good morning, sunshine." He moved in and kissed her on the cheek. "Allow me." He pulled back her chair and looked ever so pleased with himself. *Allow me?*

Beverly would never believe they were *just friends* if he carried on like that. And why did he have to look so handsome in his T-shirt and smell better than the bacon and croissants? Beverly's questions had tied her stomach in knots. Michael maneuvered her chair into place as she sat down, and then, he bounded around to his side of the table.

"Morning, Beverly." He drew in an exaggerated breath. "Everything smells wonderful. I'm famished."

"Did you have an extra helping of vitamins this morning?" Savannah kept all trace of chirpiness out of her voice. No need to fuel Beverly's suspicions.

"Ah! I see I caught you precaffeine." Michael's gaze flicked to Beverly's face. "She's like a bear with a sore paw if she doesn't get enough coffee before nine."

"Right." Beverly swiveled and headed for the kitchen. "I'll get the coffeepot."

"I'm not grouchy. I'm just not as full of jumping beans as you."

"I'm looking forward to our day. I hope you wore your walking shoes, sunshine."

Recalling yesterday's sore feet, she'd prepared better this time. They didn't exactly make the best fashion statement with her shorts, but comfort came first. "I did. There's a walk we can take to an antique bookstore close by. But can you keep the enthusiasm on the down low until after the coffee arrives?"

Michael shrugged. "Say 'Please.'"

"Pleeeeeease."

"Okay, I'll simmer down. First, pass me that bacon, will you?"

"Please."

"Touché." Not taking his eyes off her, he arranged his napkin on his lap. "Please. And thank you."

After nabbing a couple of pieces of crispy bacon, she passed the plate over.

Beverly entered with a steaming pot of coffee. "Safe to approach?" She grinned at Michael.

"Approach at your own risk," Michael said.

Savannah lobbed her linen napkin and hit him in the face, which sent his loose hair flying. His chuckle coaxed a smile from her lips. This man. What was she going to do without him once their week was over?

By four in the afternoon, she may have changed her mind about needing more adventures with him. Savannah hid behind Michael while he spoke to the coachman sitting on the carriage in front of a fancy colonial hotel. She was glad Beverly couldn't see this, because she could just imagine the smirk on the woman's face. The horse tossed his large head and snorted at her as if to mock her trepidation. She liked horses but from afar. And this massive white Clydesdale was one of the larger breeds.

It was her idea to go on a horse-drawn carriage ride, but it was Michael who suggested they drive to downtown Niagara-on-the-Lake. They'd spent all day exploring orchards, vineyards, and local attractions. She was more than ready to put her weary feet up.

But first, she had to get into the carriage without coming too close to those enormous hooves. Now that the reality was here, she questioned her own sanity. What had she been thinking?

Michael handed the man their fee and turned to her. "Ladies first."

She wiggled her finger at the substantial hindquarters still yards away. "I'd rather not get too close to them. Can you just"—she shoved Michael between her and the horse—"stand right there?"

He glanced over his shoulder, half smile on his face. "Why?"

"Have you seen the size of those hooves? They're as big as dinner plates."

Michael gave her that "I think you're overreacting" look, the one he'd always given her when she got herself all flustered. Nick had just frowned at her fears. Michael, however, had always been kind enough to humor her or joke about it—depending on how brave he felt at the time.

From his perch, the cloaked coachman held the long reins and a scary-looking whip. "No need to fear this gentle giant. Never kicked anyone in all my years."

She eyed the distance to the carriage, bending her knees like an Olympic sprinter waiting for the starter's gun to go off. She wouldn't take any chances.

Before she could execute her maneuver, Michael scooped her up, stepped into the open carriage, and deposited her on the white tufted seat. "We're in."

She could have sworn she heard the coachman mumble over the pounding of her heart, "About time."

Michael draped his arm along the back of the seat. She hesitated to snuggle in, but they were in a quaint old town, so might as well enjoy the full fairy-tale experience. Relaxing her muscles, she settled in beside him to enjoy the ride. His body heat warmed her, keeping the cool afternoon breeze at bay. She rested her hands on her thighs, conscious of how close they were.

He'd lifted her like she weighed as much as his backpack. She knew the truth. After all the delicious meals on this trip, she'd have to sign up at a gym when she got back home. Now, that would be a new experience. Maybe if she asked one of the ladies at work to join her, she'd be able to manage it.

"What's going on in that head of yours?"

Michael's breath, so close, activated an array of goose bumps all the way up to her shoulders. She rubbed her arms. "Oh, I was thinking about... Never mind."

Michael reached for the blanket to cover their exposed knees. She wasn't about to admit how snug the waistband of her shorts fit. He could eat all day and still look as gorgeous as a cover model. For all she knew, a six-pack hid under his shirt. She glanced at their legs under the blanket. His muscular thighs dwarfed her somewhat more jiggly ones. She steered her thoughts to safer ground. "Do you miss going on your runs?"

"What?"

"Well, the last time you ran was before we tried to eat waffles in Point."

His brow furrowed. "Why would you be thinking about that when we're in a beautiful carriage, touring the old part of town?"

"I'm sorry." She ignored the heat of his leg pressed against hers. "I got distracted."

"Come here." He tucked her under his arm and rubbed away the last of her goosebumps. "Better?"

"Yes, thank you." She smiled at him and met his gaze. In his eyes, she saw warmth and safety—and something else, which caused flutters in her belly.

"You can take in the view or gaze into my mesmerizing eyes," he said, lowering his voice. "I'd suggest choosing the eyes."

"While I admit I'm spellbound, it would be a waste of all that money you handed Mr. My-Horse-Never-Kicked-Anyone-Before if I spent the whole forty-five minutes looking at you."

She could feel his breath caressing her cheek, and her gaze darted to his lips. A lock of hair blew across his face, and she reached up to brush it away. He was rather striking to look at. The lines around his eyes implied a man who laughed often and loved life. "Besides, I can look at you anytime—for free."

"That you can, waffle woman." His eyes sparkled with mischief and eagerness.

The rhythmic *clip-clop-clip-clop* of the horse's hooves faded as they studied each other. In only a few days, he'd become one of the dearest people in her life again. She'd forgotten how much she'd missed him, and a surge of gratitude overwhelmed her.

"Thank you for..." Where did she begin to explain how much he meant to her? "For being you."

Michael swiped the escaped tear from her cheek with his thumb and kissed her forehead. "Happy?"

She nodded, managing a smile. He gathered her and held her while she fought to regain control of the emotions shuddering through her. There was nowhere she'd rather be. She leaned into him, the blanket pulled up to her waist. This was so like Michael, calm and rock solid, trustworthy, and—by the heartbeat thumping under her splayed hand—very much alive.

CHAPTER 13

*H*YDROGEN, *HELIUM, LITHIUM, BERYLLIUM, BORON, carbon, and was it nitrogen?* Going through the list was the only way Michael could forget the magnetic pull of the woman in his arms and how right she fit there. She made him a better man, and she inspired him to reach for more, to be more.

Reciting the periodic table wasn't working. He may have to recite the dictionary, too, if the frantic beating of his heart was any indication.

Reminding himself she was Nick's wife might work. Nick would have wanted him to take care of her, but Nick wouldn't approve of his current thoughts and feelings every time Savannah looked at him. Then again, they were both adults, and he wasn't the impulsive teenager she'd once known. Still, with every ounce of willpower, he fought against his dreams, holding them in check, before he did something stupid. Like kissing her. She was still mourning, and he'd give her the time she needed to heal.

"Beverly said there's an antique bookstore somewhere around here. Can we go?" Savannah angled her face to meet his gaze, her bright eyes doing crazy things to his insides.

"Sure. We may have enough time before the show starts."

Savannah sat up and leaned away from him. "What show?" He resisted the urge to tug her back into his arms since the distance was helping him regain his thoughts and self-control.

"When in Niagara-on-the-Lake, you absolutely have to catch a show at the Fineah Theater. I've phoned ahead and got tickets for tonight's show."

"Is it fancy? I can't go to a show in shorts." She waved a hand toward her covered legs. Legs he'd stolen way too many glances at today.

"We're having dinner before the show. But we'll drive back to the Serendipity B & B so you can freshen up first, so whatever you wear to the pub will be fine for the theater, too."

She settled back into his arms, and he rested his chin on her head. "I hope you like nineteenth-century plays."

"You mean sixteenth-century—if you mean Shakespeare?" She mumbled into his chest, a hint of laughter in her voice.

He shuddered. "Thankfully, none of those were on. The show starts at eight, and we're booked to see a play about a long-nosed musketeer and his stammering friend. They said there would be a sword fight or two."

Savannah popped up and grasped his shoulder. "I've read the play. I loved it. I saw the movie version with a French actor. Gérard someone. Have you seen it?"

"No, but the lady at the ticket office said something about musketeers. I thought it might be bearable." He'd been thankful for the lady's recommendations. He wasn't too familiar with the theater, but remembering that Savannah had been in the drama club, he figured she'd enjoy it.

Savannah wrinkled her nose. "If you feel that way, we don't have to go. We can go back to the B & B, and I'll beat you at chess."

"No, you won't. I've been practicing."

She released him and folded her arms. "With whom?"

"Ever heard of online chess?"

"It's not the same thing." She frowned and bit her lip. "Are you sure you want to go?"

"Yes."

Savannah's face was radiant. She craned her neck and kissed him on the cheek, then nodded. "Thank you," she whispered before snuggling back into the crook of his arm.

He gazed at the colorful gardens as they passed yet another inn. *Hydrogen, helium, lithium…*

* * * *

After a satisfying dinner, sitting in a theater chair may not have been the best idea. He shouldn't have finished the fries Savannah hadn't eaten. The lights dimmed and the curtain opened. He thought he'd have a hard time staying awake with a full stomach, but it wasn't long before his attention was divided between the drama on stage and the woman in the chair beside him. Just after intermission, in the dim light, Savannah laced her hand with his. He didn't know what to make of it. Was she sending him a silent signal? Women were generally confusing enough—but this was Savannah, who took confusing to a whole new level.

The figures pranced and recited on the stage, holding her full attention. The long-nosed musketeer stumbled and fell. "I have defeated my final enemies: falsehood, prejudice, and compromise—"

The wounded musketeer's cousin knelt beside him, weeping. "I love you. Don't leave me!" She kissed him. He took his last theatrical breath and collapsed in her arms.

The play had cut too close to the quick. Not once but twice in the drama, the distraught woman had lost the love of her life through death. And just like the Frenchman, Michael had hidden the truth of his feelings from the woman he loved.

He hadn't known his choice in plays would be akin to rubbing salt in Savannah's emotional wounds, or he'd have chosen another show.

The vermilion velvet curtain unfurled and fell from top to bottom, and the audience stood, applauding the cast and calling for a final bow. Michael couldn't stand with them; it was wrong, like he was abandoning Savannah to face her inner turmoil alone.

Savannah sobbed in her seat, her dripping nose, wet eyelashes, and glistening eyes causing a deep ache within him. Yet earlier in the carriage, she'd been thrilled with his choice. Mascara tinted her tear-streaked cheeks charcoal gray. He kissed the back of Savannah's hand. "I'm so sorry. I had no idea—"

Then, she looked at him, and time stood still. "He loved her all along." Her gaze roamed his face as he fought for control and her words echoed through him. Her words had sounded almost like a question. Did she know the truth about how he felt? She couldn't possibly know...

Michael stood, pulling Savannah to her feet as everything and everyone faded. He wrapped his arms around her as she sobbed against his shirt. He may not have an elongated nose, like the musketeer in the play, but by hiding his feelings, he'd allowed his best friend to woo and marry the love of his life. He'd placed his friendship with Nick and Savannah above his own needs. At least, that's what he'd told himself all these years.

He'd been a coward. Afraid of rejection, afraid if she had to choose between them, she'd choose Nick. So, he hadn't given her a choice. He'd left before she knew how much he cared. Yet unless he wanted to be like the Frenchman with the long nose, wasting even more time away from the widow he loved, he needed to rethink his strategy and perhaps risk his heart. But would Savannah ever see past her love for Nick to see him waiting in the wings for a chance to love her?

Standing against him, Savannah tilted her face. Could she see his anguish? He couldn't hide his feelings any longer. Savannah reached up and cupped his face in her hands. "Michael."

She'd never said his name that way before, with such longing. His heartbeat hitched. Her eyes reflected his bewilderment. Standing on tiptoes, her hands on his shoulders, Savannah gathered him into her embrace until they were nose to nose, eye to eye, and heart to heart. "He should have told her how he felt."

A shaft of pain pierced his already-unsettled heart. "And he should have kissed her in act one instead of hiding his feelings."

The truth of what he'd said slammed into him the same time Savannah's lips met his. He wasn't sure who made the first move, but emotions rolled over him as her lips communicated her turbulent emotions. Words couldn't capture the pain, regret, and hope their deepening kiss conveyed. They both knew loss and might be afraid of second chances, but caught up in the moment, he felt the kiss infuse him with healing and solidarity. Tears mingled, salty and sweet. Her lips moved in sync with his in a passionate dance, so unlike their kiss on the dance floor at the dreaded reunion.

Reality surpassed his dreams of what this moment might be like, and it shook him to the core. He was losing his mind as well as his heart. Savannah had kissed him, and he was kissing her right back, like he meant it—like she was his. But she wasn't. She'd always belong to Nick. He loosened his hold on her and willed his blood to cool. And he would always regret not telling her about his feelings all those years ago.

At last, they stood with their foreheads together. She'd taken his breath away.

"What just happened?" he murmured, his voice hoarse.

"I..." Savannah buried her face in his shoulder while he held her. They'd both been caught up in the moment, swept up in the drama on stage. What else could it have been?

By the time Savannah emerged from his arms, they were the only two left in the dimmed theater. An usher waited for them to exit. Savannah sniffed and cleared her throat. "They really should provide tissues for these shows."

"I agree. And I think we should get you some water. You must be dehydrated from all those tears." His words coaxed a smile to her lips. "I think we also need a tub of double white chocolate ice cream, two spoons, and a good game of chess to top off the night. What do you say?"

* * * *

Sleep wasn't coming easy tonight. That kiss. His response. Her only regret being that it ended too soon. Savannah grabbed her pillow and buried her burning face. "Ugh! What did I do?"

Michael had been nothing but kind and considerate, and now, she'd gone and ruined it all—giving him all sorts of ideas about them being an actual *thing*. Their agreed-on *thing* on the road back to Point was a pretend thing, for Claire's sake. Now, she'd gone and kissed him and likely given him hope of a *thing* she wasn't ready to embrace. And why hadn't he stopped her? Judging by the look on his face when they'd finally come up for air—no, it couldn't be. Did he have genuine feelings for her?

Savannah had read her share of romance novels, but none of those kissing scenes conveyed the depth of her emotion while in Michael's arms. It wasn't that she was starved of affection; it was the intensity of her feelings that scared her most. Could they be more than friends? No. She absolutely couldn't fall in love with Michael. He had been Nick's best friend, for goodness' sake.

Nick would feel betrayed, wouldn't he? The two men were so different, and she felt guilty for comparing them, like one would compare apples and bananas. Nick had been good to her in his way, and he'd loved her as best as he could despite the circumstances. Michael was funny, kind, protective, thoughtful, and very much alive. It was all so confusing. Yes, Nick was dead, but she wasn't. It wasn't as if she'd forgotten Nick and dishonored the life they had together. She punched her pillow, releasing her pent-up emotion.

She hopped out of bed, needing to move, and peered out of the curtained window into the garden below. The streetlight cast a soft glow, which filtered through the tree leaves, painting dappled shadows on the lawn. "Oh, Father God, what do I do now?"

It was well past midnight, and except for the nocturnal creatures below, everyone was asleep. She drew the curtains and turned her back on the tranquil night.

How was a girl to resist a guy who remembered her favorite flavor of comfort ice cream and let her beat him at chess? Again. So unfair.

And the worst part—she didn't regret kissing him. Not one bit. The thought made her stomach knot and her palms clammy.

She pulled her suitcase out of the closet, lifted it onto the bed, and unzipped it. Time for her to go home—back to her life and to reality. She'd start packing now and tell Michael she wanted to go back to Point in the morning. No way would she let herself sound rash and impulsive. She'd explain it all and he would understand.

She rehearsed her speech as she threw her clothes into her suitcase. "I shouldn't have kissed you. It was a mistake." She stalked into the adjoining bathroom, grabbed her toiletries, and caught sight of her reflection. Her hair stuck out in all directions and framed her flushed cheeks. Her eyes were shimmery and—frightened?

"What if I lose my oldest and dearest friend?"

She sank to the cool ceramic floor, clutching her hairspray and shampoo. Cold fear gripped her and she blinked back tears. Even worse, was she being like that character in the play—the pitiful cousin—running away to hide in a convent, er, library and missing out on life? It was too much to face right now.

No more. She was done with heartache.

And no more stolen kisses and adventures. Those belonged between the pages of a book, not in her life.

It was time to go home.

CHAPTER 14

B EVERLY'S FRESH-BAKED BLUEBERRY BREAKFAST MUFFINS tasted like cardboard the next morning. Michael hadn't come down yet. Instead, a perky young lady sat opposite Savannah at the breakfast table and introduced herself as Tiffany. The woman's fiery red hair, tied back in a messy bun, accentuated her petite freckled nose. She was the athletic type, all sinews and defined muscles.

Beverly bustled in with a fresh pot of coffee, and Savannah held out her cup for a refill.

As Beverly topped her cup, Savannah sighed in gratitude. "Thank you. Smells amazing."

Tiffany put her hand over the mug in front of her. "Not for me, thanks."

Who was this exuberant without caffeine in the morning? Savannah schooled her face and stifled a scowl. Tiffany's "I've been awake since the crack of dawn" energy brought on a dull throb in Savannah's temples.

She sipped from the steaming cup, hoping the caffeine would go straight into her bloodstream.

Beverly nodded, set down the coffeepot, and turned to the side table for the pitcher of chilled water. She did better at coping with the spirited guest than Savannah, smiling as she poured a glass of water and handed it to Tiffany. Lemon slices and ice cubes bobbed as the water sloshed in the jug. "Would you like some green tea?"

"Yes, please. That would be great. I want to get a run in this morning before I meet up with some friends. Are there any off-road running trails around here?"

Beverly tucked a wisp of hair behind her ear. "Let me see—there is one through the orchard, and there is one between the vineyards a few miles further out. I'll get Bruno to show you on the map. I'll be right back with your green tea." She turned on her heel and disappeared into the kitchen.

Savannah stifled a groan. Tiffany would be, oh, so perfect for Michael. The thought turned her stomach.

The woman reminded her of Claire, all perfect and toned. Savannah reached for the bacon and piled it on her plate next to the hash browns. "Shall I pass you the bacon?"

Tiffany wrinkled her nose. "No, thanks. I'm vegetarian."

Of course, she was. Savannah took another fortifying sip of coffee.

Beverly burst through the swinging doors, a mug in hand, and set it and a plate of green leaves and a halved avocado drizzled with something in front of Tiffany.

Tiffany picked up her fork and stabbed the avocado. "We have plans to go zip-lining. Then, if we can find a decent-sized cliff or gorge around here, we'll go rock climbing."

Savannah groaned inwardly. Tiffany was the sort of woman who'd be perfect for Michael, all outdoorsy and adventurous. There was no rational reason Savannah should be grateful he was late for breakfast, but she was.

Savannah pushed her untouched plate aside and stood. "I'm sorry. I'm going to step outside for a bit. Excuse me." Abandoning her coffee cup and her breakfast, Savannah ducked into the living room and headed for the back porch, eager for a calming breeze. She pushed open the French door and stepped out into a paradise garden bursting with color and greenery. Maple trees trembled in the restless air, shading annuals with residual dewdrops shimmering on their leaves and blooms. She inhaled and closed her eyes to better examine her emotions and order her thoughts. She'd made her decision, and Michael needed to know. But where was he?

She opened her eyes and smoothed the creases from her forehead with her fingers. She'd get more wrinkles if she got into the habit of frowning. She wanted to go home. A flash of blue feathers drew her attention to a birdbath under the red ornamental maple tree. A pair of blue jays dipped their beaks into the rippling water. Savannah slowly moved toward them, not wanting to scare them off. She inched closer, determined to enjoy the moment since she didn't have a phone or camera on hand. She sidestepped toward the large oak tree that would shield her with its low-hanging branches. Her movements were slow and measured. The feathered pair ignored her.

Savannah put her palm against the furrowed gray bark of the old oak tree. This stout tree seemed to lend her its serenity, and she leaned into it, her eyes on the frolicking birds.

The leaves rustled overhead, whispering their hellos, and a squirrel chittered on the branch above her.

The blue jay pair finished their bath and hopped to the lip of the birdbath before flying off. Savannah rested her cheek on the wise old tree. She'd have to face Michael sooner or later. Last night, during their chess game, he'd acted as if nothing had happened. Maybe women threw themselves at him on a regular basis. Like Claire had. Shameless. She wasn't like that. It was the performance, her grief, and his nearness that had pushed her over the edge.

Wisdom. That's what she needed. And a good dose of courage. Her mother always said, "'n Boer maak'n plan."

She'd tried to explain it to Nick and Michael. Loosely translated, it meant "A farmer makes a plan." Afrikaners muttered this saying when they weren't ready to give up, determined to find a creative solution to whatever problem.

Her problem was telling Michael she wanted to go home without hurting him. Their pact to leave without regrets still stood. At least, on her end. The intensity of her feelings for Michael scared her. She would regret leading him on, which would lead only to letting him down in the end. She could never live up to being the kind of woman he deserved. Keeping their no-regrets pact meant leaving now in order to avoid more painful regrets later.

Her fingers traced the grooves on the weathered bark. Before she made any rash decisions, she needed to know the truth. What was he thinking? She slid her hands around the thick trunk of the tree, its bark rough and tactile beneath her fingertips.

Would her fingertips meet? She extended her arms. She pressed her body against the robust old tree and reached around. Her fingertips collided with something decidedly nonherbaceous.

She jumped back. Her bloodcurdling scream sent squirrels scurrying and birds fleeing. Bruno burst through the door, a frying pan in his hand. Beverly followed close behind him, her eyes wide.

Savannah shuddered. It wasn't cold like a snake or a toad. It was warm and soft. She pointed a trembling finger at the tree. "There's something behind the tree."

* * * *

Could a man get any peace? The shrill scream had interrupted his solitude and made his eardrums throb. He'd ventured outside to think. And to put off confronting Savannah. Now, Michael had no choice but to give himself up. He groaned. Why did she have to pick now, of all times, to hug a tree? So much for his hiding place.

Bruno's bearded face appeared. "Well, I'll be—bamboozled." He waved a frying pan. "It's not a something; it's a—someone." Bruno's grin showed off his pearly whites, which Michael took as a good sign. Savannah peered over Bruno's shoulder, and Beverly popped up on his other side.

"Michael?" Their voices were a damning choir to his battered ego.

Michael covered his face with his hands, pretending he couldn't hear the chattering tourists traipsing down the street on the other side of the hedge. "I was just..."

"McCann! Why are you behind that tree?" Savannah's tone, far from teasing, only intensified his discomfort.

"I can explain."

"I can't wait to hear this." Savannah stomped back to the patio. He stepped out from behind the old oak and followed her to the patio, where two chunky slatted wooden chairs stood in the morning sun. Savannah sat, then pulled her knees up to hug them, making the oversize wooden chair her cocoon.

Beverly chuckled. "Come on, Bruno." She ushered him toward the French doors. Looking over her shoulder at them, she nodded. "I'll bring a fresh pot of coffee."

Michael gingerly lowered himself into the slatted chair beside Savannah. He ran his hand through his hair. "I guess it's time we stopped skirting the issue."

"You can start by apologizing for scaring me half to death." A golden strand fell over her face, and she tucked it behind her ear with some force.

"What do you mean? I was in the backyard first."

"Did you see me?" Her gaze, hard and cold, fixed on him.

"Yes." He slid farther down into his chair. "I knew we needed to talk, but I wasn't ready, so I..."

"Hid behind the tree." She pinned him with a glare that could roast marshmallows.

"I learned from the best." He dodged a smack to his arm, but Savannah's weak smile was like the sun peeking through a storm cloud.

Beverly brought a tray with a carafe and two mugs, set it on the low table between them, and scurried away. She'd included a plate of cookies—he'd thank her later. His stomach growled because he'd chosen solitude over breakfast.

The silence lingered long after Beverly had gone inside. Michael poured their coffee. He reached for a cookie, but Savannah shooed him away. "How can you eat?"

"What do you mean?"

"Elephant in the room? Pfft. More like the Big Five have camped out, too."

"The what?" What was she talking about?

"In Africa, they consider the Big Five to be the main wild game—the lion, leopard, rhinoceros, elephant, and the Cape buffalo."

"Savannah, it's not so bad." He was desperate to see her smile again. If he kept the conversation light, the elephant would go away on its own. He had a suspicion that she'd come to the conclusion that *the kiss* had been a mistake and was readying to hightail it out of here. Oh, the irony! "So, you won at chess and ate most of the ice cream. I won't hold it against you."

Savannah glared down her nose at him. "Not what this discussion is about."

"I'm kidding, but can I at least have a cookie? I can't think straight with my stomach gurgling."

"Not my fault you missed breakfast. Here." She shoved the plate at him. He balanced it on his lap and saved a cookie from sliding off.

"What were you really doing out here?" So much for skirting the issue. Savannah's wide gaze locked onto him. He sighed. He was at a loss as to how he'd break through her barriers. Maybe the way to a woman's heart was also through her stomach? Worth a try. He offered her the plate. "Come on. Have a cookie. Have you had breakfast?"

Savannah glanced sideways at the buttery cookies. Her fiery glare fizzled as her shoulders slumped. "All right." She nabbed a cookie, then bit into it. "Hmm, these are good. I abandoned a plate of bacon to come out here."

"Are you serious?" Making light of the truth could last only so long. By the look on her face, the elephant was only growing larger the longer he stalled. Before he chickened out, Michael squared his shoulders. "Look. Let's be honest. We've needed to have this conversation for days, and last night—well, it happened so fast. I didn't know how to react."

"Not used to women kissing you in the theater?" Her eyebrow shot up. Was it a challenge or a plea?

"There was this one time I kissed the new girl in town in the back row of the movie theater.

"You can't count that. We were fourteen, and you kissed me on the cheek. Goodness. That movie was boring."

"Not a police-martial-arts-action-movie fan, huh? Nick and I were. And Nick was with Claire. Remember?"

"Like it was yesterday." Savannah put her mug down and leaned forward. A ragged sigh shook her slender frame. She rested her head in her hands. "How did two decades go by so fast?"

Michael placed the plate on the table. He had to man up and tell her the truth. He sipped the scalding brew before putting it aside. "I don't know." He reached for her hand. "Let's talk about the next three decades." He pulled her onto his lap. Savannah's eyes widened; her lips parted. He stilled her words with his finger on her lips. "Shh. Just listen."

The way she settled into his arms bolstered his nerves more than any words she could have said. "I'm sorry about how I handled last night. You opened your heart, and I didn't know how to react. The thing is, I've dreamed of kissing you like that since we were teenagers. When it finally happened I...I didn't know what to do. It's not how I pictured it." Yet it had fueled a night of restless dreams of a future with her he dared not hope for.

Savannah shifted in an attempt to scramble away. He smoothed away the frown from her face, and she calmed in his arms. "Since we were teenagers? I don't understand. Why didn't you tell me?"

"When I left Point, I never thought I'd see you again. You were marrying Nick, and I needed to get away. I shoved my feelings deep down. I tried to live my life without you. I'd reached a small measure of contentment, and then…"

"The reunion?"

"Yes, and I can't shake the feeling that…"

"If this thing—whatever it is—goes wrong, we'll lose our rekindled friendship?" She settled back against his beating heart.

"Is that what concerns you the most?" His heart sank. He'd been hoping for more than friendship, rekindled or otherwise, even if she'd always compare him with Nick. Now, he stood the risk of losing both. Michael shook his head. "For me, it's like Nick's looking over my shoulder, judging my intentions toward you. Trying to shake the feeling that he's about to walk into the room at any moment hasn't worked. It's not that I want to forget him—he was my best friend."

Savannah sat up and faced him. She reached for his cheek, and he caught her hand in his and pressed it to his cheek as if to seal the memory of her touch in his mind.

"I know. He missed you when you left. We both did."

He worked to swallow the lump in his throat. "It's just… I don't know if I can compete with the memories you've made with him."

"You and Nick are…were so different. There's no comparison." There. She'd tried to put his fears to rest. "Besides, you and I made special—new—memories this week, haven't we? We reconnected—as friends. You made me laugh more this week than I've done in the last three years combined."

"Yes, I know, but we've been living in a bubble. What happens when we go back to reality? When you go to

Ithaca and I go to Detroit? When I have to fly out on a rescue mission with an hour's notice? Can you handle that, Savannah?"

"I don't know. I..." She dropped her hand and gazed out over the garden.

The silence stretched between them, taut and fragile.

"Tell me the truth, Michael. Did you leave Point because of me?"

"It's complicated. I was young and stupid." His heart ached at the memory of how hard it had been to say goodbye to Savannah after Nick broke the news that they were engaged and how he'd pretended to be happy for them both. His only saving grace back then was knowing—or at least, believing—that Savannah was happy. He hoped she'd understand why he'd given up on them without a fight.

"And stubborn."

Michael smiled, not refuting that. "Remember the night when I came to your house with a box of doughnuts?"

"I can't forget. We were so nauseated from swinging on the porch swing after eating them all."

"That was the night I was going to tell you how I felt, but then, Nick arrived to hang out. I saw how your face lit up at seeing him, and I couldn't bring myself to make you have to choose."

"Michael, I'm sorry." Tears shimmered in her eyes. "I had no idea."

All he wanted to do was keep her tears at bay for the rest of her life. Dare he hope? "Twenty years later, here we are."

"Yes, here we are." She sighed and relaxed against his chest as if she belonged there. "So, what happens now?"

He shifted her slightly so that he could face her better. "I still don't know how you feel about this—about us."

"Can we ever be a couple? Can you live in my world, Michael? I don't go jet-setting all over the world. My job keeps me anchored to one spot. You'll eventually grow to resent my lifestyle and my need for stability and predictability. After years of not knowing if that was the last day with Nick, I need…" Savannah's body tensed in his arms. He braced himself. "I loved Nick with everything I had. Losing him was…is the hardest thing I've had to face." She studied his face, as if she were committing each laugh line and feature to memory. "If something happened to you on the job…" Her tears spilled over and ran down her cheeks. "I can't go through that again."

"Would you ever be ready to take the risk?" He held his breath, knowing that this was the make-or-break moment for them.

"I don't know. The thought of… No, I… Not yet. Maybe someday."

"I understand." At least, it wasn't never, but still, his heart, touched by searing disappointment, labored within him. "The memories we've made this week have been like vivid colors in a black-and-white world."

"You always did brighten my world, Michael. We'll always be friends, no matter what. Right?"

"Of course." He held her close and cherished the moment because he had a feeling this moment would have to last a lifetime.

"Michael, I want to go home."

Wounded by her words, he longed for the day when she would consider a place with him to be home. *Oh, please, God.*

"Right now."

Her words were like a knife twisting in his gut. He'd hoped for one more day, but he'd take one more hour if that was all he had.

"Please. This is too hard right now. But please, promise you'll stay in touch."

"Always." He coughed and eased her off his lap. "That takes care of the elephant." He shot a quick glance at her lips. "But what about the rest of the wild beasts?"

A blush rose on her cheeks. "We must tame them, McCann. We must tame them."

CHAPTER 15

WHEN HE'D TOLD THEM THE NEWS, Beverly and Bruno hadn't made a fuss over their sudden departure, and for that, Michael was grateful. Beverly turned to Savannah and handed her a brown paper bag for the road. "If you're ever back on this side of the border, please, come and stay with us again."

Beverly's kindness to them both had him swallowing a lump in his throat. "Never say never, right?"

Michael wedged himself into the driver's seat of Savannah's pint-size car one last time, and they pulled away, waving at Bruno and Beverly as they went.

The only good thing about their trip south was that he no longer had to pretend he wasn't besotted with the woman beside him, who captivated him in every way. Her mind was fascinating, and her smile did things to his equilibrium that would otherwise be attributed to vertigo—in the best way.

But since they'd left the B & B just after nine o'clock, the sparkle in her eyes was missing. At first, he thought it was her grief, but now, he wasn't so sure. Maybe she needed more caffeine.

Michael steered into the drive-through lane of a famous Canadian coffee-and-doughnut place and ordered a double-double coffee for himself, while Savannah asked for a steeped tea. Her silence hung heavy in the tiny car, almost as strong as the scent of their hot drinks but not quite as appetizing. It was as if she'd given up, resigned herself to stay as she was.

How could he make her see what she was doing to herself even if he wasn't in her future? If only they could talk about it... A few miles closer to the border, he spotted a scenic viewing area that would work perfectly. If he waited too long, he'd lose the chance to make things right. Once in Point, they'd part ways, but he couldn't face that separation without answering the nudge in his spirit.

He pulled off the road and came to a stop. "Let's see what goodies Beverly sent while we enjoy our drinks." He opened the car door.

Savannah sat, staring ahead with the brown paper bag in her lap, unmoving. Michael grabbed their steaming drinks out of the cup holders and shut the car door with his foot. He wasn't giving up so fast. No way would he let a despondent woman intimidate him. If there was anything his training had taught him, it was to distract and calm.

He set their cups on the picnic table and headed back to Savannah's side of the car. Failing his other tactics, he'd bribe. "You just gonna sit there?" He opened her door, nabbed the bag, and trotted back to the picnic table. "If you want me to share whatever's in here, you'll have to get out of the car."

"Michael McCann, I'm in no mood for your shenanigans. I'm staying in the car."

He hopped onto the table and sat down, his feet on the bench. "What? And miss out on this view?" He'd seen it on the job before. When people were in pain, they couldn't see past themselves. Tunnel vision is what he called it.

Michael unfolded the paper bag and held it to his nose. "Mmmm. They smell amazing. And they're still warm."

Savannah squirmed in her seat. He pulled out a chocolate chip cookie, wafted it her way, and sank his teeth into it. "These are the best I've ever tasted—ev-ver." He threw in a groan of pleasure for good measure and hid his smile as she turned her head.

Savannah jumped out of the car and narrowed her eyes. She reached for the bag. "Okay. Hand over the cookies and no one gets hurt."

Michael held the bag out of her reach. On her tiptoes, she swiped at it. The eventual appearance of her grin shifted something inside him. Underneath that veneer of sorrow was the old Savannah he had always known—intelligent, funny, and slightly quirky.

Relenting, he handed her the bag, and she fished out a cookie, soon joining him in expressing her admiration for Beverly's cookie-making skills. "I suppose you are going to ration me to one cookie now, too?" Savannah said, reaching for her tea.

"If we don't want to ruin the suspension in your car, I think we'd both better stick to one cookie."

Savannah giggled and glanced over his shoulder. "You weren't kidding about the view."

She settled next to him on the picnic table, her elbow inches from him as they sat, nibbling on their cookies. A chickadee sang out as the Niagara River glistened in the midmorning sun. The breeze teased the grasses into a rhythmic dance.

Michael was at a loss as to how he was going to start the conversation. Every sentence he rehearsed in his mind sounded wrong.

After setting the half-full bag of cookies out of reach, Savannah turned to him. "Okay, McCann. Spit it out."

His eyebrows gave away his surprise, the traitors. "How did…"

"You always get all broody when you have something on your mind. Spit it out."

"Me? Broody? Like in a good way or…"

"Focus, Michael." She huffed and wagged her finger his way. "Don't get distracted. Just get on with it."

"Anyone ever tell you, you're one bossy lady?"

Savannah grinned. "A few university students, perhaps."

"Look. I don't know how to say this, so I'm just going to jump right in."

Savannah rolled her eyes, likely in jest, but in her eyes, he saw apprehension and — could it be? — fear. He'd have to choose his words well. *Give me wisdom, Lord.*

"After last night, I promised myself I'd never hide my true self again, so what I'm going to tell you is me doing that. When I left Point all those years ago and spent a few wild years living it up during college with the climbing crowd, there were some things I did that I wasn't proud of. I was selfish and reckless, living from one thrill-seeking adventure to the next. It took a severe fall and months in the hospital to bring me to my knees, but at the bottom of my desperation, I had a God moment. I found purpose and meaning. God has promised never to leave me or forsake me. And I know God keeps His promises."

Savannah fiddled with her fingernails, avoiding his gaze. The urge to reach for her hand almost knocked him off his seat. But she'd played the "just friends" card, and he'd honor that, so he tucked his hands under his thighs.

"Look at me, Savannah. Do you still believe that? Where is the Savannah who dragged me to youth group and annoyed me to no end with the intensity of her faith?"

She lifted her chin and met his gaze. "He's not out of my life, Michael. I'm trying. There is a lot to process, and in time, I'll be back where I was. But first, I have some things to figure out."

"And you think God's happy waiting for you to figure out that He loves you?"

"He loves me?" She pinned him with a glare that could singe his eyebrows. "How does a loving God deny me a husband and baby? Why? Why, Nick? Why not me?" She lowered her voice. "And what now?"

The intensity of her feelings washed over him like a riptide. He had no idea the pain she must have been through. Life wasn't fair. *But God is.* "God doesn't expect you to have everything figured out before you come back to Him. Being single again is one thing, Savannah, but being single—widowed—without God in your life, well, that's a path I don't think you truly want to walk down."

The stormy look in her eyes intensified. "Look. I don't need you to fix me, McCann!"

He knew that. He just needed to ruffle her feathers enough, push her out of her nest, so that she would fly again—want to fly again.

"You can't fix it, either. Only God can."

"Look. I appreciate your concern. I do." Savannah straightened her shoulders. "But life gets messy sometimes, and I'm done with the crying. I'm done with feeling bruised all the time."

He opened his mouth, his words at the ready, but she raised her hand. "Wait. Let me finish." Savannah reached over, grabbed his hand, and turned it face up. He forced himself to concentrate on her words rather than her fingers as she traced a circle on his palm.

"I don't think you know what it's like to be locked behind a wall of steel just so that you can breathe again and not feel pain. This circle is like that barricade."

She put her finger in the center of his palm. "These few days have been my foray out of that hidden place, with you. It was a big step for me. But I can't stay out there forever. You can't keep me safe out there." She folded his fingers into a fist with both her hands as if to preserve that special place, those memories, within his hand. Then, she kissed his hand and withdrew.

"The only problem with that, Savannah, is that if you don't feel pain, you also don't allow yourself to feel joy, love, and peace." He searched her face for a sign that he was getting through to her. "Just like the bereaved woman from that play last night—she thought she was safe from the pain by hiding away, but she also missed out on all the good things, too." Not to mention the love of a good man...

"But it's not real life, Michael." The intensity of her gaze, full of pain, took his breath away. "It's fantasy."

"Fine. I get that. But that's not what I'm saying. I'm not talking about this—about us. I'm talking about your faith. Don't you think God can handle your questions? Do you think He hasn't experienced grief or pain? He has; He did. Could it be that God is grieving over losing you? Missing you?"

Savannah leaned back and crossed her arms. "What do you mean?"

"I know what it's like to miss someone you love, to crave their attention, to wish they'd have space in their lives for you." He swallowed the lump in his throat. Those words sliced way too close to his core. He knew that truth with every fiber of his sorry being. And he'd made a promise never to hide the truth from her again.

Savannah dropped her hands to her sides and gazed into the distance. "I never thought of it that way." Her voice held a certain wonder.

"You are wrong if you think I don't battle with fear." Michael leaned closer and put his hand on her shoulder. She turned her beautiful face to him, and it was all he could do not to pull her into his arms. "We are far more alike than you'll ever know."

She held his gaze for an instant, and then, something shifted. She hopped off the picnic table and headed for the car. "Come on. Let's hit the road before I eat another cookie."

The conversation was over. But he wouldn't have to live with the regret that he'd stayed silent. What Savannah did with his challenge was up to her now. And God. They'd have to figure it out for themselves.

By the time he dropped his bags at his feet that evening and dug in his pocket for his front-door key, he was hungry and exhausted. The buzz of the city only intensified his irritation. He'd found trouble in Point after all, yet he'd never forget his time with Savannah or the memories they'd made. But for now, he'd unpack his things, tame his runaway heart, and leave Savannah in God's hands.

Could he do it? Could he give her the space that she had asked for, that she needed? Would she ever give him a chance? He'd already resisted texting her a dozen times, but surely, sending a friendly text was okay?

Michael pulled his phone out of his pocket.

MADE IT HOME SAFELY. LET ME KNOW WHEN YOU GET HOME.

IF YOU EVER NEED RESCUING, I'M YOUR MAN. ALWAYS.

There. He'd leave it at that. Boy, was his faith being tested with this one.

"Lord, she's Yours." He turned the key and walked into his empty apartment. "Take care of her."

CHAPTER 16

SAVANNAH RAN HER FINGER OVER THE spines of the hardcover reference books in the second aisle of the Adelson Library. They reminded her of the collection on the bookshelves at the B & B that she'd never gotten a close look at. She'd come home and settled back into her predictable life, yet a week after her return, the memories of her time in Canada lingered close to the surface.

Right there, in the resource section of the library, Savannah could almost smell the melted chocolate and cookie dough in the brown paper bag that Beverly had packed. Her stomach growled.

She glanced at the clock. It was almost time for her break. Maybe she'd take a stroll out to visit the blue heron sculpture she loved, with its wings spread as if it were about to take flight. Somehow, it always lifted her spirits, like an old friend wishing her well, inspiring her. If she had enough time, she'd eat a snack and take in the view of the river. But it wasn't the river view she'd shared with Michael, nor were the birds the ones he'd been so proud to show her at the aviary. Her heart ached at her reluctance to let him too close to her.

The thought that she was drifting, while Michael had become more grounded, struck her. She pushed thoughts of his dimpled smile from her mind. It was his kindness and gentleness that had done her in. Her defenses couldn't stand against that for long.

Her mind went back to the heron sculpture. Would she ever be ready to fly again? Take risks? Give her heart away again? Why couldn't Michael have turned out to be an accountant or something, with the only risk being paper cuts and coffee spills? No. That wasn't who he was, and to be anything else would be like clipping the wings of a beautiful bird. Like the hyacinth macaw he'd taken her to see. She'd been glad to spend time with one up close for once in her life, but that beautiful bird deserved to fly free in its natural habitat.

Memories of Michael and Nippy flitted through her mind like a movie. How long had she been standing beside the bookshelf, daydreaming? She had to pull herself together. She glanced at the list of books she needed to gather. She pulled the gilded volume of Austen literature off the shelf for the English lit professor, added it to her book cart, and thought about how the main characters overcame their pride and how things worked out for them. Was she being unfair to Michael? Had she misjudged him? He really wasn't the prankster and troublemaker he once was. She sighed. There was no way around it.

Still, she'd chosen to move on without him. So now, she'd have to start small, make new friends here in Ithaca, and nurture the friendships she already had.

Savannah missed Beverly and Bruno, who had become unexpected friends. They'd been so kind to her. Savannah hated to admit she even missed Beverly's prying questions... She covered her mouth with her fingers to hide her smile. Library patrons would think she'd gone and lost her mind. But the memory of how Michael had said goodbye to Beverly and Bruno and squeezed his athletic frame into the driver's side only made her want to giggle.

Michael had asked her whether she was ready to hit the road with a smile on his dear face. Trust Michael to make the best of the situation. He was one of a kind. He'd texted her to say he'd arrived home safely, but she hadn't heard from him since. Checking her phone for the time, she did some quick math. It had been six days and sixteen hours and...forty-two minutes.

Savannah tucked her phone into her pocket and scanned the list of remaining books she needed to retrieve from the shelves. Why would someone write a thesis on the peculiar behavior of the Ecuadorian long-wattled umbrella bird? She pulled the heavy volume from the shelf and set it on the book cart next to the clipboard. She pushed her cart over to the biology section and scanned the shelves, but she couldn't focus on the numbers. Somewhere in the library, someone sneezed, upsetting the silence for a moment.

She and Michael were doing the right thing, weren't they? Scenes from their time together replayed in her mind, their moments of respite from reality tucked away along with her memories of Nick and their life together. Could her memories live there, side by side, all separate and tidy?

"Hello, Savannah." A familiar voice cut into her thoughts.

She spun to face the newcomer. "Mrs. Delaney!" Savannah covered her mouth with her hand. "Sorry," she said, lowering her voice. "I'm just so surprised to see you. You're far from the mystery-and-suspense section. Did you miss it?"

Mrs. Delaney's smile lit up the room. Despite her need to lean on her cane occasionally, her zest for life put people half her age to shame. Savannah included. "Oh, no, Christine told me you were back here. It's lovely to see you, my dear. Now, tell me about that high school reunion of yours."

"I'll admit, it was strange being back in Point, so familiar and yet so…bittersweet." She leaned against the bookshelf. "Everything reminded me of when Nick and I were young and idealistic."

"Did you put things to rest?"

Her speech to her former classmates about living life to the full had brought a measure of closure in that area. Although she wasn't doing so great herself on that front. "Yes…"

Mrs. Delaney raised her eyebrows and leaned toward Savannah. "And?"

"And no. It's complicated, Mrs. D." Savannah did her best not to grimace.

"I see. Just as I thought." Mrs. Delaney wiggled an accusatory finger at her. "A handsome man?"

"Yes, handsome, kind—and annoying." Savannah grabbed her clipboard, checked the book title off her list, and turned her full attention to the old woman. "You were married for fifty years, Mrs. Delaney. I need some advice."

"Not all men are the same. My Norman was something else. One in a million."

"Michael is like that, too, but we decided that although our paths converged for a time at the reunion, our lifestyles were too different. He's an on-call extreme rescue worker based in busy Detroit. I'm a research librarian surrounded by college students. We couldn't be more opposite in what we want from life. He understood. As hard as it was, we both knew we couldn't make it work—not without ruining our rekindled friendship. You know, as teenagers, we were pretty close. He was my best friend before…before Nick. Did I do the right thing?"

The gray-haired woman leaned on her cane and tilted her chin, peering at Savannah over her bifocals. "You *both* decided it wouldn't work?"

"Yes and…"

"No? I thought so. Keep your options open, Savannah. If that handsome man of yours really loves you, he'll keep. Until he figures things out, promise me you'll not lock yourself away." Ouch. Those words hit close to home. Except, the way they'd left things, she was the one who had to do the figuring out.

"You need to get out and be with others. Being alone isn't good for anyone." The old woman patted her arm.

Had Mrs. Delaney been talking to God about what to bug her about? "As fond as I am of you, you need someone your own age to talk to." She waved her cane in the air, and Savannah ducked out of its way. "I have my bingo and book club..."

"I appreciate your concern." *And meddling.* "I'll try."

"As long as you're trying, I'll be content with that." Mrs. Delaney patted Savannah's hand. Knowing the older woman, though, this wouldn't be the last she'd hear of it.

"Did you see the new arrivals shelf?"

"Yes, and Christine directed me to a new series I hadn't heard of with female sleuths who solve mysteries."

"They must have come in while I was in Nia—away."

Mrs. D tapped her cane on the floor. "Aha! My sleuthing nose can smell something." She leaned toward Savannah, both hands on her cane. "What are you not telling me?"

"You're probably smelling these old books. After all, there's nothing like the smell of a well-used book." Mrs. Delaney would wheedle it out of her eventually, but right now, she had work to do. "I need to pull two more books and get them all to the front counter. How about we catch up tomorrow?"

Nothing like putting off for tomorrow what one wanted to avoid today.

* * * *

Michael inched into position, looking down at the man semi-buried and squirming in the ditch below him. The late-afternoon sun threw shadows across his face. *Sometimes stupidity and trying to save a few dollars puts you right in the middle of a pile of dirt.*

"Grab on to the rope, and we'll pull you free." Michael signaled to his men manning the ropes to hang tight.

The man's eyes were the only part of his face not smeared with dirt. The unstable ditch had already partly collapsed and buried the man up to his knees. If they didn't get him out fast, the crumbling trench he'd dug to pilfer from his neighbor's gas line would collapse and become his grave.

Michael tugged on his own rope, making sure it was secured to his three-point harness. Owen and Benjamin were in position at the anchor point, ready to haul them to safety on his signal. It was a reassurance he never took for granted. Each time his team risked leaking gas lines or being buried alive or found themselves in danger to rescue civilians, he relied on their loyalty and trustworthiness.

The man blinked the dirt from his bulging eyes. "My feet are trapped under my shovel." The man whimpered, writhing in his dirt trap. "I dropped it when the dirt fell in on me, and now, I'm stuck."

"Stay calm." Michael infused his voice with as much calm as he could. "We will get you out." They didn't have time to waste. As if the risk of a broken gas line weren't enough, a steady stream of dirt cascaded into the ditch and threatened to bury him even more. Digging out the man's feet wasn't an option. "Are you wearing boots or shoes? Can you wriggle your feet enough to get them free?"

"I'll try... My laces aren't tight."

Michael stepped down into the ditch and maneuvered slowly to avoid disturbing the crumbling sand and causing a cave-in. He sniffed the air for signs of gas leakage and was relieved to inhale nothing but dust.

"My boots are off, but my legs are too tired to pull myself free." Tears made tracks through the dirt on his face.

"You see those men over there? The rope is attached to an anchor point, and once the line is secured around your waist, my guys will pull you out." Michael heard the plop of clods as they sprinkled onto the board they'd erected to bolster the interior. Too much movement could trigger a cave-in. "Don't budge. We'll pull you out." He took the end of the rope in his gloved hand so that he'd be ready to wind the rope around the man's waist.

Michael reached out to the man with the rope in hand. "Once I get this around you," he said, keeping his voice calm and slow, "we'll pull you up on the count of three."

Eyeing the edge of the ditch overhead, he gasped at the flow of dirt that rained down and rushed to fill the empty spaces like grains in an hourglass. Clods of dirt hit his helmet. They were out of time.

Michael lunged for the man, wrapped his arms around his chest, and locked his right hand around his left wrist. "Now!"

The rope went taut, and his muscles strained to maintain his grip in a tug-of-war for the man's life. With a jerk of the line, Owen and Benjamin hauled them both out of the pit amid cascading dirt and gravel. The shifting soil slammed into the ditch, burying the boards they'd rigged to stabilize the site as the earth settled back into place. A cloud of dust hung in the air.

Michael coughed and stumbled to his feet, kicking the soil off his pants and boots. He reached out and helped the other man stand. "Are you okay?"

The man nodded and stood with his head hanging low, his gaze on his now-bare feet.

A second later, and they'd both have been buried alive. They'd had only hundredths of a second to spare.

"What's your name?"

The man's gaze darted to Michael. "S-Stan." He was free, but he looked shaken—and guilty. The stricken man glanced at the police cruiser and officer who held back curious onlookers. "Will I get into trouble?"

"Well, Stan, will you try this stunt again?"

He shook his head, and his eyes filled with fear and remorse. "It almost cost me my life."

"I think your wife will have something to say about that, too."

Michael turned him over to the waiting medic, who'd check him over before handing him back to his frantic wife, who'd been the one to call for help. As far as Michael could see, Stan's only true injury was to his pride.

Owen Richardson, always the first to lend a hand, rushed over from where he had been manning the crane. "That was cutting it close."

Benjamin—Owen's brother—and Johnnie, the rookie, sauntered over to check on him. Owen brushed the dirt off Michael's back and shoulders, creating another cloud of dust.

"You're making things worse, O." Michael coughed and sputtered, shoving Owen away.

Owen held up his hands in mock surrender. "Suit yourself. Just trying to help."

Johnnie nudged Benjamin and nodded toward Michael. "Is he always this grouchy?" There was no smile on Johnnie's face to suggest he was joking.

Owen tilted his head like he was forming an opinion. "Only when he's trying to pretend he's fine."

Michael crossed his arms. Owen seemed sure he had all the answers, but he needed to keep his assumptions to himself.

Johnnie took off his helmet and ran a hand through his shoulder-length hair, letting his locks flow free. The corner of his mouth hitched up. "So, it's not the fact that there's dirt in his ear?"

Michael glanced at his watch. Their shift was over. "I *am* fine, and do you guys mind not talking about me like I'm not standing right in front of you?" To disprove their grumpy-pants theory, Michael forced a laugh while he pulled off his gloves.

"He probably won't come." Benjamin smirked and shook his head. "He'd have to lower himself to hang out with us ordinary folk."

Michael waved his grimy hand in front of Benjamin's face. "I'm right here."

Benjamin elbowed his brother and nodded like it was a done deal. "I bet you twenty dollars he wouldn't last an hour."

"Hello." Michael stepped between Benjamin and Owen. "What are you talking about?"

"He's in a bad mood. Has been ever since he got back to Detroit last week." Owen turned to Johnnie. "He'll find an excuse to leave within twenty minutes."

"I'm not in a bad mood. I won't leave. I guarantee it." They were ganging up on him. He wasn't about to be outsmarted by the three men he trusted with his life. True, he'd been sulking over Savannah, but a man was allowed to lick his wounds once in a while. "So, where are we going?"

"We're going to Sheena's."

"Okay." Michael shrugged out of his harness. He had never heard of it, but they didn't have to know that he was clueless. Plus, he'd been feeling out of sorts. A night out with the guys might help shake it off. "I'm in."

"Unless you have something more important to do?" Owen looked all innocent, like he wasn't making a jab.

"Look. I said I'd be there." He busied himself coiling his rope.

"Be there?" Owen chuckled. "You're driving."

He stowed his rope and unclipped his helmet. "First, I need to hit the shower."

Owen didn't even try to hide his smirk. "Oh, yes, you do, Mike."

They loaded up their equipment and scattered back to their vehicles to head back to base.

Once the men had showered and dressed in their regular clothes, they all piled into Michael's four-by-four. Apparently, he was the designated driver. Since he'd pretended to know exactly where it was, he was glad when Owen slipped him the address on a small sticky note, further cementing his suspicions that the guys were up to something.

Sheena's turned out to be an unobtrusive little bar and grill tucked away in downtown Detroit, serving fried foods and offering live music. Not too bad. At this rate, he'd last more than twenty minutes, easy. The place was packed for a Thursday night—must be the fish and chips special they were having.

Once their attention was no longer centered on their menus and filling their stomachs and once their drinks had arrived, there was a brief lull in conversation.

Owen cleared his throat. "So, Mike, what happened at the reunion?"

Michael forced his hand to relax around his glass. "Nothing." Maybe if he counted the lightbulbs on each fixture, he wouldn't recall a pair of luscious lips taking his breath away in row two of the theater.

Owen peered at him. "How has 'nothing' gotten you all discombobulated?"

Michael raised his chin and sniffed. "Do you know what that big word means, O?"

Over Owen's shoulder, Michael saw a woman set up a microphone stand. Michael flagged down the waitress. "What's happening onstage?"

"Thursday is karaoke night." She said it like everyone should know this. Including him. She bustled off to serve another table, while an intolerable thought wormed its way into his mind.

"Wait." Michael regarded his crew, who were supposed to be his friends. "You guys knew it was karaoke night?"

"You promised not to leave." Owen grinned. "And if you do, Benji owes me twenty dollars."

Their server arrived with arms laden with burgers and fries.

"So, we have to sit here and watch people sing eighties songs into the microphone." He could do that long enough to watch his *friend* lose his dollars. Why, he'd confound them both and stay for two hours. He glanced at his watch. That was only another ninety-five minutes or so.

Benjamin snagged a fry and dunked it in a blob of ketchup. "And we get to enjoy the good ones and chuckle at the bad."

"Unless you'd rather tell us about your trip back to Point. I mean, you are being tight lipped about the reunion." Owen drank the rest of his soda and pushed his glass away. "Cindy thinks it's because of a woman."

Owen had stepped over the line, bringing Cindy into it. "Since when do you discuss my life with your wife?"

"Hey, she figured it out all by herself after church this weekend when you weren't your usual chipper self." Owen leaned in. "I think the prickly demeanor may have given you away, my friend."

Michael's throat went dry. No way was he going to talk about Savannah. He hadn't yet untangled his feelings. One moment, he was certain he'd done the right thing, and the next, he was bent on running back to her and begging her to reconsider. So, he'd lost a few nights' sleep and was grumpy. What of it? He'd get over it eventually.

His silence would only confirm their suspicions. There was no choice but to employ diversion tactics. He needed something to shift their attention from his miserable love life. One thing would work.

"Would prickly do this?" He strolled across the room to the stage. He stifled a smile, silently apologized to his elementary school choir teacher, and grabbed the microphone. He ignored the confounded looks on Owen's, Benji's, and Johnnie's faces.

If his eyes weren't deceiving him, he could see money changing hands over whatever other bet they'd cooked up at his expense.

Sometimes, stupidity landed you in a pile of dirt. Sometimes, it landed you with a microphone in your hand, belting out the lyrics to your favorite boy band hit, horribly out of tune.

CHAPTER 17

SAVANNAH SETTLED INTO HER CAR AND headed for home after her Friday shift at the library. The new book she'd ordered was sure to be on her doorstep, a thought that had her treading a bit heavier on the accelerator. On the lookout for a speed trap, she eased her foot off the gas pedal and smiled, thinking about Michael and their run-in with Officer Jenkins.

An ache settled in her stomach at the distance between her and Michael. She'd waited to hear more after his initial *I made it home* text, but there'd been nothing from him since. She'd struggled to find the right words to reply, so she'd waited until she had something relevant to say. So far, she'd come up with nothing.

Savannah turned the key in the lock of her front door and picked up the package on her doorstep. Was this destined to be her future? Every day. For the rest of her life?

She took a deep breath, then fled into her air-conditioned ground-level rented apartment before she started sneezing from all the pollen. Their apartment was one of the two with a separate entrance from the rest of the building with a ramp for Nick's wheelchair before he'd gotten too sick for her to care for him herself.

The daylight hours lengthened as summer stretched out ahead of her. Most university students were home with their families, which meant the library traffic had been subdued. She didn't like it. Too much time to reflect. She needed to be busy. Maybe she should get a cat.

Mrs. Delaney's words cycled around in her head. Was Mrs. D right? Did she lock herself away with her piles of books?

Savannah dropped her keys into the wooden bowl on the front hall table. The package tempted her to get lost in the pages of the book within it. She tucked the package out of sight in the coat closet and shut the door. Mrs. D was right. Time to find a hobby. Savannah caught sight of her reflection in the hall mirror and made a mental note to book a hair appointment. Her locks were getting out of control. Nothing drastic—just a trim.

It was time she made her own happiness and stopped waiting for it to knock on her door and shout "Ta-da!"

She needed to take a leap of faith and push her boundaries. Nothing crazy. She didn't have to go skydiving or take Michael up on his suggestion of a mountain hike. She could catch up with old friends. Evelyn and Catherine had stopped asking her to join them on their nights out after she refused four or five times with the excuse of being too busy with volunteer work at the library. Would they be surprised to hear from her after all this time?

The trip to Point had taught her a valuable lesson. She needed good people in her life—like Beverly and Bruno. They'd opened their home and their hearts to her, and she treasured the memories of their warmth and kindness and how quickly she'd grown attached to the couple. How she wished she'd had more time to spend in conversation with them, but it had been her choice to leave early. All the more reason to find similar friends here or reconnect with those she'd neglected.

Savannah hung her purse on the hook by the door, and led by her growling stomach, she headed for the kitchen, where the fridge yielded uninspiring leftovers. Regret stung as she remembered exploring new places with Michael and their long conversations over delicious foods and new flavors.

A fleeting wish for a deeper relationship flickered like embers in a firepit, but she applied an extinguisher to that before it burst into a runaway flame. Falling for Michael was not a safe choice for either of them. She'd end up breaking his heart—again. She couldn't ask him to change, to give up what he loved for her. And as noble as Michael's rescue career was, how could she live plagued by the fear that something would happen and he'd be lost to her forever?

Michael could be somewhere right now risking his life. Better to lose a friend than a lover. Still, despite her best defenses, her heart hadn't come away unscathed from their reunion.

She slammed the door on her unappealing fridge and errant thoughts. It was time to move on. And making her own way meant accepting her future and taking steps to make it a better one. Starting with friends.

She caught sight of the blank calendar on the wall. She needed to reconnect with those who'd stood with her through Nick's illness. If Evelyn was still meeting with the girls for their weekly nights out, she'd join them. Nick had always encouraged her to go, but she'd stopped when he moved to hospice care.

No time like the present. Savannah dialed, needing to hear a familiar voice. "Evelyn. It's Savannah. How are you?"

"Savannah! You've made my day. It's good to hear from you."

"I've meant to call." For all of five minutes, but still, it was the truth.

"What's up?"

A whole load of nothing was up, and that was the problem. "I was wondering if you and the girls are still having your girls' night out."

"Of course. Still on Sunday nights. Husbands and significant others, beware. I'm sorry, Savannah. How insensitive of me. I didn't mean—"

"It's okay, Evie, really." Savannah opened the cupboard and took out her favorite mug.

"I feel awful. Please, say you'll come back. We've missed you."

"If you'll have me."

"Pfft. Nonsense. We're always ready to welcome lost sheep back to the fold. In fact, a new girl tried our group for a few months, but it didn't work out."

"Too wild?" Savannah flicked on the electric kettle and leaned against the counter.

"No. She had some questionable ideas of what our girls' night out should look like. Before it got awkward, she lost interest and ditched us. The girls will be thrilled to see you."

"So, same place, same time?"

"Yes, and don't be late. We have so much to catch up on."

"We do. I'll tell you about my adventures on Sunday night." At least, a few of them.

"Adventures? Sounds intriguing."

Just how much was she going to tell the girls? She couldn't keep dear Michael to herself for long. The girls could sniff out a secret better than a bloodhound in pursuit of a fox.

Through the phone, Savannah heard another voice.

"Where are you?" She tossed a bag of tea into her mug and sat down at the kitchen table.

"At the pediatrician's waiting rooms with Matt. That was the nurse."

Memories of doctors' offices with Nick flooded back, bringing a feeling of unease. "Is everything okay?"

"Yes, it's just a routine checkup. They're ready for us. I'll talk to you later. Oh, and wear jeans and flats."

Savannah disconnected the call and poured the steaming water from the kettle over the tea bag. Her mother would have a conniption if she saw how she made her tea without a proper teapot and without putting milk in first. What her mother didn't know wouldn't hurt her. Living life on her terms meant brewing her tea however she pleased. And eating popcorn or ice cream for dinner if she wanted to. No one was here to judge that decision, either. She stirred, fished the tea bag out of the cup with a spoon, and dropped it into the garbage. A few drops of milk perfected the brew—even if her mother would disagree.

Savannah sipped the fragrant beverage, the distinctive taste of bergamot lingering on her tongue. "Mmmm, good."

Her words echoed through the hollow spaces of her kitchen. Despite that, her lips curled into a grin. She'd done it. She'd taken a step, albeit into the mildly comfortable. She'd be with friends and not strangers. It was time she ditched her pile of books for real people, at least on occasion, but that had to count for something. So what if it was more like a shuffle of faith than a leap? It still counted. Baby steps, baby steps.

A flicker of hope burned deep within her, warming her to the core.

She was ready to begin living again. She'd show Michael that she wasn't as *lost* as he feared. She didn't need him. Okay, who was she kidding? She didn't *need* a man to be whole, but she sure did enjoy being with him.

And now, she was going to enjoy being with her other friends.

However, after she climbed out of her car two days later at the rendezvous point, the warm, fuzzy feelings fled once she heard what the girls had arranged.

"We're doing what? Whose idea…" Savannah's voice died in her throat. Evelyn's booming laugh did nothing to calm Savannah's racing heart. "Someone will lose a few fingers or toes!"

Lucy raised her hand, her smile wide. "My idea. I think it's a brilliant one. You don't have to wear plaid. It's not a rule."

Evelyn held up her hands to halt Savannah's protests. "Calm down. It will be fun. Catherine will be here any second, and she's all in. Although I can guarantee she'll be wearing plaid all the way down to her underwear. She gets quite into our excursions." Evelyn could not be more opposite in temperament to Savannah, but they'd formed a bond despite their obvious differences.

"Ladies! I don't care if we all wear plaid from head to toe. There's no way I'm getting in a room with you to throw axes at anything." The air around Savannah was stagnant and stifling.

"Oh, Savannah, they'll have an instructor. It's perfectly safe." Evelyn waved off her fears as if shooing a fly.

"My idea of safe is sitting around a table, drinking milkshakes. Not flinging sharp metal objects at a…at a… What do we throw the axes at?"

Evelyn put her arm around Savannah. "It's the latest thing. When Lucy suggested we go, I thought it was a great idea."

"This wouldn't have anything to do with disproving the 'this group is not wild enough' theory?"

"Not at all." Evelyn grinned and turned to Lucy. "There's Cathy. Let's all go in my car. It'll be fun."

It will be fun. Famous last words.

Savannah could drown in the palpable excitement rolling off Lucy and Catherine, which did little to still her trembling hands. Too soon, all four of them stood side by side behind the painted blue line on the floorboards, where they waited for their instructor.

Behind a wire safety fence, a group of men hollered and fist-bumped one another, their axes making loud thwacking sounds as they cut into the wooden board. She'd never held an ax, let alone thrown one at a wooden board marked with dizzying red circles. Her dad had cut firewood for bonfires and for their indoor fireplaces using a sturdy old ax. Except these axes were smaller and sharper, and she had visions of dropping one and slicing her toes off. A person could take her eye out if she swung it the wrong way.

Evelyn shuffled them around, rearranging their order like a sergeant major, prodding them with her finger. "Cathy, you go first, then Savannah. Lucy and I will watch you two; then, we'll go next."

"How about I wait with you and Lucy goes first?" The earthy smell of sawdust and wood shavings did little to calm Savannah's nerves. She had the perpetual feeling of being on the verge of sneezing.

"Savannah, you and Cathy are similar in height. Lucy is closer to my height. Safety first."

Lucy and Evelyn both shopped in the kids' department for their clothes. "You have a point."

Savannah eyed the wooden boards they'd be attempting to hit. On them were three painted circles, the target being the red one in the middle. Catherine peeled off her yellow-and-black plaid shirt, which reminded Savannah of a bumblebee, and tied the sleeves at her waist, leaving her red T-shirt and bandana exposed. Lucy and Evelyn, dressed in jeans, drew the line at wearing steel-toe boots. Instead, they wore cute sparkly sneakers—likely also from the children's department. Savannah wore her strappy flats, which exposed her painted toes. Further proof of how out of her element she was. She should have worn her sneakers like she'd done when touring with Michael. A pang of longing rolled through her.

Maybe if she kept her mind off his endearing smile, she'd be able to breathe easier. "How did your appointment with Matt's pediatrician go?"

"For once, she had a good report. She said he's doing great on the new meds. We've been monitoring side effects since we've begun treatment of his ADHD."

"That's great. Does he read much at home?" Maybe she could recommend some books.

"Not unless it's on a screen. We've been waging the war against excess screen time—it's difficult."

Lucy groaned like she'd eaten a sour apple. "We're having the same issues with Stacey and Sarah. They're down to three hours of electronics a day, but it's hard. By the time bedtime rolls around, I collapse into bed. Most nights, Gerry has to remove the book to prevent a book-shaped dent on my face. He says he can tell I'm not reading anymore when I snore."

Catherine leaned in. "That is why Bob and I are never having kids. I need my sleep."

Her friends would never know how much Catherine's words were like a knife twisting in an already-gushing wound. How could Catherine know the effect her words had? Savannah and Nick had dreamed of a family, but the one time before his treatments when she found out she was expecting, a miscarriage had ripped that dream from her. They'd kept their tragedy to themselves, except for their parents. Then, Nick had taken a turn for the worse, and really, they hadn't expected him to battle for so many years. The cancer kept coming back. Her biological clock, well… ticktock, ticktock.

Catherine nudged her. "Look. Here comes the instructor."

Wearing a black shirt with two silver axes on the front, crossed to form an X, he had a beard that lent him the air of a lumberjack. "Good evening, ladies. My name's Tom. I'll be your instructor and host for the night. First, we'll have a lesson. Then, after a few practice shots, your tournament will begin. I'll oversee and keep score. Questions?" He didn't sound like a redneck lumberjack. She'd have pegged him as an office worker, except for the beard.

"A tournament?" Savannah poked Evelyn's arm, giving her the evil eye.

Tom nodded and took the clipboard from a hook on the wall. Someone had tied the pen on with a fraying piece of twine. "I see you've decided on your teams. Names, please."

Evelyn pointed to each lady. "I'm Evelyn Harper. This is Lucy Adams, Catherine Deeks, and the one with the grumpy face is Savannah Sanderson."

"Before we go in, I'll do a safety check." Tom pointed to Savannah's feet. "I'm sorry, but you must change your shoes. If you don't have alternative footwear, we have some you can rent. Come this way." Savannah's cheeks burned. "Um...sure."

"Follow me." Tom stalked off in the direction of the rental booth.

Savannah glared at Evelyn, who just shrugged. "Oops!"

Probably a good thing she'd not mentioned plaid and axes, or I'd never have agreed to come out with the girls.

Savannah followed Tom's broad and muscular back to the rental counter. So much for baby steps. More like a gargantuan leap out of her comfort zone. By the time she laced up the clunky ankle boots, she felt queasy, her palms slick with sweat. Lucy's chatter grated on her already-fragile nerves. Savannah pasted on a smile and took up her position next to Catherine. Her one goal—to go home with all her fingers and toes intact.

"Come on, Savannah. Don't worry; you'll be fine." Catherine sniffed. "Just pretend you are throwing a book at the wall."

Savannah gasped in horror, causing the trio to dissolve into fits of giggles. Tom demanded their full attention through his instructions for safe and effective ax throwing. Catherine turned out to be a natural, cutting the board on her second throw. Savannah's fifth throw bounced right off the board.

Tom came and stood behind her. "Back up one step, Savannah." His bulky frame almost eclipsed the light hanging from the rafters above them. "Now, hold the ax loosely with your right hand. You want the handle to slide out of your hand."

The heat of his body radiated onto her back, and Savannah fought the urge to move away. Tom's large hands covered hers as they held the handle of the ax. Then, Tom guided her arms back, her elbows pointed toward the rafters, and together, they threw the ax. Adrenaline pumped through her veins as the ax slid out of her grasp and rotated until it bit into the wood at the edge of the red circle.

"Almost a bull's-eye." Tom's voice, close to her ear, was husky and much too flirty. It felt wrong, not like when Michael helped her and spoke into her ear, just like he'd done at the boat railing. What was it with men? Tom saw a woman in need of help and some exposed toes, and suddenly, it was a license to flirt. Maybe her heart was already taken. She'd show him. She'd hurl that ax so dead on that he'd back off.

Her next throw without Tom's help was straight and true, thwacking into the panel dead center and sending splinters flying. "Whoa!" The chorus of voices sent another spike of adrenaline into her veins.

Evelyn applauded and held out her hand for a high five. "I think you got the hang of it now. Well done. Now, pass me that ax; it's my turn."

The next morning, Evelyn sent a photo of Savannah and Catherine with their trophy and axes. Savannah couldn't stifle the pride as she remembered each exhilarating ax throw and nailing the bull's-eye almost every time. It wasn't a fluke, either. She'd hit her mark over and over.

Michael would have loved every second. Savannah saved the photo, then forwarded it to him.

YOU'LL NEVER GUESS WHAT MY "FRIENDS" MADE ME DO. AX THROWING! I ADMIT I WAS TERRIFIED TO BEGIN WITH, BUT IT WASN'T SO BAD ONCE I GOT THE HANG OF IT.

HOPE WORK IS GOING WELL? ☺

* * * *

Glancing at the clock, Michael had thirty minutes before he'd leave to tackle Monday morning rush-hour traffic so he could be on time to begin day one of the two-day training he was giving at the fire station. Training sessions were the less glamorous part of his job but essential to keeping his skills in top shape and passing them on to others. He loved his job, but only the best training would translate into the best decisions on the field. When a crisis came up, it was his training and the readiness of his team that set them apart. He had a reputation, and he'd worked hard for it.

What he hadn't been prepared for was how much he'd miss Savannah. How could a few days with her have turned his world upside down? She was there, in the back of his mind, visiting his dreams. He hadn't slept well in the eleven nights since he'd gotten home to Detroit. He was used to being in control, but the emotions swirling inside left him unsettled. Owen, Benji, and Johnnie had called him grumpy. Okay, so he'd admit it—they were right. He was like a bear with a sore paw—not that he'd come close to one, but it was a saying, so it had to be true.

Michael's phone sat on the kitchen counter next to his empty bowl of cereal. He switched it to silent and shoved it in his pocket before he caved and called Savannah.

He was trained to fix things, rescue people. Only, he couldn't rescue Savannah, and by the way his battered heart beat rapidly at the thought of her, he was in greater need of rescuing than anyone. And this time, he couldn't fix the situation. When he'd put Savannah in God's hands, he'd meant it, but his control issues kept popping up, tempting him to take it all back and fix things. Back in Canada, he'd challenged Savannah about her faith, and here he was the one failing to trust. As a rescuer, it was hard to let someone else do the rescuing. His gut felt like he'd swallowed a brick. That was the root of the grumpy-bear thing.

His hair fell into his face. "Urgh!" He gathered it back into a ponytail. His hair was annoying him. Another thing he'd lost control over. Maybe he'd stop by the barber on Tuesday night on the way home, or if they were too busy, he'd go during his day off on Wednesday.

Another look at the clock, and it was almost time to go. Looking for a snack to pack for his lunch, he opened the fridge and peered in. Aside from half a carton of milk, nothing but leftover pizza from the night before and a half-used carton of eggs were edible. He spotted a container at the back of the fridge. When he opened the lid, the pungent smell of rotting leftovers hit him. He gagged. He dumped the food, container and all, into the garbage can under the sink and waved the smell away. "Disgusting!"

Michael tied up the bag so he could drop it in the dumpster on his way out. Time to get his act together. Time to pin down a plan. He pulled his phone out of his pocket, opened the notes app, and tapped out a list of items he needed. Milk, chicken, veggies. No, scratch the veggies—he'd get some carrot cake. He smiled. Savannah would have something to say about that last item.

He noticed the icon for a missed text message and swiped left to check it. He hit View. From Savannah. *Finally!* A message and a photo. Savannah and another woman stood in front of a trophy, holding axes. His breath hitched. Her smile and the sparkle in her eyes were mesmerizing. He was so far gone—who was he kidding? He tapped out the beginnings of a reply and then deleted it. At a loss for words, he shoved his phone into his pocket and headed for the door.

Maybe he'd sign up for a few extra shifts, keep busy, and continue to give Savannah the space she needed. From the photo she'd finally sent, she seemed to be getting on just fine without him, and he was having a hard time convincing himself that he was happy for her.

CHAPTER 18

"**W**E'RE DOING WHAT?" SAVANNAH'S VOICE HITCHED up an octave.

Evelyn crossed her arms and rolled her eyes. "Here we go again."

"Someone could fall to their death. Whose idea was this anyway?"

Lucy bounced on the balls of her feet like a kid in a doughnut shop, making her blond curls bob. "Mine, again."

Evelyn held up her hands to halt Savannah's protests. "Look. Wasn't the ax throwing fun? And you did great. So, relax. Catherine will be here any second, and she's all in. Although I can guarantee she'll be wearing all the gear needed to summit Mount Everest. She gets quite into our excursions."

"So you've said." Savannah's words dripped with sarcasm. She really should have known that the girls would cook up something like this after last week's fiasco. At least this time, she had sneakers on and her comfy yoga pants.

"Ladies! There's no way I'm getting in a room with you to dangle from ropes and likely break a leg or something." The air around Savannah was stagnant and stifling.

"Savannah, they'll have an instructor. It's perfectly safe." Evelyn rolled her eyes.

"My idea of safe is sitting around a table, drinking virgin cocktails. Not scampering up a wall like that superhero."

Evelyn put her arm around Savannah. "It's the latest thing. They've added rock climbing to the Olympics, so it's all the rage. You did great at ax throwing; this will be fun."

A sense of déjà vu descended on her at those famous last words. On the way, she came up with the perfect excuse as to why she wouldn't be making the next week's outing. She'd host a book club at her house and invite some of the ladies from church. She could serve carrot cake with extra icing. What's the most trouble she could get into in the safety of her home surrounded by bookish people?

As soon as they arrived at their destination, Savannah was convinced that Evelyn and the girls were trying to kill her. Nothing else explained it. Savannah's eyes traveled up the wall. Colorful shapes littered the sandpaper surface, like a child had thrown lumps of colored putty that had stuck and hardened. She wasn't going to trust a misshapen blob screwed to the cement when her life was on the line—whether two feet off the ground or two hundred.

"When exactly did our plan to see a movie change into this?" Savannah waved her trembling hand at the climbing wall.

"The other girls wanted to do something more active than sitting in chairs, wolfing down buttered popcorn, and I could stand to lose a few pounds myself."

Savannah had to agree with that notion. With all the food she'd eaten in Canada resulting in a tighter-than-usual waistband, she could use some exercise herself—but perhaps with both feet on the ground.

Evelyn gathered her hair in a ponytail and turned to Catherine. "Savannah's about to have a panic attack. I told you this might not be the best idea."

Catherine peered around Evelyn, her eyes narrowed. "Savannah, you got this. Just go back to your wild and carefree childhood. Embrace your inner child, not some stuffy old grown-up who has forgotten the fun of climbing."

"It's not like we had safety gear when we were kids," Evelyn muttered, not taking her eyes off the wall. She pointed over her shoulder. Savannah turned to see a row of empty benches along the far wall. "If you're too scared to even try, you can sit over there and watch me beat Lucy to the top."

"Not a chance. I accept the challenge. I'll climb to the top of this thing. You'll see." She wasn't about to go all yellow bellied in front of the girls.

"It's not a competition, Savannah. Just have fun." Lucy's puckered brow gave away her concern.

A familiar feeling bubbled up inside Savannah. Michael had always liked to uncover her competitive side.

Catherine bit her lip like she was holding back a comment or a laugh.

Either way, she'd show them. And she'd show Michael. A pang of regret zinged through her thumping heart. Her cowardice had pushed Michael away. She could be climbing beside him, but she'd put herself on the bench out of fear. Time enough to think about that later.

Savannah wiped her damp hands on her pants. "I'm ready." Well, she wasn't really, but she was as ready as she'd ever be.

A young guy who smelled of bubble gum tapped the oval ring holding her rope to the harness as if it would reassure her it was locked in place. "See. The rope is sturdy. You have an autobelay which will catch your rope and hold you, and it can't come loose."

Savannah studied the rope. It went straight above her to where it fed through a pulley system. Eyeing his skinny arms and knobby knees, she remained unconvinced the young teenager had the brawn needed to scale a ladder, let alone a climbing wall. Swallowing hard to get rid of the lump in her throat, she glanced at the benches.

Savannah wished she hadn't eaten that extra slice of pizza. And the birthday cake from her coworker's fiftieth birthday party during their lunch break. Maybe that extra weight would be too much for the rope, and she'd end up in a mangled pile on the rubber floor. She shuddered, handing back the rope she'd tugged to thoroughly test its strength for herself. The harness around her hips brought to mind how toddlers must feel in those pull-up diapers.

The instructor checked the autobelay device, then stopped chewing his gum. "Okay, you can climb now. Don't worry. Just take it slow." Next to her, a five-year-old lowered himself off the wall, swinging like a mini wrecking ball, giggling all the way down. If he could do it, surely so could she. Considering that Evelyn's shoes were at eye level and Lucy and Cathy were almost halfway up, taking it slow wouldn't get her to where she needed to go.

As she put her toes on a bean-shaped blob the young guy told her was a foothold, Savannah's heart beat faster. She stepped up. The other foot left the ground, which produced a heady rush. Savannah leaned her forehead against the wall and got her breathing under control. *Don't look down; don't look down.* But she couldn't resist. She glanced down and gasped. She was only half a foot off the floor. *Oh, come on, Savannah. That's pathetic.* She needed to do what Catherine said—be that child, embrace that child. Her snarky little so-called inner child was rolling on the floor, laughing at her for making it only six inches off the ground. She could just imagine the mildly supportive smile—but still a smirk—on Michael's face if he could see her now.

Savannah took another look up at the rubberized shoes her friends wore. The same friends who were climbing like a spider had bitten them. Wriggling her toes in her rented climbing shoes, she pressed her lips together and took a deep breath. She would not be left behind.

She reached for the triangular green handhold and pulled herself up. She kept her body as close to the vertical concrete surface as she could. Her thigh muscles strained and trembled as she stepped up to the next foothold, almost skinning her nose in her attempt to find it. Savannah reached over her head for another green handhold, and her nail split as she grabbed on. She put her finger in her mouth to soothe the sting.

Michael would hardly call a climbing gym a worthy challenge, not like a mountainside or rock face, but, hey, to her, it might as well have been El Capitan in Yosemite. If Michael were here, he'd be thoroughly disgusted that she'd worry about a broken nail while her friends were acing the whole climbing thing. Even if it was an indoor wall.

A spark of determination sprang to life, burning in her belly and spreading through her being. Why did she care what other people thought? She was doing this for herself, not the girls—and not for Michael, who had completely ignored her for days. He hadn't even responded to her ax-throwing photo. That stung worse than her broken nail.

Savannah pushed up to the next thin toehold and balanced her big toe at an angle, ignoring the ache in her arms. Yes, she'd do this for herself. Not for a man, not for a friend. One handhold and one foothold at a time. She ignored that she sounded like a puppy panting after a long run, a growing feeling of pride spurring her on. She would beat the other girls while she was at it.

She took a deep breath, then pulled, stepped, and strained until she was close enough to reach out and touch the top of the wall. Catching her breath, she dared not look down. She tilted her head, her eyes on the painted purple roof, and let out her fear in one blood-chilling whoop. "I did it!"

Her moment of victory was short lived. How was she supposed to get down? Savannah froze, the adrenaline spike in her veins causing her head to spin. She squeezed her eyes shut. A sound much like a mewling kitten stuck up in a tree agitated her. Perhaps the trapped animal was on a ledge. After the third mew, Savannah snapped her lips shut. The sound came from her traitorous mouth. All the courage she'd used to get to the top had run dry. She opened her eyes and gritted her teeth against the pain in her calves as they trembled on their footholds. She'd got up; she could get down. Maybe.

"What's she doing?" Cathy's voice floated up from what sounded like far, far below.

"I don't know. Were we supposed to go that far? She's the highest climber here." Evelyn sounded...surprised. No, shocked.

Had she outdone herself and impressed her friends? Now, it was even more important she not make a fool of herself—or fall to her death. What would Michael say if he knew she was dangling off a wall? Thoughts of him distracted her. Again. What would he say if he knew she was in a fix because she hadn't paid attention while their gum-chewing instructor gave instructions? She'd missed the part about how to get down—she'd been thinking about Michael. Why did she care what he thought, anyway?

Everyone in the gym would be watching her, and it made her skin crawl. Maybe one of them would be kind enough to yell something useful instead of standing around and talking about her like she couldn't hear.

"You can come down now." Cathy's words floated up to Savannah.

Not helpful. But how? Too high to see how anyone else did it, Savannah couldn't bring herself to peer at those lower. How was she supposed to watch their movements for clues without risking a glance? She clung to the climbing holds, willing her hands and toes to hang on just a little longer. She inhaled and exhaled to clear her thoughts. Little spots danced in front of her eyes; her breaths came in bursts. She would faint and fall off the wall and flatten the lot. Served them right for making her do this.

The surrounding sounds faded while blood pumped through her temples. Fear wound its icy tendrils around every fiber of her being and paralyzed her.

"Savannah. Savannah." The voice of an angel called to her.

"Savannah, snap out of it." Calm and soothing at first, the voice had turned demanding.

The voice came from next to her. How?

"Savannah, can you hear me?"

She nodded, careful not to look down. She'd pressed herself as close to the wall as she could. A scrawny arm came into her one-eyed view. She was sure she could smell fruity gum. Really? They sent the bubble-gum kid up to save her?

"You can come down now." She was thankful he wasn't chewing, or she'd be tempted to let go with one hand and fish the offending gum right out of his mouth. The instructor dangled beside her from the rope the five-year-old had left.

Still, she was moments away from death, so she swallowed her pride. "I forgot how you told us to get down. I was...distracted." Even though high above her friends, she whispered her confession.

"All you do is let go, and the rope will catch, and you'll go down. You don't have to do anything."

"What?"

"All you have to do is let go."

"I'm sorry. Could you repeat that?"

"Just let go."

"You're crazy!"

"Calm yourself. Take a deep breath." Gum Boy reached over and put his hand over hers, where it had a death grip on a misshapen pink blob.

"Take your hand off me." Savannah resisted the urge to slap his hand away.

"I'm trying to help you."

"Are you going to pry my hands off these holds so I plunge to my death? Is that your plan?" Her forearms were in on the plan. They trembled under the strain, and her knuckles turned white. Maybe her high-pitched comments were freaking the guy out. They were freaking herself out. Did he think she was deranged?

She took a deep breath and forced herself to think. Maybe if she pretended she was still six inches off the ground, she'd push through the fear. Children pretended a lot, right? Catherine would be so proud of her.

"Sorry. I want to do it myself. See those girls down there? They're my best friends. If I want to face them with any self-respect, then I have to do this on my own."

"Okay. I understand." His calm voice was straight-up annoying. Couldn't he work up just a bit of panic to make her feel better about herself?

"Shouldn't someone be holding my rope?" So, they were trying to kill her—all of them. Maybe all that hyperventilating fed her brain with the oxygen she needed to put those facts together. She wasn't going to give in, not this time.

"No. You're on an automatic device, which means you just have to release it and you'll go down." There was no trace of mockery in his voice, only calm reassurance.

How many times had he been required to talk down a spooked thirtysomething woman such as herself? "So, I just have to let go of the wall with my hands..."

"Hold on to the rope attached to your harness and keep your feet on the wall, until you feel the pulley system catch you. Then, you can relax and enjoy the ride down. The magnetic pulley system will do the rest."

"What if it doesn't work?" She risked a peek at the instructor, who was holding on only with one hand. *Show-off!*

"You'll be just fine. You can do this. Just let go and relax."

He sounded like her pastor in one of his sermons about letting go and letting God. Had God sent her an object lesson to illustrate His point? Was she holding on too tight to everything? Maybe it was time for her to give up an inch of control. Relying on that magnetic pulley system was a good enough start. She'd build up to the big leaps of faith later.

"Okay, I'm ready."

"She's coming down," Bubble-Gum Dude said to her friends below.

Savannah took a deep breath, leaned back, and released her grip. A fleeting feeling of free-falling had her stomach lurching. She was going to die.

Then, she felt the pulley system engage and felt the tension on the rope. Her heart flipped in celebration of her victory. The colored holds whizzed by as she fast approached the floor. Had she climbed that high, all by herself?

By the time her feet touched the padded floor, her mouth hung open. She'd clambered farther than she'd expected.

By the hoots and hollers that greeted her and the three pairs of arms around her neck, she guessed her friends were happy she was safely on the ground.

"Can we go to a movie next time? Please."

Evelyn exchanged glances with Cathy and Lucy and dissolved into giggles.

"Of course, we can. I'm so proud of you," Evelyn said between snorts.

"From now on, we're calling you Spidey Woman. You almost gave us a heart attack." Lucy placed her hand over her heart to prove its distress.

"So, you weren't trying to kill me?" Savannah grinned, unhooking her harness and rope with the help of her bubble-gum-chewing hero, who smiled at her and winked. Only he knew how afraid she'd been.

"We thought you were trying to give us all heart failure. You were only meant to go halfway. Next thing we knew, you were at the top." Cathy pointed to the ceiling.

Savannah looked up. Pride at what she'd accomplished washed over her. If she'd realized just how high she'd climbed, she may have gone into cardiac arrest herself. But she'd done it. She'd climbed forty feet up a vertical obstacle course. And then, she'd faced her fear and let go. And since she'd faced all that, she might as well admit the rest of it.

"The climb wasn't that bad. I only forgot how to get back down and thought I'd be stuck up there all night." Savannah gathered her friends for another hug. "Now, let's go eat. I'm starved."

By the time they retold the story over dinner, Savannah could laugh at herself. On her drive home, she reflected that this trying-to-live-again thing was going to be a challenge. But it was worth it because the experience—albeit terrifying for a few moments—was a personal victory and she'd survived. And by the end of the night, the heaviness of loss had lifted.

Nick would have wanted her to enjoy each day, even if he wasn't here to share them with her. Cancer had stolen his strength and, with it, his ability to give her what she needed emotionally. It wasn't that she blamed him exactly; he'd been fighting for his life. She'd put her needs on hold for so long that she'd have to relearn how to connect with them. To feel like she was allowed to dream, to let someone hold her.

In his last months, Nick had often pleaded with her to live her best life for him. Did he know what he was asking of her?

It was time she stopped wrestling. She'd do her best. To honor Nick's memory. She just wished Michael could have been a part of that learning to live again beyond their short trip to Canada. Her dream of a family had died when Michael went back to his perilous lifestyle.

Savannah's silent drive home along the familiar roads of Ithaca brought stiffness to her overused muscles. Would Spider Woman's calves hurt as much? Was she going to end up like Jacob, who wrestled with God until daybreak and came away with a new name and a limp?

How long was she going to struggle with God? The thought brought uneasiness to her soul. She could no longer deny that she had to find her way back to God, without relying on her friends or her excuses. For the first time in a long time, just like at the climbing wall when she conquered her fears one plastic bump at a time and then trusted in a rope enough to let go, the feeling that God was smiling warmed her. She felt His love through her friends, and maybe, just maybe, her little stumble out in faith—her tiny object lesson of letting go on the climbing wall—was the first step in bringing her faith back to solid ground.

Under the light of the moon, Savannah's heart lifted. *His mercies are new every morning.* The thought soothed her tired soul. "Okay, Lord," she whispered into the night, "I'll take it one day at a time." It was time to let go of the pain and reach out even more to reconnect with the life she'd lost when Nick's illness turned their world upside down.

By the time she flung herself into bed, she was ready for sleep. But a ding from her phone prompted her to sit up and turn on her bedside light. Maybe Michael had texted her back.

Evelyn had sent the group photo they'd taken with their young climbing instructor along with a note: MOVIE NIGHT NEXT WEEK. BRING POPCORN.

Thank goodness! Along with her relief about a tamer night with the girls, Savannah couldn't stifle pride as she remembered how she'd overcome her paralyzing fear and let go.

Michael would have loved every second of the climb as she overcame her fears. Before she could second-guess herself, Savannah forwarded the photo to him.

BEHOLD THE ROCK-CLIMBING CHAMPIONS. NEXT WEEK, WE ARE WATCHING A MOVIE, SO NO PHOTOGRAPHIC EVIDENCE NEEDED FOR THAT. HOW ARE THINGS ON YOUR END? ☺

Savannah switched off the light and settled back into bed. Shadows danced around her as the lights from passing cars created shadow ballets with leaves from the oak tree outside her window. Being on the ground floor had its perks, especially with the manicured garden outside her windows, cared for by the custodians, giving her the illusion of her own private garden.

She wasn't sure whether Michael would see the photo tonight. "Lord, please, look out for Michael," she mumbled into her pillow. "Protect him. Keep him safe."

She fell asleep thinking of his twinkling eyes and his touch on her cheek.

CHAPTER 19

THE FIRST MONDAY IN JUNE HAD dawned clear and bright for her drive in to work. Who knew that one used the same muscles to haul large books off shelves that one used to ascend climbing walls? Savannah winced as she pulled a bulky book from the shelf.

"Are those for me?" A male voice halted Savannah's progress down aisle one of the reference section at the Adelson Library.

She turned to find the man gesturing to the full cart of reference books and audiobooks. Savannah shoved her glasses back up her nose while clutching a trio of books about African birds. This man couldn't be the professor she was waiting for, who'd requested the book about the Ecuadorian long-wattled umbrella bird a couple of weeks ago. What was his name again? For one, this man's short-back-and-sides haircut, a little longer on top, was trendy.

That stylish look continued all the way down to his tailored pants and pointy dress shoes.

"Were you looking for Christine? She's next door in the multimedia room." He must have come over from the art and drama department and mistaken her for the youth and drama librarian. No, that couldn't be it. She hadn't worn artsy scarves and beads. No trace of flair in her ensemble today—or any day.

"The lady at the front desk pointed you out—are you the research librarian? I'm sorry. I'm new in town. She said you'd have my reference material." He wiped his palm on his tailored pants and then shoved his hand in her direction. "Radcliffe."

His warm fingers were soft, but his handshake was firm.

A loud throat-clearing beside her and the thump of a cane made Savannah smile. "Ah! Mrs. Delaney. I didn't see you there." The lady had a way of lurking around corners and then appearing at the oddest times.

"Nice to meet you. I haven't seen you around here before." Mrs. Delaney gave the new guy a once-over from top to bottom, nodded, and then turned to Savannah. "I just wanted to remind you about our Scrabble date tomorrow night, dear."

"Yes, of course. I'm looking forward to it."

"All right, then. I'll leave you two alone." Mrs. D patted Savannah's arm and left with a smug smile on her face while clutching a collection of twelve short stories about a certain mystery solving nineteenth century detective.

Savannah watched her trundle off. She'd bet ten dollars that Mrs. D's exceptionally fast exit to the next section with the assistance of her walking cane was to allow some matchmaking. Matchmaking that she didn't need or want.

"I didn't mean to interrupt." The man ran his hand through his hair and studied the carpet.

"Oh, no. Mrs. Delaney and I share a love of fiction. She usually comes to me when she can't find a book."

"It would seem many people do—myself included."

"Happy to help." As she rolled the book-laden cart toward the checkout desk, she glanced at her list. She had only one book left to find. Among the stack of bird books on her cart were a few about African elephants. Michael would be nudging her at the mention of elephants right about now if he were here. "Forgive me for asking, but the long-wattled umbrella bird?"

"It's for my recreational reading actually. I always wanted to be a biologist. Thank you for making my search for these resources easier."

"Ah, that explains it, and you're welcome." The list of books on tropical birds—and elephants—didn't quite fit his look.

"That explains what? I don't look like a biologist?"

His piercing gaze brought on a hot flush. "Not really." She waved her hand, and her breath caught in her throat. Her ring finger was bare. After planting some annuals in the two large pots at her front door, she must have forgotten to put her wedding rings back on. She'd worn them to ward off interested college professors, but she knew she couldn't live that way forever.

A faint frown furrowed his brow. "I must work on my biologist look, then." His dimpled grin only made her cheeks burn more. Professor What-Was-His-Name-Again was flirting with her. In the library. In aisle one. And she was sure Mrs. D wasn't missing a thing from her hiding spot in aisle two. Savannah could see her eyes sparkling between a large book on Amazonian amphibians and a volume of *Aviaries and Bird Sanctuaries of the World*.

"Maybe if you combed your, um…hair differently, you'd have a better shot at it." Sometimes, her mouth just had a mind of its own. She hoped she didn't sound insulting.

"You don't like my hair?"

"No, I do. But it's much too trendy for a biology professor."

His brown eyes twinkled. "You think I'm trendy?"

"That's not what I said. But if you aren't a biology professor, then you're not writing a thesis on birds." She stopped and scanned her clipboard for the last item on her list. She grabbed the book off the shelf, clutched it to her chest, and leaned back against the bookshelf.

"No, I'm not. My true interests lie in biology even if I teach in a different field. If I'm not pulling off the biology-professor look, then can you guess what course I teach?"

Ah! Maybe she was right, and he *was* an art and drama prof with a bird-watching hobby. "Not after knowing you all of two minutes, no. I'd need to gather more clues." That did not come out the way she'd intended. She wasn't trying to encourage the man.

"Right. That's only fair. When does your shift end?"

Oh no! Now, what had she gotten herself into? She wasn't looking for a boyfriend. And if she were, there was only one living man whom she'd ever consider. "I'm working all day, but I'm about to have my coffee break, so I'm not sure—"

"Perfect. How about we grab a coffee and you can gather your clues?"

How was she going to backtrack without hurting the man's feelings? "That's kind of you, but I…"

"Hardly know me."

Still not looking for a boyfriend.

"I know. I get it." He leaned toward her. "Like I said, I'm new in town and on campus, and I could do with a friend."

Mrs. Delaney's words from weeks ago were like a poke in the ribs. Maybe if she focused on being a friend to someone else, she'd stop feeling sorry for herself. Could Mrs. D be spot on? She needed to stop being self-absorbed and help a stranger.

"Well, if you put it that way. One can never have too many friends. Let's get these books checked out for you."

"Great. Sorry. Did you tell me your name?"

"Savannah. And…I'm sorry I didn't catch your first name."

"Donavan. Donavan Radcliffe."

They took care of the checkout process and headed out the library door with two tote bags of books. Savannah soon found her hands curled around a chunky ceramic mug of java. The soothing smell of coffee and cinnamon permeated the air despite the arctic air-conditioning being pumped into the building. The professor had chosen a table tucked away in the shop's corner, next to a shelf of tempting sachets of whole roasted coffee beans, where Mrs. D couldn't spy on them.

Mrs. Delaney would be so proud. Savannah was out socializing with others. Check. Out with someone her own age. Check? The professor could be around her age. She wasn't sure—yet.

"So, you're new on campus, Dr..." She was turning out to be a horrible friend since she couldn't even remember his name longer than sixty seconds.

"Please, call me Donavan. I wanted to escape from the craziness of the city. Although the campus was in the Boston theater district, the pace was hair raising, and I wanted a quieter life. When the position at— Wait. I can't tell you which campus yet. That will interfere with your intrepid clue gathering."

That's it. He must be from the art and drama department.

"Boston? Let me guess. Did you come from that fine arts school and museum at the university?"

He raised an eyebrow. "An armadillo has more artistic ability than I have."

"Okay, then. What about technology? Did you come from that institute in Boston? What is it called again?"

He shook his head and added a packet of sugar to his coffee. "Nope, not a techie, either. But you're getting warmer."

"It's freezing in here." Savannah bounced her legs to generate body heat. In one fluid movement, Dr. Radcliffe hopped up, shrugged out of his jacket, and draped it over her shoulders. "They think we're hunks of meat in the freezer department, don't they?"

"Thank you." Savannah pulled the jacket around her shoulders. "I usually come prepared. I'm still a little out of routine. Vacations will do that to you."

"Were you somewhere warm, like the Bahamas?"

"Not an exotic destination, no. Ever heard of Point? It's almost directly west of here but south of Rochester and southeast of Buffalo. If you drive by and blink for a second, you'll miss seeing it. It's a tiny town."

"Not familiar with it—sorry. Do you have family there?" Dr. Radcliffe tore open another packet of sugar and added it to his cup. Michael had done the same thing. What was it with men and their need for sugar? She had to stop comparing the professor with Michael.

"Not anymore. My parents moved years ago. I went back to my high school reunion."

Stirring in the sugar, he kept his eyes on the swirling liquid. "Let me guess—you graduated in…2000?"

"Close. So, not the arts or technology. What about the medical field?"

"I can't stand blood and pain. I stick to metaphoric kinds of pain, in a way." Those dimples appeared again. The man had an endearing smile.

"That's it—you must be in law."

"Good guess. My parents thought I'd make a good lawyer. Too many arguments and counterarguments as a teenager might have cemented the deal. How did you know?"

"Process of elimination." Savannah sat back in her chair and adjusted his jacket around her shoulders. It smelled of linen and what must've been his cologne.

"Truth is, this whole teaching thing is a new gig. I gave up my law practice to teach." Dr. Radcliffe leaned forward, elbows on the table, hands around his mug of sugared coffee, just like Michael, but the hands were academic, not rough and strong... *Urgh!* She *had* to stop thinking of Michael every second of the day.

"Now, you've solved the mystery. Tell me about you?"

"I'm a research librarian working in three different university libraries—but mostly at this one. When I'm not working in the research department, my guilty pleasure is reading romance novels." She sipped her coffee, the hot liquid thawing her from the inside.

"What genre? Contemporary or historical?"

Savannah sputtered and coughed. The professor handed her a napkin and stood. He patted her on the back until she caught her breath.

She wiped her watery eyes and composed herself. Michael had teased her about half-clothed men on the covers, but then, his eyes had glazed over when she got long winded in explaining that she didn't read those kinds of books and why. This man wanted to know more about her beloved romance novels? First time for everything. Wow. "I'm sorry. Guys rarely ask me that. They usually glaze over and change the subject."

"Do they? I don't see why men can't read. Although not romance, I'm into the suspense-and-mystery genre. From what I observed, I have something in common with your Mrs. Delaney." Wow. He'd done better remembering names than she had.

"She'll be delighted." And Savannah would never hear the end of it.

When they ran out of small talk, Savannah thanked the professor for the loan of his jacket. "It was nice to meet you, Dr. Radcliffe."

At the end of her shift, as she drove home, she thought the professor was pleasant enough, in a friendly sort of way, but she'd made a point to avoid sending any nonverbal messages that might be misunderstood. In fact, now that she'd decided to attend church again, she'd introduce him to some of the guys, if he was the churchgoing type.

She'd enjoyed Dr. Radcliffe's company. No sparks flew; no zinging chemistry developed to complicate things. Although he was still a stranger, she'd welcome a friend who didn't threaten to turn her world upside down.

Except he had also reminded her what she was missing.

Fireworks.

CHAPTER 20

TWO WEEKS AFTER OVERSEEING THE TEDIOUS training with the fire department, Michael was glad to spend his Wednesday off with Owen surrounded by nature in Wisconsin instead of in the city with its honking horns and screeching tires. They'd taken a couple of extra days off on account of the nine-and-a-half-hour drive to Sturgeon Bay from Detroit. But the drive had been worth it.

From the top of the Potawatomi Tower, Michael's view from seventy-five feet in the air was impressive. The June sun glistened off Sturgeon Bay in the distance. He overlooked a sea of varying shades of green as the trees danced in the breeze between him and the distant water. If only the tranquil scene could calm his inner struggles.

Michael traced his finger along the long-forgotten letters etched into the sun-bleached wood. Every available inch of the tower displayed names carved into the weathered gray wood—in remembrance of love declared or claims staked. But there was no "Savannah + Michael 4 Ever" scratched into the wood.

Owen stepped onto the top step that led to the lookout and turned his face into the wind. "Ah, a breeze. Nice." He dug in his backpack and pulled out his water canteen. "Amazing view. And to think this structure was made in 1932, almost entirely out of wood."

"Yeah."

"Hey." Owen looked at him dead on. His brow puckered. "It's been almost four weeks since you got back from New York. Are you ever gonna tell me what's eating at you, buddy?"

Michael winced at Owen's candid approach. He was trapped—no karaoke to save him this time. "Can I ask you a question, O?"

Owen swigged his water. "Ask me anything." He wiped the back of his hand across his lips.

Michael turned to face him, hoping for insightful answers from his longtime friend and teammate. "How does Cindy feel about what you do?"

"She thinks it's cool. Why?"

"So, she doesn't worry about you, that you'll get hurt?"

"Yeah, but we talked about it. There's no more risk in what I do than in crossing the street. We don't take unnecessary risks, and we're not thrill seekers. Once she got that and realized what we actually do is far removed from the Hollywood version, she was happy. Plus, she said every time I leave, she puts me in God's hands."

"She's a smart woman." Michael whacked Owen's shoulder. "How did you land such a gem?"

"Hey, I ask myself the same thing all the time."

They grinned at each other like adolescent boys who'd discovered that chocolate was the way to a woman's heart.

Michael ran his hand through the short hair that he was still getting used to. "I suppose you want to know what happened at the reunion, huh?"

"Dude, I think talking about it will help you figure things out. Cindy says guys don't know how to communicate, so blame her for the recommendation. But yes, I want to know, if only so you can lighten up and get back to your old self."

"Have I really been that bad?"

"Truthfully, yes."

Ouch. Not even trying to sugarcoat the truth.

Michael twisted the lid off his own water canteen while collecting his thoughts. Time to get some objective wisdom, even if it made him look foolish in the process. *Here goes.*

He cleared his throat. "I've never told you this, but in high school, I had a major crush on this girl. She loved my best buddy. So, when I saw the writing on the wall, I skedaddled out of town as fast as I could. They were engaged, and I couldn't stand it. We never talked about it, but I think Nick knew how I felt, and it strained our friendship."

Owen's eyebrows shot up. "Let me guess. She was at the reunion?"

Michael nodded. "Not only that; Nick had died of cancer." He gazed out over the water so he wouldn't see the reaction he was sure he was about to get from his buddy. "So, I did a stupid thing. I kissed her. Well, she kissed me first, but it doesn't matter. I wanted to kiss her, anyway."

Owen snorted. "Wait. This happened at the reunion?"

Michael groaned. He'd have to tell Owen everything. "No, the kiss happened after I convinced her to spend a week with me, touring Niagara Falls." He recalled his little sea nymph clutching the railings of the boat on the Niagara River.

Owen thumped him on the shoulder. "You didn't!"

"Turns out my feelings for her never really went away, and now that Nick's gone, it's even more confusing. Like my buddy's still there and she's always gonna be his girl."

Rubbing his hand over his chin, Owen turned to look at the vista. "But how does she feel about the whole thing?"

"I thought I knew where things were headed. We had dinner at a fancy restaurant, and she almost stopped my heart in her killer dress—I almost messed it up big time then. We got talking about regrets and moving on, and I thought she was open to the possibility of a future together."

Michael leaned against the railing. He could still see Savannah's face, her lips saying "No regrets, remember?" He'd been mesmerized by them, taken captive by the notion that one kiss could communicate his feelings better than his mangled and disjointed words ever could.

"Michael, can you cut to the part that's bothering you? We have a hike to finish."

"So much for the sympathetic friend, huh?" Michael laughed. "I take it your version of communication and Cindy's are a little different."

Owen's eyes sparkled. "I like the summary; she likes the unabridged version."

"Fine. After dinner, I couldn't sleep. I snuck up the stairs at the B & B where we were staying and stood outside her door."

Owen's low whistle was like a stab in the heart. "What happened?"

"I lost my nerve." Michael hung his head, averting his gaze. "What was the right thing to do? Knock on the door, then kiss her senseless and maybe scare her away, or not let my feelings show, only to lose her anyway? When she asked me about suspicious noises on the stairs, I chickened out and feigned ignorance. I couldn't take the risk. I wanted to give it more time. Then, we went to the theater, and she—"

"Wait. You went to an actual theater? As in, real actors in tights on a stage?" Owen's grin widened.

"Hey, don't diss it until you've tried it." He could still feel the emotion that had washed over him as the drama unfolded.

Owen nodded and waved his hand for Michael to continue.

"So, at the theater, she kissed me, and it blew me away. But by the next morning, she had second thoughts, and it was over before it began. But I can't get her out of my mind."

"Who walked away, then?"

"Both of us. After losing her husband, she's afraid my job is too risky. And I couldn't handle being compared to my high school best friend. But letting her go is the stupidest thing I've ever done, other than run away from Point. I should have stayed and fought for her. Now, Nick isn't there anymore, and I..."

"You're intimidated by your best friend's ghost?"

Had the air around him been sucked away? "I guess I am."

"That's messed up, man. No wonder you've been a grouch."

Michael forced his chest to expand and drew in a shaky breath. "We're supposed to stay friends, but it's killing me. Just over a week ago, she sent a photo. Her girlfriends had taken her rock climbing at an indoor gym. I'm happy for her—she's afraid of heights—so that must have been a big deal for her, but I didn't know what to say. Looks like she's moved on—"

"Without you." Trust Owen to state the obvious.

"Yeah, and I can't count the number of times I've started to send her a message and then deleted it. I'm afraid my feelings will show through." What kind of friend promised to stay in contact and then didn't?

"I think a brisk hike along the Ice Age Trail is what you need to clear your head."

Maybe Owen was right. And he'd been praying about it, but he was having trouble leaving the whole thing in God's hands. Some exercise and sweat would do him good. He watched a chipmunk scamper to the top of a tree, his thoughts lingering on Savannah.

He turned his back on the scenery, needing to get one last thing out in the open. "That's not the only issue. I think she's struggling with her faith. I guess losing a husband can shake the foundations."

"What makes you say that?" Owen drizzled a small stream of water onto his face.

"When we were in Point, at the service—it was a cobblestone church she loved. Anyway, she seemed on edge and fidgety. Distracted even."

Owen tilted his head. "Maybe the pews were uncomfortable? Did you ask her about it?"

Michael released a long, slow breath. No use hanging on to one more regret. "Yes, but she balked. It's just that I'm not sure she can see past the rebellious and reckless teenager I was. I'm not sure she can see the change in me. I'm different but the same. You know what I mean?"

"Different but the same? You are making no sense. You know what I think? I think you are assuming a whole lot without going to the source. Ask her."

"I get it, O. The faith part is one thing, and we talked about it a little. That part's up to God. But I never really told her how I felt about her, just hinted and hoped she understood." The most frustrating part was he couldn't do anything to fix it. "I'm more in love with her now than I ever was, and I let her go...again. But if I ever get to talk to her again in the flesh, I'll tell her."

With one last glance over his shoulder at the scenery, he stowed his canteen in his pack. *Time to move on.* He tilted his head toward the stairs. "Let's go."

They planned to follow the trail from the eastern terminus at the shoreline, all the way south until they reached North Duluth Avenue, where they'd stashed their bikes. A four-mile bike ride back to where Michael had left the truck would help work out his frustration.

As they started up the trail, Michael's phone vibrated. He looked at the screen. Disappointment washed through him when the number displayed wasn't Savannah's.

"Yes, this is McCann."

"Sheriff Tanner here." The gravelly voice brought Michael to attention. "Sorry to bother you on your day off, but we need you and your team in Teton County ASAP. We've got some hikers trapped in a flooded cave. How soon can you get here?"

"We're out on a hike in Wisconsin, but there's an airstrip a mile south of here. It's the Door County Cherryland Airport, and we can be there within the hour."

"Hold on. Let me see if I can send a helicopter to get you."

Michael covered the phone with his hand. "Ready for a five-hour helicopter ride, O?"

"What?" Owen rocked back on his heels. "Now?"

Michael nodded.

"Can you be ready in ninety minutes?" the sheriff asked after some commotion on the other end of the line.

"Sir, my team is based out of Detroit. They'll have to be briefed on the situation and picked up first."

"No problem. I have their details on file. I'll take care of it; just be at the airstrip."

"Thank you, sir." He punched the end-call button. He'd soon be busy enough to keep his thoughts of Savannah at bay. They'd skip the shoreline hike, hoof it to his jeep, and grab the bikes on their way to the airfield. The jeep should be safe parked there for a few days.

He turned to Owen. "We're going to Wyoming. Get Benjamin on the phone. Tell him he'll be getting a briefing call so he'll know what gear to get together. And have him give Johnnie a call. The helicopter will pick them up in Detroit. Benji will know what to do."

* * * *

Time was running out.

Michael crossed his arms and faced the sheriff in the rain. Although it was eight o'clock in the evening in Teton County, Wyoming, the warm rain made the air muggy. They had about fifty minutes of daylight left before they'd fire up their generators and spotlights. Dense droplets fell from the sky, making miniature muddy rivers on the sun-hardened ground. In places where vegetation failed to protect the exposed earth, the rain scoured the mountainside, bringing down pebbles and sand.

Sheriff Tanner was in charge of the scene, and in that position, he commanded respect. Except the way the rain collected in the sheriff's wide-brimmed hat, then cascaded off the edge like a waterfall when he tipped his head was at odds with his position of authority. "Do you have a contingency plan, McCann?"

Michael gritted his teeth at the questions leveled at him by the stalwart county sheriff. It wasn't unusual to have his skills and experience questioned before the head of a rescue signed him on, but it was as if the rain had washed away his confidence and left him vulnerable. Each question became a personal attack. Logic told him he was irrational, but Michael's equilibrium had been off ever since he'd returned from Point last month.

"We always do." He glanced over at the members of his team under their shelter, already hard at work preparing for what lay ahead. "Given the complexity of this rescue, we have two in place. And we'd like to get started before it really is too late." The teams would plan for a rescue mission until circumstances pointed to a recovery.

"Hmm." Sheriff Tanner nodded, and another sheet of water tipped off his hat onto Michael's boot.

Why the older man insisted on standing in the rain next to his vehicle made no sense when there was a portable shelter just three feet away, where local volunteers were setting up makeshift kitchens to feed everyone that had come to help with the search. Michael stepped back under the overhang of the tent and waited for the next deluge of questions.

"I checked you out, and you have many successful rescues under your belt, McCann. There's no doubt about that. My concern is the lack of contacts on your emergency list. Not only that; there's only one name. A Thelma McCann. And if I'm not mistaken, she's your late grandmother." Sheriff Tanner lowered his eyebrows. "What if something happens to you in there?"

"My grandmother Thelma raised me. I have no other family." Given his longing for what was out of reach, the truth of the matter stung.

Sheriff Tanner's eyes narrowed. "That makes this list invalid. Loners get into trouble, McCann. It's not a good sign."

The sheriff's words were like a slap in the face along with the driving rain. "I'm single and unattached *because* I put all my focus and energy into what I do." A fact he hesitated to admit, but like it or not, it was the truth. Savannah was the living proof of that.

"Everyone needs a sounding board to process the tough stuff we face. Can you guarantee you have the mental strength and stamina to handle this rescue? Teamwork will be the critical factor." Sheriff Tanner leaned against his SUV. He held a plastic-protected file in one hand and rubbed his cheek with the other. The emergency lights from the vehicle splashed onto the sheriff's stony face, making clinging droplets glisten in the intermittent flashes. Neither man would back down an inch.

"You've obviously checked my record, so you'll know I've trained for this." Michael resisted an eye roll. "Check my record more if you must."

"I have. Now, look. It'll be a tricky one, McCann. I need to make sure those hikers have the best chance for survival—while mitigating unnecessary risk to the rescuers. How can a man like you have a blank emergency contact list?" He pinned Michael with a piercing gaze that would make veteran search and rescuers cringe. "On paper, your reputation is good, and you come highly recommended, but—" The sheriff's car radio blared static, and a garbled message cut off their conversation.

Michael let his nerves settle. "You question my skills as a technical rescuer because of a next-of-kin list?"

"I know it sounds that way, but if something happens, I need an emergency contact. I'm accountable to my superiors as much as you are to yours. Come on. You know how this works."

The incessant *swish-squeak, swish-squeak* of the SUV's wiper blades grated on Michael's frayed nerves. Hours had passed since the rain caused the initial flooding that prompted Teton County Search and Rescue responders to call for help. He'd since brought his support crew and all their equipment in the helicopter to Jackson Hole.

"My men and I take calculated risks within the ordered chaos. And we've worked together as a team for years. These guys work at a level of trust few experience. They risked their lives for each other. I'm not alone out there. And together with your medical team and the local volunteers, you can count on us."

Sheriff Tanner nodded. He stood tall and handed Michael the transparent plastic folder. A pen clipped inside it gave it some weight. Michael stood his ground and looked the man in the eye. The sheriff's gaze held a challenge, as did his, no doubt, like steel blades in combat. He could almost see sparks fly.

"I know about your climbing accident. Now, I need to know it won't happen again. Put one current name on your emergency contact list, and you're good to go."

"Yes, sir." Michael dipped his head in acknowledgment, his cursory smile as fake as the enthusiastic tone in his voice.

Sheriff Tanner took shelter behind the tinted windows of his vehicle in response to another radio call, and Michael clenched his jaw. Would his days as a reckless youth ever cease coming back to bite him? Hadn't he turned his mistakes around to help others? He'd worked hard to build a good reputation. Wasn't that enough?

The clock was ticking. Every minute they wasted on higher-ups with their interrogations, paperwork, and lists lessened the odds of survival for the trapped hikers. He scribbled a name and number on the sheet. God willing, they'd never have to make the call. Michael knocked on the tinted window.

The window slid down, and Michael handed over the paper and pen. "Here you go, Sheriff." He saluted the man as he drove off.

Michael rejoined his crew. "Okay, men, listen up." In the waning light, they huddled around the rudimentary map used by locals for their annual cave-rescue training exercises. Owen lit the gas lamp so they could better see.

"Here's what we know about those in the cave. There's an unclaimed car in the parking lot with out-of-state plates. Which means they are not locals and aren't familiar with the terrain."

Benji raised a hand. "Has anyone filed a missing-persons report?"

"Not yet. Suspected entry point is here at daybreak, where four pairs of boots were found."

Johnnie shook his head. "Why would they take off their boots before going into the cave?"

"Who knows?" Owen shrugged. "We'll have plenty of time to ask them once we get them out alive. Maybe they were resting and something made them go back into the cave."

"What?" Johnnie's eyes widened. "Like a wild animal or—"

"There's no way to tell." Michael pointed out the path to the entrance of the cave. "The rain wiped out all footprints and any tracks. Sherriff says the cave goes in about twenty-four feet before it narrows to a passageway leading deeper into the mountain. The locals say there are many constrictions and the cave is like a maze."

Benji traced a finger along the passageways on the map. "Without route-finding skills, these amateurs could be stuck in there without food or water for days."

"Exactly." Responsibility weighed heavy on Michael's shoulders. "Our biggest concern is that the cave floor dips substantially before elevating again. It's an unmapped muddy cave known to fill with water in a storm like this. If that's the case, their exit is likely blocked."

Benji's face puckered as he scowled. "So, there's a very good reason that cave isn't on the normal map for the public to see."

It wasn't Michael's first time in uncharted territory. Michael eyed the map and then looked out over the terrain, imagining the cave entrance below them. "Be prepared to float out injured hikers if the water level is low enough. Otherwise, we'll have to swim them out.

Owen, make sure we have all we need in case that happens."

"Got it." Owen nodded. "But how up-to-date is that map?"

"It's a year old, and any rockfalls or changes in the water flow since then could make it tricky. Also, they say there's a sinkhole higher up that feeds the runoff water into the obscure cave. You need a certain amount of skill in route finding and have plans in place to go spelunking in this area. By all indications, the group had none of that, nor did they check in with the park office."

Johnnie straightened his shoulders. "Whatever it takes, we'll get them out. When do we move?"

Michael liked that kind of attitude.

"At daybreak, we make our way here." He pinpointed the spot on the map and pointed downhill to where a temporary shelter had been erected near the gorge. "We repel down, then head into the cave, where they will have already set up a tarp with our diving gear and supplies."

"I've already made sure we have spare wet suits." Trust Owen to be ahead of the game.

"Great. All right, men. Once everything has been double-checked and moved to the staging area for the locals to lower down into the cave, see if you can squeeze in some shut-eye tonight."

Johnnie, the newbie of the crew, bent over the oxygen tanks, testing the regulators and mouthpieces. Michael appreciated his give-all attitude, but he'd still have to keep a close watch on him until he gained more experience. He needed to know Johnnie worked under the same set of ethics as the rest of the team. He gave Michael the impression of being a bit wild, reminding him of his younger days. Maybe it was his long hair and tattoos.

Michael tugged at the knots on his rope-covered steel cable and tested his climbing equipment one more time. He mentally reviewed everything his team needed to accomplish at daybreak. It was rare for him to combine his climbing, caving, and diving skills in one rescue, but trapped hikers in a flooded cave left little choice. They'd exhausted all other options. Their best bet would be to extract the survivors by using a rope and harness to haul them up the side of the cliff—if they could get them out safely through the water back to the entrance.

With his crew checking equipment, the only thing left for him to do was wait. He stepped into the doorway of the tent to check on the weather. In the tent next to theirs, a local crew was finishing setting up their base of operations, where they'd administer medical services to deal with injuries. A blond woman broke from the group setting up spotlights and headed their way. "Well, if it isn't my favorite rescuer."

Michael towered over the five-foot powerhouse. She was small but feisty. "Gillian, what in the world are you doing in these parts?" He pulled her just inside their tent for a soggy hug.

"You're dripping!"

Johnnie stuck his head out from behind a stack of supplies. "Gillian?"

The woman swung around as Johnnie stepped around the tarp-covered compressor.

"Gillian! What are you doing out here?" Johnnie stood with his arms by his sides, his eyes wide and his jaw slack.

"It's been years." She pointed a thumb over her shoulder. "Are you with these guys?"

Johnnie shrank back into the shadows. "I...we. Um, yes. Michael recruited me almost a year ago."

Gillian turned to face Michael, her brows raised.

"Johnnie is working as Benjamin's buddy. Great to have you on this with us, Gillian." Michael grinned at the paramedic. It was nice to see a friendly face.

Johnnie mumbled and scurried out of the tent toward their borrowed pickup truck.

"I heard they called you in. You are looking a lot better than when my dad and I first met you, dangling off that tree like a Christmas ornament."

"I owe my life to the quick actions of your dad. How is he doing?"

"He's great. Looking forward to retirement. Took me a while to recognize you with that new haircut."

"My helmet fits better, too. I thought I'd go for a more respectable, less wild-mountain-man look. Do you like it?"

He ducked his head so she could see the style better.

Gillian ran her hand over the short spikes. "You look perfectly respectable, unlike Johnnie over there with his mop. Speaking of which, I didn't expect to find him here." She stepped into the light. "Then again, I transferred out here about a year ago. Needed a change."

"How do you know Johnnie?"

Her eyes sparked, then cooled. A slight frown furrowed her brow. "It's complicated. Let's say we grew up together."

"Girl next door?" Michael asked, lowering his voice. Just like the girl he'd known even though she'd lived three blocks away instead of next door.

"Something like that," Gillian whispered. "It's history."

"I sense there's a story there. Maybe someday, you'll tell me about it. Anyway, it's good to see you. We go in at first light, so now that we have our game plan, I'm hoping my team can get a couple hours of shut-eye. We'll have to catch up when it's all over."

"You can buy me a coffee—how's that? Our crew has four rescue stretchers standing by, but try your best not to need us, okay?" With a general wave for the whole group, she retreated into the shadows. Her quick departure left questions hanging in the humid air.

Johnnie returned with their spare oxygen cylinders and positioned them on the pallet to keep them off the muddy ground. Outside, the rain abated to a misty drizzle.

Michael stepped closer. "Johnnie, is there something I should know about you two?" he asked, lowering his voice so the others didn't hear.

"No." Johnnie tucked his hair behind his ears and nodded at Michael. "We're cool."

"Look me in the eye and tell me Gillian being here means nothing to you."

Johnnie's shifty gaze told him all he needed to know. He'd have to keep a close eye on Johnnie and adjust their plan so the kid's rattled state wouldn't pose an unnecessary risk to the operation. Every member of the team had to be 100 percent focused and committed. Including himself. He wouldn't give Sheriff Tanner reasons to doubt him further.

While he was used to memories of Savannah intruding on his thoughts and invading his dreams back in Detroit, here she was an unnecessary and potentially dangerous distraction. There was no room for emotion when it came to hauling people out of tight spots unscathed. He had a job to do, and he'd do it well.

CHAPTER 21

THE COMING DAWN TURNED THE SKY gray as they waited for the sunrise over the mountain, and the air was heavy with anticipation. Michael stood under the tarp with his men around him, each with a paper cup of steaming coffee in hand. He ran the plan through his mind one more time.

Owen tapped Michael on the shoulder, interrupting his thoughts. "A local news channel got wind of what was going down. They've set up their cameras and microphones on the other side of the gorge. The undersheriff is going over there now to tell them to back off." Good old Owen. Not letting anything get past him.

"Thanks. Let's stay clear, and hopefully, they'll leave us alone." Michael had no intention of allowing the news crew to interfere with their operation.

He drained the last of his coffee and tossed the cup into the nearby trash can. "Just one last thing before we head out."

All eyes turned to him, determination and courage evident in their wide and steady stances—despite the circumstances. "Keep your ears open at all times. If you hear anything change—wind direction, a sudden downpour, an incoming rush of water—the sooner we all know about it, the safer we'll be."

Owen crushed his empty cup and lobbed it in the trash. "Weather report says the rain will let up for a couple hours, then start up again around noon. Hopefully, it will hold off long enough for the cave to drain and the water levels to recede."

Michael's gut had been churning ever since he asked Johnnie about Gillian. A change so late in the game was always risky, but he never ignored his instinct. "Johnnie, a change of plan. You're with me."

Johnnie nodded, a smile tugging at his lips. "Benjamin and Owen, you'll be pairing up instead. Any objections?"

"Owen had better be right about the weather. I'm not a fan of mud." Benjamin shot Owen a mock glare.

"All right, you guys. No time to waste. Let's show the sheriff how it's done." Michael fist-bumped each man, meeting their gazes in silent camaraderie. They turned toward the gorge, and the faintest feeling of unease slithered down Michael's spine and halted his stride. Should he pray?

"What's up?" Johnnie's voice came from behind.

Michael waved at Owen and Benjamin. "You two, wait here. Owen, check the scuba gear. We'll need it. Johnnie, follow me."

Michael and Johnnie switched on their high-performance headlamps. Their dual beams pierced the darkness. Bat's wings fluttered, and little rodent feet scurried in response. Johnnie didn't flinch—a good sign that he, too, didn't fear vermin or the protected insect-eating mammals who fought their own little war for survival against fungal disease in these parts.

Guided by the way-finding rope used by search and rescue during their failed attempts to reach the hikers yesterday, they waded into the silty water until it reached their thighs. The dank, earthy smell was less pungent than in the permanently flooded caves he'd been in before.

"Let's go back for the scuba gear and wet boots. If the map is close to accurate, the water only gets deeper from here."

After retracing their steps, they met Owen and Benjamin at the mouth of the cave. "Suit up. We're going in." Michael changed out of his wet pants and set his hiking boots aside to dry under the tarp. He tugged on his wet suit and footwear that Owen had laid out next to their tanks, thankful it would give him a measure of protection against the ever-present risk of hypothermia. Rainwater in a cave would lower his body temperature too fast and render him useless for the job. Although the exterior of the mountain had warmed significantly in the June sun, it wasn't warm enough in these conditions.

As their heads bent over the map Michael had traced on waterproof paper the night before, Johnnie handed each man an extra waterproof flashlight.

"According to search and rescue, the path-finding ropes they'd followed before they'd had to turn back when the water got too high go all the way to the first chamber. Although the ropes probably go all the way to chamber three on their training map." Michael moved his finger along a line on the map. "About two miles."

Owen scooted closer. "My guess is that the hikers are in chamber one. The elevation is higher than here." He stabbed the map with a finger of his gloved hand. "If so, they'd be on level ground."

"That's best-case scenario, although I'm not sure how the locals would not have found them there. But if the hikers ventured deeper into the mountain, then they could be past chamber three. We need to plan for that and hope we don't have to push further. The map only goes to chamber three—then we're into uncharted territory. It's been over twenty-four hours, and who knows what state the survivors are in? Benjamin, do you have the emergency food and water supplies in your pack?"

"Right here." Benjamin patted the waterproof bag. "Once we have proof of life, the radio for medical help is under the tarp. The medics will be down stat. Best case, we have bumps and bruises. Worse case..."

Michael factored in all possibilities while hoping for the best. The time for talk was over. He shouldered his tanks and other dive equipment. "Johnnie and I will lead. Owen and Benji, give us five minutes, then follow the rope." Michael rested his hand on the rope reel strapped to his belt. "We'll lay a new line if we go off course, but make sure you stay focused. Let's move."

Four beams of light penetrated the darkness as thigh-deep sludge became chest-deep water. The cave ceiling remained high, giving them sufficient headspace as they pressed on. If the water level stayed manageable, they could float the hikers out, but Michael didn't like the undercurrent tugging at his feet.

Taking care to keep his gloved fingers on the line as the icy water reached chin height, he paused to put on his fins and glanced at his team. "Going under. According to the map, the cave veers off and dips before it climbs and opens into a cavern."

"Chamber one, right?" Johnnie snapped on his fingerless gloves and positioned his dive mask over his face.

"Fins on, men. Let's hope we greet some hikers when we surface."

Suspended grains of sand and debris danced in the shaft of light from Michael's headlamp, making it difficult to see even the bubbles from his regulator—mere inches from his face. With one hand on the line, he ran the fingers of his other hand along the opposite wall of the cave. The corridor narrowed until it was a few inches wider than his shoulders. After taking a deep breath, he maneuvered through. His equipment scraped along the wall, and the rope in his left hand turned upward.

If he were a novice diver, he might get freaked out right about now. Instead, Michael moved smoothly through the upward-slanting tunnel until the route leveled in front of him. He broke the surface, then pulled himself out of the water onto a sandy ledge to his right. He removed his mask and sniffed the stagnant air as Johnnie popped out of the water and hopped onto the ledge next to him. He was relieved that the rookie handled that tunnel with poise.

Michael pointed his light to illuminate spectacular stalactites suspended from the high ceiling, glistening in the beam. Water dripped down the sides of the cave. He swept his light over the chamber, searching for objects that had been left behind, signs the hikers had rested there.

"Chamber one." Michael swallowed hard. "No sign of survivors."

He glanced at his watch. Even by moving quickly in the water, they'd taken an hour to swim through the tunnel, being careful not to knock their tanks loose on the overhanging rocks. To hike on foot would have taken longer.

"Hear anything?" Johnnie whispered into the eerie silence.

"Nothing."

Only the sound of Owen's and Benji's bubbles surfacing broke the silence. The two popped up, removed their masks, and looked around.

Benji's tone was grim. "Guess we'll visit chamber two next."

* * * *

After another cold and murky swim, albeit not nearly as cramped or as long as the first tunnel, Michael surfaced and removed his mask and regulator. He found chamber two as empty as chamber one. Even the bats rated it unfit to hang out in. He eyed the rock formations overhead in the light of his headlamp. Being clocked on the head by a rock presented less of a threat than hypothermia in these cold and wet conditions. He had seen it before—survivors who overcame the odds only to succumb to the effects of the prolonged cold. Still, some of those formations were suspect.

Owen, Johnnie, and Benjamin surfaced, their light beams bobbing in the darkness and creating menacing shadows. Once they removed their fins and hooked them to their belts, they waded on in their wet suit boots. The others waded behind him and Johnnie through the icy current that was gaining strength. They'd have to swim even harder against the current as they continued. They needed to pick up their pace. Unease niggled at his consciousness. The danger to his crew was mounting with no sign of life to justify their risk.

Michael glanced at his watch. They'd been in the cave for over two hours. His hope that chamber three would offer up their refugees dimmed like the waning light at dusk. How had the hikers gotten this far? And why? People didn't just wander this deep into a cavernous mountainside without knowing what they were doing.

Owen tapped him on the shoulder. "You think they got disoriented? Thought they were headed to the exit?"

"Maybe. I wouldn't want to be in here without footwear, though. This whole thing makes no sense. Watch your heads." Michael reached up to steady himself on the low-hanging jagged rock ahead of them and ducked under it.

"Hey! Wait up." Owen's headlamp highlighted the protruding rock that Michael had just ducked under. A streak of deep red stained the rock where his hand had touched.

Michael held his fingers up to the light. They were red. He brought them to his nose and sniffed. The still-detectable metallic smell confirmed his fears. Blood. And it was fresh. Not the sign of life they were looking for. "Looks like the hikers came this way, and chances are we'll need to deal with an injury as well as hypothermia. Not good. Let's move."

"They can't be far," Owen said to the group. *Always the optimist.* Michael loved that about O, always keeping morale high.

The passage twisted deeper into the mountain, and the gradual incline caused the water to drop to waist deep. All four stooped to avoid hitting their heads on the rocky roof. The passage opened into what must be chamber three. They'd reached the end of the area covered by their map, so Michael folded it, unzipped his wet suit, and tucked the damp map inside. He turned to his men. "Here's where the lines end. Ready?"

A collective grunt confirmed they were. Michael began laying a line where the annual training team's guide ropes ended deep in the mountain. His new line would guide his team farther into the cave. His nerves zinged with anticipation. How far would they have to venture into the heart of the mountain? "Let's press on."

One behind the other, they made slow progress as they climbed the winding passageway up toward what must be another chamber. Their calves sloshed through the receding murky water, making more noise than man-size washing machines on spin cycle.

Once they were on dry land, Michael tested each foothold for safety as they scrambled up and over jagged rock formations and down into the opening of a large water-filled sandy cavern, the beams from their headlamps bounced off the craggy cave walls. Michael surveyed the area. The stagnant air stank of sweat and urine. He'd been in enough caves to immediately know when something was different. He stopped and held up his hand to halt the others. "Wait. Quiet."

A faint sob sounded up ahead. Michael's heart raced, and a smile spread across his face. "Hello?" His voice boomed and bounced around the chamber.

Sounds of scrambling and scuffling reached him, and three wide-eyed faces appeared like meerkats from a hidden alcove, blinking as four beams of light found them.

"We're here to get you out. Is everyone okay?"

"We're here!" Three gravelly voices answered in unison.

Michael tied off his line and stepped down into the icy water. He advanced through chest-high water toward the huddled hikers, scanning their bodies for injuries, careful not to shine his light directly into their eyes. He was close enough to see they were standing, dressed in muddied T-shirts and shorts, seriously underdressed for their ordeal.

"One at a time."

"We're okay, but Andrea's not," said the redheaded guy sporting five-o'clock fuzz, who looked like he was in his forties. "She hit her head. Can you help her?" He waved toward where they'd been huddling.

Ah, so, there *were* four hikers like the sheriff suspected. Michael motioned for Owen and Benjamin, who'd waded into the water behind him, to clamber onto the sandbank while he retrieved the map and handed it along with a pen to Johnnie. "Update this, will you? If she needs medical help to come to her, we'll have to go by an updated map."

"Right. I'm on it."

Beside the redhead, a teenage boy and girl huddled together. The young man's arm encircled the shivering girl's bony shoulders, and Michael dug a couple of thermal blankets out of his waterproof bag and tossed them to the shivering pair. While the young man unwrapped his, the girl's gaze followed Michael's every move, and her chin trembled as silent tears rolled down her face.

Owen unfolded the foil blanket and tucked it around the teenage girl. "What's your name?"

She tore her gaze away from Michael and frowned at Owen.

"Her name's Tina." The young man pulled her closer.

"Tina. Everything will be fine. We'll get you out of here." The girl nodded, accepting the warmth of the blanket and his words with a weak smile. Owen certainly had a way with kids and teenagers. They gravitated to him as if he were a rock star, a trait for which Michael was grateful.

Owen disappeared into the alcove where they'd said Andrea was while Benjamin retrieved water bottles from his pack and handed them to the disheveled hikers. The trio grabbed them like he'd handed them nectar from the gods. "Slow down," Benjamin said. "Small sips. Don't chug it."

Three sets of eyes looked at Michael as if to say, "Is he for real?"

Michael grinned. "If you haven't had fresh water since yesterday, take it easy."

Owen reappeared, but he avoided eye contact with the hikers as he hopped back into the water and waded over to Michael.

Uh-oh, he knew that look. "What's her status?" Michael asked, lowering his voice.

Owen turned his back on the others. "We can't move her, Michael. Her vitals are weak." He scrubbed a hand over his face. "If we can't get Gillian and her crew in here, then we'll need a spinal board and a neck brace. It doesn't look good. The shirt wrapped around her head is saturated, and it's obvious she's lost a lot of blood. I didn't get a look at the wound, but…"

Michael's mind kicked into high gear. Their options were limited. "Find out if those three can swim. If they can, you and Benji get the two best swimmers to the entrance of the cave. You'll have to buddy up and share air. Johnnie and I will stay with the others until you come back. Fill Gillian in and accompany her back here. She'll know what to bring."

Owen's brow furrowed. "You think they'll be able to swim through the tunnel?" he whispered.

"They have to." Michael turned away from the rest of the group. "It's not a long way underwater, and you have a spare regulator."

Owen nodded, but his eyes said otherwise. Michael could tell he wasn't convinced.

"You've got this, O. Benjamin's done this before. Give him the lead if you have to." Michael rested his gloved hand on Owen's shoulder and squeezed before sharing his reasons that this plan was the best option. "We're running out of time. The return trip will take almost four hours. More rain is coming. These three are already showing signs of hypothermia. Tina's the worst, but despite the boy's bravado, he's not far behind. We have to get them out of here—and fast. Once they are out, they can be treated for their various scrapes and cuts."

"Right."

"First, we need more light." Michael pulled an impact glow stick from his pack and hurled it into the dark recess of the cave. It clattered and came to rest on the rocky cave floor, where it cast a soft blue glow. He handed another to Owen, who carried it to Andrea's location.

"That should keep the shadows at bay for eight hours, more than enough time to get everyone out of here safely." Michael wasn't as sure as he sounded, but his words would give the hikers the hope they needed.

Owen joined his brother. "Benji, are you ready for a swim?" Michael caught his teasing whisper.

Benji glanced over at Michael, his jaw tense like he'd already guessed what this plan was. Michael gave him a reassuring thumbs-up and sloshed over to Johnnie. He double-checked the updated map before nodding his approval.

Michael and Benji bent over the map, their heads almost touching. "You'll have to guide these hikers back to chamber two, then through the narrow passage. I say take the teenagers out first. The girl's body temperature is low."

Johnnie's finger hovered over the map. "Think they'll make it through here without panicking?"

"Never underestimate the will to survive. Owen and Benjamin have talked kids in worse shape through tighter places. If they panic, Owen won't go through with it. The water is too high to float them out, so there goes that plan. Then, we'll go to plan C."

"Which is?" Johnnie lifted his head, and their gazes met.

Michael kept his gaze steady. "We pray for a miracle."

CHAPTER 22

SAVANNAH SHOT A SECRET SIDEWAYS GLANCE at Dr. Radcliffe as they walked toward the library parking lot. Running into him just outside the coffee shop where she'd popped in for a bite to eat and to buy a bag of cookies for her rare afternoon off with Mrs. Delaney had been a pleasant surprise. Perhaps they could be friends outside her research-librarian duties after all. Things between her and the professor couldn't be more perfect or more different from how Michael affected her. Clean-cut, the former lawyer wore a navy blazer and jeans, far too dashing to be a professor, yet—nothing.

No heart palpitations when he smiled. No thoughts about him at random times of the day. No dreams about kissing his lips. No hidden emotional landmines. Thank goodness.

She did her best to get on with her life without Michael. But every morning, her feeble prayers for the strength to accept her lonely fate seemed to bounce off the ceiling. Still, at least, she was trying. However, her accidental meeting on campus with Dr. Radcliffe didn't distract her enough.

She patted her pocket. Yep, her phone was still there. She fished it out. No messages, no notifications. Nothing. She huffed and shoved it back in her pocket.

The professor removed his sunglasses. "May I ask you a personal question?"

"Sure." Savannah slowed until she stood face to face with the professor in front of a bronze statue of some long-gone ornithologist.

"Are you satisfied with where your life is going, Savannah?"

Had he read her mind? "Why do you ask, Professor?" She tucked a strand of hair behind her ear and peered at him through lowered eyelashes.

"Please, call me Donavan."

Savannah wasn't comfortable being on a first-name basis with handsome single men—well, except Michael. *Doctor* seemed too medical after all she'd been through with Nick and his illness, so she balked at saying the word, even if it was accurate. Just *Radcliffe* got too close to that teasing banter she shared with Michael. Although calling him *Professor* wasn't right, either, since she wasn't his student. But it was the best option since she didn't want him to get the wrong idea.

"Savannah, we only just met a week and a half ago, but in the last couple days, you've been restless and distracted."

"I have?" She cleared her throat. "How so?"

"It's like you're somewhere else. Not present with me. You check your phone like you expect an important text, then look desolated when you don't see what you were hoping for. At least, that's what I thought at first. But it's been days and you still do it."

"What? Librarians can't get important text messages?"

"They can, but you've been obsessively checking your phone. It's keeping you agitated, like a cornered raccoon."

"Pfft. I'm not obsessive just because..." The lie died on her lips. "Do I really come across as obsessive?"

Dr. Radcliffe's gentle smile coaxed a grin of her own. "Are you sure you want me to answer that?"

"Maybe not."

"What's up, though? Are you being blackmailed or threatened?" Genuine concern mixed with a smidgen of teasing furrowed his brow and raised his eyebrow. "Should I worry?"

"No!" Savannah placed her free hand on the professor's forearm. "Nothing like that." She shook her head. A strand of hair loosened itself from her ponytail and blew across her face.

The professor gently tucked the strand back in place. Such a tender gesture set off alarm bells because it was something Michael had done often. Had she given him the wrong impression? She snatched back her hand and wrapped her arms around her middle, jostling the bag, releasing the aroma of chocolate and warm cookies. The scent reminded her of another bag of warm cookies shared with a man with a pair of mesmerizing blue eyes.

She sighed.

Might as well tell him the truth. "It's a long story. Remember that reunion I told you about the day we met?"

"I remember." Dr. Radcliffe led her by the elbow to the park bench below the bronze statue. "Come on. Let's sit."

Savannah settled next to him, balancing the bag of cookies on her knee, and turned. "You had guessed the high school had our twenty-year reunion, but my late husband made me promise to go in his absence. I ran into his best friend, Michael, who also happened to be one of my closest friends. In fact, he and I were closer friends until Nick swept me off my feet. Anyway, it was great to see Michael again. It was comfortable and familiar. We even took an impromptu trip to Niagara Falls to explore. Let's just say things went well. At least, until he basically told me he had always been in love with me but Nick's memory stood between us."

"He broke your heart?"

"Not exactly. I think I may have broken his. We both came up with reasons it would never work. Honestly, I thought we were doing the right thing. I convinced myself we were acting as mature adults; then, we committed to keep in touch and stay close friends."

"And he hasn't texted…and you are second-guessing the whole thing."

Savannah studied him through narrowed eyes. "Are you sure you studied law and not psychology?" Dr. Radcliffe had an appealing smile. Pity it wasn't as stunning as Michael's. She missed that smile with a physical ache.

"You're not the first woman to ask."

Here was another man who could laugh at himself.

"It's more complicated than just a high school crush." So, she was perhaps more than halfway in love with Michael. Had she always been on some level, and now, was her love finally blooming only to wither on the vine?

A restless breeze rustled the wild grass along the pathway, causing the nearby flowers to bob and buckle mirroring her own agitation. She bet the bees were having a hard time clinging to their petals.

No regrets, right? That was a promise they made. That and to keep in touch…so she would keep on texting even if he didn't reply.

"It's understandable that you'd be extra cautious about making another commitment. Sorry. I think my solitary hours spent watching talk shows are showing, huh?"

Savannah grinned. This man had such a strong sense of empathy. A weight lifted from her shoulders. What a treasure to share her heart with him. Evelyn and the girls would never understand. They'd jump to the wrong conclusion and suggest retail therapy—a practice she'd rather not be coerced into.

"Doctor—Donavan, you will make some lucky girl a wonderful husband one day."

"Why, thank you."

Was the professor right? Was she second-guessing herself? No, her feelings for Michael were true; absence had made them stronger. The only thing she was second-guessing was why she'd waited so long to text him in the first place. If only Michael would let her know he was okay. Maybe hint that he missed her, too? Tempted to check her phone again, she resisted because she had an audience who'd already called her an obsessed raccoon. She needed to get a grip and accept that Michael could forget more easily than she could. She could, however, glance at her phone to check the time. Right?

"I need to get going. I have the afternoon off, and I'm having tea and cookies with Mrs. Delaney."

He took her free hand and pulled her to her feet. He shoved his sunglasses back on his face as the sun dipped lower in the sky. "I'll see you around." He waved goodbye with a cheery smile lingering on his face.

She picked up her pace toward her car. Mrs. Delaney was one to raise an eyebrow if she was even a minute late. Before long, she was seated on Mrs. Delaney's floral couch.

Who'd have thought a lady with doilies on every surface of her home would become so dear? Nine doilies in the living room alone. Savannah had counted them twice on her first visit to make sure she wasn't seeing things. They were the crocheted kind, made from fine cotton strands. Mrs. Delaney had made her one. It was tucked away in her linen closet, and she brought it out only when Mrs. Delaney visited.

Savannah settled into the wingback chair. The clatter of china teacups from Mrs. Delaney's kitchen reminded her of afternoons spent with her mother in Florida before the reunion and before life got complicated—also known as Michael.

A ginger tabby cat trotted into the room. He looked her up and down, deemed her worthy, and ambled over to sit at her feet. "Hello, kitty. Aren't you a handsome boy?"

The animal inclined his head as if to say, "Duh! Glad you noticed."

She rubbed him under his chin. The tabby jumped onto the arm of the chair and nuzzled her face. A rumbling purr confirmed his pleasure, and he curled up on her lap like it was newfound territory.

Nick had wanted a dog. He'd never said as much, but Savannah suspected he wanted to ease the pain after the miscarriage. Then, after Nick's diagnosis, they'd dropped the idea. But Savannah had always wanted another bird like Henry. Except that reminded her of Michael, so perhaps she'd pick a pet unassociated with either of the men. Like a sweet, easygoing, cuddly cat.

Was this her life now? Were tea parties with gray-haired old ladies to be the highlight of her week? Then again, the episode at the climbing gym had been a highlight. Cold sweats broke out whenever she thought about how she could have fallen to her death. With this trend, she would die either of boredom or of fright.

"I'm so glad you and Teddy are getting along." Mrs. D held a cup of steaming tea inches from her nose. "Here you go, dear."

The cup rattled in its saucer as Savannah placed it on the doily-covered end table. "Thank you. You said you had something important to ask me?"

"I'm going to India, Nepal, and thereabouts. I need someone to take care of Teddy while I'm away. Can you do it for me?"

"Sure—are you going by yourself?" The eighty-four-year-old walked with a cane and had no qualms about traveling halfway across the world at the drop of a doily.

Apart from immigrating with her parents from South Africa to the States, Savannah's big adventure had taken her barely into Canada. She stifled a moan that threatened to expose her shame. Mrs. D hadn't let age stop her. At almost half Mrs. D's age, Savannah had stagnated. She'd put her life on hold and hadn't quite figured how to get it unstuck. Then, Michael had turned her world upside down. Stuck and upside down—and confused. Yet she hadn't felt so alive as when standing near the rushing waterfall or holding the macaw or laughing at the sight of him folded into her tiny car. Almost the same sensations she'd had after being shoved out of her comfort zone to throw an ax or climb a rock wall. Hmm. So, maybe the somewhat tingling and painful feeling of being upside down was actually her coming back to life after the fog of grief? Was upside down actually right side up? Something for her to ponder later.

"I'm going with Andrew and Gladys from the bridge club. They've invited their friend Mr. Sanders." Mrs. Delaney handed Savannah a folded stack of papers. "That's our itinerary and some contact details if you need to get hold of us. I've included instructions on which weather channels Teddy likes."

Now, she'd heard it all and sunk to an ultimate low. She'd be keeping company with a TV-watching cat for a month. The three-page document detailed their extensive trek across numerous countries. She unfolded the notes. "This is quite an expedition. You'll be touring all these exotic cities—Mumbai, Kathmandu, Mandalay, and Bangkok, ending in Vladivostok, before flying back home via Paris. Is it safe?"

Mrs. Delaney sat, perched on the matching chair, sipping her tea. "Is what safe, dear?"

"I'm sorry, Mrs. D, but unless you travel with someone who knows the pitfalls of developing countries, you could fall into danger."

"The only danger I'm in, dear girl, is to fossilize here at home because people think I'm too old to enjoy life."

"People?"

"My nephew kicked up a fuss." Mrs. Delaney stood and waved her cane. "He stands to inherit, and he would rather I not spend my last penny on traveling."

"Your last penny?" This reminded her of the life-insurance policy sitting in her bank account that she was too afraid to spend.

"Now, now, it's just a figure of speech." She leaned over and petted the sleeping cat on Savannah's lap. "Teddy and I are just fine. Aren't we?"

Teddy's purr engine rumbled back to life. Savannah could feel the vibrations all the way to her core. "When do you leave?" She reached for her tepid tea.

"I meant to mention it earlier, but you were with that new professor, so I thought I'd mention it later. Then, I had a senior's moment and forgot to mention it at our Scrabble game. But I leave this afternoon, dear. In fact, the taxi will be arriving in about twenty minutes."

Savannah almost spat bergamot black tea all over the sleeping cat. Tea dribbled down her chin as she sputtered and caught her breath. "So soon?"

"I've always been of the mind that once a plan is in motion, one must act on it in good time. I've planned this for months. I didn't want to mention it too early in case you tried to talk me out of it." Mrs. Delaney forced a laugh. "I've learned that opportunities pass you by if you hesitate. I'm too old to gather any more regrets."

Mrs. Delaney's words stung Savannah like a flick from a wet towel. She regretted plenty. And what was worse—she'd chosen these regrets. She'd walked away from the grandest adventure of her life when she asked Michael to take her home. Living with regrets based on her stupid choices was like a Dead Sea's worth of salt rubbed into her already-raw wounds.

"Now, tell me about Dr. Radcliffe." Mrs. D's fingers paused on the handle of her teacup. She leaned toward Savannah, her eyebrows raised. "He seems like such a lovely fellow."

The professor? His face hadn't been the one that popped into her mind moments ago at the mention of regrets. She wasn't thinking about his lips on hers nor whether he was allergic to cats. Dr. Radcliffe—Donavan—bless him, was calm, polite, and loyal. His only fault? He wasn't Michael.

"He's a good friend."

"Mm-mm-mm. I saw him hanging around the research section again this morning." Her voice lilted like she was asking a question and not merely pointing out the obvious.

"Really, I bumped into him outside the coffee shop. He has some interesting reading habits. Did I tell you he was a lawyer?"

"Are you trying to change the subject?"

"No, but there's nothing to tell." There was no hiding from Mrs. D's laser-sharp scrutiny, but she had nothing to hide when it came to Donavan Radcliffe. She straightened her spine and looked Mrs. D in the eyes.

"Savannah, dear." Her face softened. "Does he know there's nothing to tell?"

"What do you mean?"

Mrs. Delaney arched her brow. "Has he developed feelings for you?"

"Pfft. He hasn't. I'd know."

The meddling woman raised her cup, attempting to hide her smirk. "Like how you knew about Michael having feelings for you?"

Urgh! She should never have let the woman pull that part of her story out of her during last week's Scrabble match.

"I don't want to talk about him." A hasty sip of cooled tea did nothing to ease the dryness of her throat.

"Oh, yes, you do. I can see it in your eyes. You've been miserable ever since you came back from that reunion. Tell me again—what happened between you two?"

"We decided it wouldn't work out." Her teacup rattled in its saucer.

"We?" She narrowed her eyes, pinning Savannah with a knowing look. "Or you?"

"Well…"

"I thought so. And do you believe it was the right thing to do?"

Savannah fought back the tears that mingled with her mascara and stung her eyes. "I miss him so much. Logically, we made the best decision, but..."

"What does your heart say?"

"My heart is about to tumble out of my chest in a million pieces." If she could go back to when she had Michael in her arms, she'd never let him go.

"Have you told him how you feel?"

"It's no use. He's not answering my texts." They'd promised to remain friends, but even that hadn't stuck.

"If you think you've given him enough of a chance, then you need to move on. Let him go." She leaned over and waved a paper napkin Savannah's way. "There's no use living in the past. Live for today and look for your next adventure. Maybe something that involves a certain professor?"

Savannah hiccupped as she took the offered napkin to soak up the tears welling in her eyes. She'd chosen stability and predictability, a choice that was proving to be unsatisfying.

Mrs. Delaney sat back and wagged her finger in the air. "Except you'll have to wait until after my trip. Teddy hates to travel."

With that, the woman set down her teacup and disappeared into her bedroom, then emerged with a wheeled suitcase. "Come on, my dear. Give us a hug."

Savannah held on tight to this woman who'd become so dear to her and sent up a silent prayer for safe travels.

The older woman stroked the fur of her cat, whispering endearments and a sniffling, "Goodbye, Teddy." A honking horn outside sent Teddy scurrying into the kitchen. Mrs. D's eyes lit up. "That will be my taxi. Goodbye, my dear."

And with that, she disappeared out the door, leaving Savannah a bit shell shocked. At the sound of the taxi pulling away, Teddy finally peeked at her around the doorframe. Knowing that the honking monster was gone and likely concluding that the coast was clear, the feline walked across the living room, nose in the air and tail swishing like nothing had happened.

"Silly cat. Come on." Savannah grinned and patted the couch next to her. Teddy obliged by hauling his chubby self onto the seat and turned to face the television. "Meow."

"I presume that's cat for 'Get on with it.'"

Savannah perched on the edge of the couch and groaned in frustration. The remote control had a million buttons. Mrs. D was already on her way to the airport and couldn't help. Teddy sat upright, his tail tucked around his body. Occupying the other end of the couch, he stared at her and waited for the television to light up. "Which button do I press, Teddy?"

His meowed reply suggested he was saying "Stupid human."

Nick had always commanded the remote control, so she'd never mastered the skill. Unlike Teddy, Savannah would rather pass the time reading a book than watching the news or the weather.

When she pressed the large blue button, the television zinged to life, but the news report seemed to be almost over. Teddy looked at her in disgust.

"We interrupt to bring you breaking news. Authorities are concerned that the return of bad weather will jeopardize the search and rescue of hikers believed to be inside a cave in Wyoming." The anchor in his black suit and navy tie sat beside a brunette in a white blouse and gray suit jacket. "Reporting live from the scene is our correspondent Randy Aiken."

Savannah sat down next to Teddy. "There you go. We didn't miss out on all the news."

Trying to decipher Mrs. D's chicken-scratch writing, she pressed several buttons, and while the channels flicked, none was the one Teddy approved of, so she ended up back at the original station.

Teddy tucked his paws underneath his body and settled in to watch the live report. On the screen, rain lashed the man's face, the only exposed part of him in his rain slicker. Holding a bulbous microphone, Randy turned away from the camera and pointed across the gorge behind him. Lines, like the ones she'd seen at the climbing gym, dangled down a rock face above a cave. "We have unconfirmed reports that the missing hikers entered the cave over there. Four rescuers went into the cave at dawn. It's not looking promising, Sheila. Authorities are concerned the deteriorating weather is putting the operation in jeopardy. The sheriff's department has refused to comment, but we are monitoring the situation closely."

Teddy licked his paws. "Not interesting enough for you, huh?" He blinked at Savannah and curled up next to her as she stroked his silky fur.

"Back to you in the studio for your regular regional forecast," Randy said above the whistling wind. A map of New York State appeared on the screen, and a lady in a suit began expounding on high and low pressures and wind speeds. None of which was of interest at all.

With Teddy napping at her side, Savannah scrolled through the channels again. She settled on a documentary about an expedition to the Okavango Delta, but her mind soon wandered back to the news report. Grateful she was dry and warm, she sent up a prayer for those stranded hikers and the men and women who were risking their lives only because others took dumb risks first.

Her thoughts went back to Michael. How ironic that Michael's job was to rescue stranded strangers like those hikers yet he couldn't rescue their fractured relationship. But his first text after returning to Detroit said he'd rescue her anytime. She'd tried to reach out with her text messages, but it was his turn now. Despite what Mrs. D might think about chasing adventure and romance, Savannah hadn't lost her self-respect.

Mrs. Delaney had encouraged adventure and romance, but Michael had left her heart in tatters. Unregulated adventures, as the news report suggested, could be dangerous. After the climbing-wall fiasco, she promised herself she would try not to control everything in her life by holding on with white-knuckle force. She could ease her grip and take some risks of her own, just small ones. Like maybe listening to Mrs. D about letting Michael go and giving Donavan a chance.

No matter what Mrs. D said, for the foreseeable future, her adventures would be limited to minding Teddy and the complicated television remote beside her.

Teddy arched his back and hopped onto the carpet. After a quick sharpening of his claws on Mrs. D's Persian rug, he trotted off to the kitchen. A few moments later, he strutted back and sat in front of Savannah to clean his ears with his paws. He then climbed back up onto the couch only to plop his ample body onto the remote. The television screen went black. Oh no! At the sudden silence, Teddy began protesting, yowling and glaring at her like she'd been the one to turn off the TV.

She didn't know how to fix it. Except she'd pushed the big blue button before. She dug the remote out from under the furry animal, accidently pressing some other buttons in her feeble attempt to retrieve the remote. She pressed the large blue button. Nothing. Now, she'd done it. Another month of this, and she'd lose her mind. And then, Teddy hissed at her. Hissed! This was a real crisis.

Whom did she know with the genetics to understand remotes?

She pulled out her phone and looked on the university website for Dr. Radcliffe's email address. She opened her email and tapped an urgent message. She glared at the cat.

"Look what you made me do." She tapped her toes, worrying that the professor would be too busy with his bird books to read his email for hours. But what was a girl to do? A broken TV and an upset tabby weren't exactly what she'd had on her wish list for the day.

Her phone dinged, and she snatched it up.

BE THERE IN A FEW HOURS

CHAPTER 23

"I CAN'T DO IT." TINA'S EYES WIDENED in the dim light. Owen and Benjamin were already in the water. Michael's hopes that they'd make it back to the cave entrance without incident crashed. They'd already been talking Tina out of a panic for twenty minutes. He stood at the water's edge, holding a flashlight over the water rippling around Owen and Benjamin.

Tina turned her face away from the water they'd have to wade through to reach their flooded escape route.

The young man—Philip—grabbed her hand. "Tina, you're on the swim team at home. Think of it as another swim meet."

"In the pool, I can see the black line at the bottom. In clear, chlorinated water. Who knows what kind of bacteria and nasty stuff is in that water?" She shuddered and wrapped her arms around herself. "What if we run out of air and I can't see which way is up? This is murky stuff—no, I can't."

"You're both competitive swimmers?" Michael's gaze fixed on Tina, but he directed the question to Philip.

"Yes. That's how we met." Philip pulled Tina closer.

"You guys have done hypoxic training, then?" Michael appealed to them as athletes. "You know you can go without air longer than the average person might think."

The teenagers nodded.

Owen's casual smile helped ease the tension. "The tunnel we'll eventually reach isn't as long as the pool you train in."

"Once we scramble over those rocks, we'll be going along the passageway where you entered this chamber. From there, each of you will swim with one of us close by you. We've got wet suits, headlamps to help you see, in addition to the rope to guide our way. I'll give each of you your own flashlight; plus, we have fins which will propel you through the water, so you know you can make it without running out of air even if something should happen to the compressed air supply." Benjamin's puppy-dog eyes and soothing voice worked their own magic. "You'll be sharing air with us, so you don't have to worry about that. Especially since I can hold my breath way longer than my brother here."

Philip stood taller with a determined glint in his eyes. Tina's head moved from side to side, and Philip cupped her face in his fingers. "Tina, look at me. You can do this. Those nerves you feel when you get on the block? You already know how to overcome that feeling. Push back the fear; control it—delay it. You can freak out all you want after we're out."

Tina studied Philip's face. "What about Andrea?"

Michael leaned closer to the pair huddled on the sandbank. "We need to get you two out first, so the faster you get moving, the sooner she'll get help."

"Do this for Andrea," Philip said.

Tina nodded. "Let's get it over and done with."

"Now, that's what I like to hear." Owen grinned at Tina and held out his hand to help her up. He glanced at his watch. "Look. It's ten thirty now, and if all goes well, you'll be eating a late lunch in the sunshine."

Michael left Owen and Benjamin to give the teens further instructions. He scrambled up the steep sandbank and into the alcove, where Andrea lay in the lingering blue light of the glow stick. Muted shadows fell across her pale face beneath her makeshift bandage. It was all he could see of her injuries beneath the silvery blanket Johnnie had tucked around her slender frame. Johnnie sat at her head, and Danny, the redhead, was near her feet.

Johnnie met Michael's gaze. In his eyes, the message came through: *Don't ask how she is in front of her friend.*

Michael gritted his teeth. It couldn't be good, but he could already see from here that Owen's initial assessment was right. They wouldn't be moving the woman anytime soon. But he needed the facts before he could come up with a plan.

He cleared his throat. "Danny? Owen and Benjamin are instructing the others on how the extraction process works. You'll want to listen in so you know what to do when your turn comes."

Michael waited until Danny was well out of earshot before dropping his gear and squatting. "Okay, give it to me straight."

"Owen was right. I'm not a paramedic, but she's definitely clammy. She's in and out of consciousness. And when her eyes open, she's confused, like you'd expect with a head injury." His grim expression did nothing to calm Michael's suspicions that the risks were mounting like a pile of rotting fish. "There's no way she can be moved without stabilizing her first. How soon can we swim Gillian in?"

"Best case, they'll be on their way in with Gillian in four hours. It should only take three hours for them to get back here since we know the way. If the weatherman's wrong and the water level drops, maybe sooner." Michael wiped away an errant water droplet that tickled his hairline. "How do you think Gillian will do coming through that tunnel?"

"I don't know." A crease appeared on Johnnie's forehead. "She's a professional, but she was claustrophobic when we were kids. I'm no shrink, but that may have had something to do with her brother locking her in a closet." Johnnie rubbed his forehead, his expression pensive. "She told me she went to therapy for it. If there's no trigger…"

"We're asking her to go above and beyond. I don't mean to get personal, but if you brought her in, would that make a difference?" Michael's heart thudded. He pushed aside his emotions when working for a good reason. But if the connection between Gillian and Johnnie could get this girl the help she needed faster, it was worth a shot.

Johnnie squared his shoulders and looked Michael in the eye. "We have history, sure, but she trusts me. I can bring her in."

"Good. So, take Danny with you now, and follow the others out. I'll stay here with her." Michael propped his backpack up as a backrest and dug out a water bottle and a flashlight from his bag. He traded places with Johnnie, sitting with his knees by Andrea's shoulders and putting a hand on either side of her head to stabilize her neck.

Johnnie stood, dug in his pack, produced a wet suit, and rolled it up. "Since we can't use this for her, we might as well use it to cushion her. You hold her head while I position this around her head and neck."

Johnnie then turned and made his way down to the water's edge. Owen met Johnnie halfway and, after a few words, gave Michael a thumbs-up. They headed toward Tina and Philip, walking out of Michael's line of sight.

As the voices and splashing faded, Michael's pulse sped up. It would be a long wait until he'd know whether they made it out. He drew in a deep breath. In the dim blue light of the glow stick, he would have plenty of time to think and pray. "Hang in there, Andrea. They're bringing help."

Andrea would need a miracle if Gillian or one of her team couldn't get through in time. But then, Michael believed in miracles. There'd been a time when he'd been in Andrea's place.

A decade ago, he'd been in Yosemite, climbing a granite rock face without a rope. Free soloing pushed the risks to a new level, and he'd gotten too confident. If it hadn't been for the tree that broke his forty-foot fall and an off-duty paramedic's quick actions, he would have died. He'd opened his eyes in the hospital with a few broken ribs, a punctured lung, and a couple of cracked vertebrae, surprised that he wasn't at the pearly gates. That day, he'd promised to make his second chance at life count. He just never realized how helpless being a rescuer could make him feel.

Andrea's eyes fluttered open. "Danny?"

"Lie still. You're hurt." Michael squeezed her hand. "You're okay. I'm right here."

"Where's Danny?" She strained against Michael's hands, her eyes wide and unfocused.

He steadied her. "Just relax. Don't try sitting up. You'll see Danny soon."

The tension drained out of her. Her eyes rolled back and her eyelids slid shut.

Michael monitored the shallow rise and fall of Andrea's chest as water trickled down the walls of the cave. There was only so much he could do.

"God, Andrea needs You. There's no way we'll get her out of here without You. Please."

Michael turned off his headlamp to save the battery. His eyes quickly adjusted to the dimmer light of the cave, and so far, Andrea's breathing remained consistent. That was a good sign.

With a guttural moan, the young woman shifted and her eyes fluttered open again. "Take it back; take it back...for the...fifteen times—"

Andrea was babbling just like Johnnie had described. Not a good sign. Michael stabilized her head and neck while she thrashed. "Andrea, it's okay. Stay still."

Her breathing sped up as her face crumpled with pain. Wild-eyed, she blinked at him. "What happened?"

"You hit your head. I know it hurts. Help is coming. Hang in there just a little while longer." Michael reached for his water bottle. "Here's some water." He got a few sips into her by barely moving her head.

Her breathing slowed to an even rate, and within seconds, she was out cold again.

Michael shifted his weight on the damp, sandy floor. His muscles screamed for relief, but he couldn't risk leaving Andrea to stretch his legs. Flexing the muscles he could move, he turned his vigil into a mental challenge. Andrea needed him to stay focused and ready should she become distressed again.

He took a small sip from his water bottle—just enough to moisten his dry throat. He'd keep the rest for Andrea. How much longer? And how would they get Andrea out? He'd turned these questions over in his mind like an unsolved 3-D puzzle. If the water level receded, they could attempt to float her out, but the problem of the narrow tunnel remained. Going deeper into the cave, hoping they'd find another exit, would be madness. The last resort. He closed his eyes and prayed for wisdom.

He couldn't tell whether the swirling, rushing water had quieted or whether he'd gotten used to the sound after listening for hours. He guessed the water in the cave wasn't just a giant puddle, but perhaps it was being fed from somewhere.

An ominous shadow, shaped much like the hunchback of Notre-Dame, moved along the wall toward them. Michael froze. Whatever cast that shadow moved between the wall of the cave and the glow stick. The hair stood up on the back of his neck. Andrea was vulnerable, and he wasn't equipped to face a wild animal. He took a calming breath and held it, straining to hear over the dripping and flowing water.

Faint scuttling and scratching gave away a tiny rodent scampering their way. The furry creature caught sight of Michael and stopped in its little tracks. His beady eyes widened as if to say, "What are you doing here?"

Michael's shoulders sagged with relief, and he released the breath he'd been holding.

The little guy's whiskers twitched in the dim blue light.

Michael smiled. "Hey, where did you get those?"

The rodent possessively clutched a branch laden with wild blackberries as if to say, "Don't you touch my dinner." He turned tail and ran back the way he'd come.

"Funny little guy." Michael's smile lingered. It was a wonder animals lived so far underground. By the look of the leaves on that branch, it was freshly harvested from an unsuspecting bush. The water had flooded the entrance to the cave, so either that thief could swim or...

Michael strained his eyes to see where the critter had gone. He sat up and felt the smile slip off his face.

There must be another way out of the cave. Maybe God had answered his prayer about a way out for Andrea after all?

He clenched his jaw. He'd have to wait until Johnnie and Gillian returned. He couldn't leave Andrea to investigate until the others returned. He adjusted his position on the uncomfortable ground to ease another cramp in his leg and searched for a distraction. In the meantime, maybe he could plan his next vacation? He'd heard the scuba diving in the Egyptian Red Sea was spectacular. He'd never been to Africa. Maybe Savannah—he cut that thought off before it could fully form in his mind.

Would he ever accept that she'd be only a distant part of his life? He'd thought he'd figured out what was best— what he needed to do. Had he made a serious mistake in walking away from their second chance at love?

If Nick hadn't sent him that unexpected email a year ago, asking him to promise to go to the reunion. Then, he wouldn't be failing to keep a pair of sparkling eyes behind tortoiseshell-rimmed glasses out of his mind. Had Nick known he was going to die? Had he guessed Michael's reasons for leaving Point? Would Savannah ever come to terms with Nick's death and be ready to find love again?

Too many unanswered questions, but they would have to wait until he could get to a phone. In the meantime, he still had to figure out how to rescue Andrea.

CHAPTER 24

B Y 4:55, TWO DISGRUNTLED MALES SAT on Mrs. Delaney's couch and stared each other down. Why were they so territorial? Dr. Radcliffe's normally perfect hair was ruffled from raking his fingers through it. Savannah stifled a grin. Imagine that. A grown man intimidated by a cat.

Teddy hadn't taken well to the man's presence in his house, let alone on his favorite couch. His ears flattened, his tail puffed, and a line of hair along the ridge of his back stood on end like the bristles of a hairbrush.

"Maybe you should sit over here." She and the professor switched places. Teddy watched their every move. Satisfied that the intruder was far enough away, Teddy tucked his paws under his body and lay down, looking more like a loaf of bread than a ferocious feline.

The professor had promised to teach her how to use the dreaded remote. How he would do that from clear across the room remained to be seen.

"This is the power button, and this is the preprogrammed channel..." Donavan pressed a button, and the television zinged to life.

"Before we go to the weather, we have breaking news from the rescue attempt in—"

"This button is for the volume...and this one..." He pressed another button, and the channel changed. Cancan dancers waved their ruffled tulle skirts, exposing fishnet stockings and heeled lace-up boots while a familiar tune filled the room.

"Wait. Go back." Savannah waved her hand.

"I was going to show you—"

She jumped to her feet. "Hurry, or we'll miss it."

Donavan frowned and pointed the remote toward the television. He punched a button with his thumb. "There."

On the screen, Randy was once again at the scene in the pouring rain. "Exciting developments here at the site of the rescue!" he said with the gorge behind him. The camera panned over the gorge and zoomed in on the mouth of the cave. "Moments ago, a rescuer emerged with a teenage girl. We are waiting for more details, but the support crew wrapped her in blankets, and medics are on the scene." Randy's voice and the howling wind blared through the speakers.

Teddy yowled and scrambled for cover.

Savannah winced and covered her ears.

"Sorry." Donavan grimaced. "I was just testing the volume button." He directed the remote at the television and pressed the volume button hard—as if doing so would reduce the volume faster.

Once it was at a normal level, the professor put the remote on the side table, gave it a pat, and slowly drew his hand away, as though it might bite him.

Savannah bit her lip to dispel a grin and settled next to Teddy again, her eyes on the screen.

"Wait. I'm being told another rescuer has just emerged and is guiding a young man to safety," Randy said from off screen. The camera zoomed in, and Savannah saw that a man in a wet suit and a teenager hugging a blanket were dragging their feet in seeming exhaustion as they made their way toward the dangling ropes.

"What were teenagers doing out there, anyway? I hope there are—"

"Sorry. Can we listen?" Now, she'd done it. She'd cut Donavan off and offended him all in one fell swoop. She'd apologize later. And since when had she referred to him as Donavan? No time to think about that now. Savannah turned her attention back to the saga playing out on screen in real time.

"Look. There's another one." Donavan pointed.

Savannah leaned forward. Randy's commentary faded as she focused on the third rescuer. Long hair stuck out from beneath his helmet, and his chiseled jaw was covered in stubble. Her heart jumped into her throat. Could that be Michael?

She focused on the third rescuer, who handed a bedraggled redheaded man off to the medics, then turned to speak to the lady who had been pointing and shouting when all the action started. Perhaps she was in charge? The camera zoomed out, and three sets of paramedics huddled around the hikers at the top of the gorge. Two of the rescuers wrapped themselves in blankets and sipped from steaming mugs. The third rescuer refused the mug, then pulled the lady medic aside, leaned down, and said something to her. The lady's eyes went as big as pie plates. Savannah wished she'd learned to read lips.

"Another stranded hiker is still inside the cave." Randy's words snapped her focus back to his report. "They've told us that a second phase of the operation will now begin to get the last injured hiker out. They must navigate significant challenges before they can attempt to do that. The rain is expected to continue through tomorrow morning, making this a race against the clock. We'll keep you updated."

Savannah stared at the screen. Was Michael involved in the rescue holding the nation's attention? She lunged for her purse and dug out her phone. She'd just send him a quick text. If he replied, she'd know he was safe at home in Detroit.

Her fingers blurred over the phone as she tapped out a message.

ARE YOU OKAY? I SAW THE RESCUE IN WYOMING ON TV.

ARE YOU PART OF THAT? I KNOW YOU HAVEN'T REPLIED TO MY TEXTS IN THE LAST COUPLE OF WEEKS. BUT I'M WORRIED ABOUT YOU.

She needed to say so much more, but for now, she'd keep it short and to the point. She added one last line. Satisfied that her message had the intended punch to prompt a reply, she pressed Send.

Donavan watched her with a lopsided grin. "It's Michael, isn't it?"

"I have this horrible feeling he may be part of that crew. I couldn't be sure, but the guy with the long hair looked an awful lot like him. If only the cameraman had zoomed closer."

"What will you do if he is?"

She shifted on her seat. "I don't know."

Donavan walked over. Teddy sat up and hissed. Donavan stood in front of her and eyed the resentful cat. "Um, could we talk somewhere private?"

Savannah pursed her lips and crossed her arms. "What can't we discuss in front of Teddy?"

"Look. We need to talk about the elephant in the room." Donavan glared at Teddy.

"I don't see an elephant. Just a grumpy cat and an indignant professor." She raised her eyebrows and looked around Mrs. Delaney's doily-infested living room.

"I can't focus with him looking at me like that. Can we go for a walk?"

"And leave him by himself?"

"Surely, Mrs. Delaney didn't say you had to be here all the time?"

"Well, no, but…"

Donavan guided her by the elbow into the entrance hall and opened the door. He shoved her outside. "I'll bring her back before midnight, Teddy!"

At his grave expression, Savannah dissolved into laughter. He glared at her, and she clapped a hand over her mouth. "I'm sorry. I've never seen a pair react to each other like you two."

When they reached the sidewalk, they turned toward the park next to Mrs. Delaney's house. Kids were out playing, butterflies flitted from flower to flower, and in the distance, a swarm of gnats frolicked in the sunlight.

"Okay, Donavan. Tell me about this elephant." She grinned, remembering the conversation she'd had with Michael about taming elephants and emotions.

Donavan cleared his throat. "I meant to bring this up before, but I'm not sure where to start."

"Oh, just spit it out, Donavan. There's no use ducking behind the bush."

He had a grimace on his handsome face. "Beating around the bush?"

"What?"

"The expression is 'No use beating around the bush.'" He slowed his steps and reached for her hand. "You're right. I'll just say it."

Seconds turned into moments. Savannah endured the agonizing wait while trying to reclaim her hand. Oh, for the love of tabby cats, could he come out with it already?

Donavan's forehead creased. He took a deep breath. "You're in love with him."

No, he can't be right. Just play dumb. "Who?"

"Isn't it obvious?"

"I presume you don't mean Teddy?" She grinned. Maybe she'd deescalate the tension with her wit.

"No, as delightful as he is, I wasn't talking about Teddy. I meant Michael."

Or maybe not. "And what makes you say that?" She was afraid to ask why it mattered to him in case Mrs.

Delaney was right about him having developed feelings for her.

"The color drained from your face when you thought you saw Michael on the screen."

"I was worried. That's all."

"That's not all. I know that, earlier today, you said you broke his heart, but can't you unbreak it?"

"Absolutely not." But, oh, how she wished she could.

"Tell me the truth. Who did you text back there? And why did you bring your phone with us as if you're obsessively waiting for a reply?"

Savannah reclaimed her hand and turned away from his piercing gaze. So, she was addicted to her phone, or rather—she was addicted to Michael.

"So, I texted Michael to see if he was all right. So what?"

"Aha! I was right." The man pumped his fist like his favorite team had just won the Super Bowl. Not the reaction she was expecting.

"I promised myself I wouldn't go running after him. If he wants to give us a second—no, third chance—then he knows where to find me."

"Can I offer some advice? Give the guy a break."

"No, Donavan, that ship has sunk."

"You mean, 'That ship has sailed.'"

"What?" She sighed. Her traitorous heart couldn't help but recall the twinkle in Michael's eye when he'd point out her mistakes...and Donavan's corrections didn't feel quite as friendly.

"The expression is 'That ship has sailed'—not sunk."

"I meant, that ship has sailed and sunk and lies somewhere at the bottom of the ocean with barnacles growing all over it and octopi sheltering within its crusty hull. There's nothing that will make me go running after him. It's too late."

"Then, why did you text him?"

"As a *friend*, I wanted to make sure he was okay." She dipped her chin and peered at Donavan over her glasses.

He rocked back on his heels. "A friend, huh? Okay, then."

"Why does it matter to you?" Savannah had to know whether Mrs. Delaney's suspicions were correct.

"It matters because I care about you." His sober expression made her skittish.

Her stomach clenched. She gathered her courage. "Donavan, do you have feelings for me?"

"I have feelings for you." He leaned closer. "I'm your *friend*."

Savannah raised her eyebrows and conceded defeat. She was no closer to the truth than she'd been before. Weary from all the emotional upheaval, she let it go.

"Now that I've had my say, let's get you back to Teddy before he scratches my eyes out. He's rather fond of you." Donavan tucked her hand into his elbow and turned toward Mrs. Delaney's house.

At least, Teddy made his feelings clear. She knew where she stood with him. The men in her life could take lessons from that cat.

CHAPTER 25

THE SOUND OF SLOSHING WATER AND echoing voices approached in the waning light of the glow stick. Shadows danced around the cavern walls. It was all Michael could do to stay in place. He glanced at his watch; they hadn't made good time since it was just after 19:00 hours.

Johnnie shoved a large bundle strapped to a backboard onto the sandy ledge and scrambled up. "Sorry. That took longer than expected. Tina needed some extra coaxing to get into the tunnel, and the backboard slowed us down on the return. Pulling it against the current took a lot of effort." He pulled Gillian up the sandbank.

"Gillian, you made it." Michael's grin must have been wider than a groom's on his wedding day.

Johnnie helped Gillian get the scuba gear off her back and ushered her toward their patient, dragging the backboard and large pack behind him.

"Hey, Michael, can't say the dive in was the most fun I've ever had. More like my worst nightmare, but Johnnie did a good job of guiding me through."

"Sorry, Gillian. There was no other way."

Gillian cracked a new glow stick and held it aloft, shedding light on her patient.

She looked over at Johnnie, who was shrugging out of his gear. "Yeah, that's what he said. Let's see how she's doing." She knelt and checked Andrea's pulse. "Has she been coherent?"

"When she was awake, she was confused or in pain. Likely both. I managed to get a few drops of water into her from time to time but not nearly enough. Her breathing is shallower but still steady." Michael grimaced as his calves cramped like they'd done off and on over the last few hours. He'd kept wriggling his toes to keep the circulation going.

"It's pouring outside, and from what I heard from the support crew, it had been for hours. The water levels through chamber three have also risen, which is why it took us longer to get back even with the rope to follow."

Not the news he wanted to hear. By the sound of things, getting Andrea out that way would be next to impossible.

Johnnie stood beside Gillian, a bag in his hand.

"Pass me that pack. I think she's hypovolemic—she'll need replacement fluids. I brought an IV and a neck brace." Gillian got to work and nodded that it was safe for him to move.

Once the neck brace was in place, Michael inched his way free, stood, and raised his arms above his head. He stretched, and one by one, his vertebrae popped back into alignment. He rolled his shoulders. "How long do you think before we can move her?"

"I've just arrived, tiger. I can't do miracles." Gillian smiled at Michael. Then, she turned to Johnnie and handed him the IV bag. "Here. Hold this. Nice and high."

Johnnie took the bag and raised an eyebrow. "Penance for making you dive through that hole?"

"No."

"What? Are you going to make me pay a forfeit?" Johnnie grinned.

"I'll think of something. In the meantime, keep that bag high and keep it still." Gillian moved the thermal blanket aside, uncovering the girl in her tank top and shorts, and swabbed Andrea's arm with an alcohol wipe.

Michael turned away. "I'll go see what else you guys brought. I'm thirsty." He turned on his headlamp and headed down the slope toward the water, not willing to admit needles terrified him. He dug a fresh bottle of water and a protein bar out of the pack Johnnie had brought. He drank his fill and savored the sweetness of the water.

With a little food in his stomach, circulation back in his limbs, and someone else looking after Andrea, it was time to explore. Climbing over rocks toward where the rodent had come from, he felt air moving. Michael followed the draft a little way and shone his light into what looked like a tunnel. He spotted a small round object. He picked it up and sniffed. It was a berry, proof his little furry friend had come this way. Michael unclipped his extra flashlight and shone it into the tunnel, then dug at the entrance in an attempt to widen it enough for him to fit his bulky frame into. His flashlight illuminated a dry and clean tunnel, which if his suspicions were correct, would be an answer to prayer. He ventured far enough in to confirm the route was a viable option and then reverse crawled his way out.

Michael backtracked to where Johnnie and Gillian had emerged from the water. Rocks were submerged where his team had first greeted the hikers. Water had risen significantly since he'd started watching over Andrea.

Time to talk to his team and decide on their exit route. Andrea's life depended on it. Courage was only a breath away from fear. Gillian and Johnnie were quite a team, and he'd be relying on them to execute the extraction.

He packed their gear, including all the tanks, into an unwieldy bundle, leaving Gillian to care for her patient. Then, he turned to Johnnie. "Help me move this toward the tunnel."

Michael was sure they'd go for his plan. He explained how he'd seen the little rodent who'd given him the idea to investigate another exit route, but when he mentioned the tunnel, he remembered too late Johnnie's comment about the medic's claustrophobia.

"You want us to follow a rat out of here?" With her hands on her hips and her nostrils flaring, Gillian reminded Michael of a bull preparing to charge.

"We can't swim Andrea out the way we came in. Even if we could put a mask on our unconscious patient and pull her through that crooked tunnel on a stretcher without causing her to freeze, the water level is not receding. Since we'd be going with the current, which by the way has gotten stronger, we run the risk of slamming her into the rocks and injuring her further. I see no other way."

He glanced at a grim-faced Johnnie, who nodded, even if it would be hard for Gillian to face.

Michael rested his hand on Gillian's shoulder. "You swam through the waterlogged tunnel. It's the same but without water. Progress will be slower, but at least, the patient will be warm and dry. You won't have to do anything outrageous. Our headlamps will light the way. If you keep yourself focused on Andrea, you'll be out before you know it. This route is safer. The incline isn't as steep even though we'll be going up and out, and we're here if you or Andrea need us."

Johnnie wiped his brow and tightened the strap of his helmet. "I'll be behind you, Gillian. I can talk you through it."

"He's done it before." Gillian's gaze locked with Johnnie's, a silent message passing between them.

Trust was a powerful thing. It was just what they needed to give them the edge against the odds.

"Here's the thing. I'm fine in water. Water gives me a different sense of space, of weightlessness and substance." She swiped her hand across her face as if to wipe away the dread. "It's the dry places that get to me."

"While you guys were stabilizing Andrea, I explored the tunnel. It's low, but as long as you belly crawl and keep your head down, you'll be fine."

Gillian frowned, walked over to where Michael stood in front of the tunnel, and peered into the hole. "Any chance of cave-ins?"

"From what I can tell, it's structurally sound. The roof is hard packed. I think a badger or larger mammal uses it to access the caves."

Gillian's face blanched. She leaned against the cavern wall, drawing deep breaths through her nostrils. Johnnie pulled her into a hug. She clung to him until her breathing evened out. She pulled back, wiped a tear, and nodded.

"No sign of any critters, Gillian." Michael dropped his official work tone, using his "trust me" voice, gentle and low. "No sign of scat or droppings, fresh or otherwise. They'd be more afraid of you."

Gillian turned back to where Andrea lay, knelt, fiddled with the tubes and straps, and checked Andrea's heartbeat. "Her pulse is stronger. We need to keep her head above her heart." Gillian placed a hand on Andrea's forehead just below the new bandages she'd applied. "She has a low-grade fever."

Johnnie put his hand on her shoulder. "Quit stalling, Gilly. We need to move."

She looked up at Michael and gave a curt nod. "Okay, freak-out done. Let's go."

"Yes, ma'am." He grinned and turned to Johnnie. "You okay dragging all the gear while I pull the stretcher?"

Johnnie slid on a pair of gloves and tipped his helmet like he was wearing a bowler hat and a tux. "Lead the way, sir."

Gillian tied a rope onto the slim stretcher and spinal board close to where Andrea's head rested. She double-checked the straps that secured Andrea to it, then stood and tightened the chin strap on her helmet. Michael knew Gillian was out of her comfort zone, but he admired her tenacity. Once they got out, he'd tell her how proud he was of the way she'd handled the strain.

Johnnie cracked a new glow stick, fastened it to the stretcher, and then hesitated. "What happens once we get outside? Everyone expects us at the other entrance."

"After we get Andrea out, we signal for the helicopter. I have a flare, so they'll find us." Michael picked up the end of the rope fastened to Andrea's stretcher, tied it around his waist, and knotted it tightly. "If you need to get my attention, tug on my rope twice and I'll stop."

Squatting at the entrance of the tunnel, Michael examined his handiwork. He hadn't told Gillian he'd already scraped handfuls of sand out of the underground passageway to widen it until his fingers were raw. He ducked into the opening and lay on his stomach; the rope tugged at his waist, jostling him as Gillian and Johnnie maneuvered the stretcher into position. They'd follow without a rope between them.

After pulling himself onto his hands and knees, he edged forward. It wasn't long before the sandy floor turned to rock. Slow and steady, he pulled Andrea behind him. Gillian would be behind her with Johnnie bringing up the rear. At least, he trusted they were. His heartbeat picked up its pace. He was pulling this off blind and wasn't able to keep an eye on those behind him.

His headlamp shone only so far, and thanks to the glow stick, Gillian would not like what he saw ahead. The roof of the tunnel dipped, calling on his skill and experience as a caver. Focusing on moving on one knee at a time, he crawled forward and felt a loose rock dig into his knee. Knee pads would have been a good idea, but he hadn't known to be that prepared ahead of time.

He lowered himself onto his belly and crawled like a salamander through the narrow gap. His helmet scraped the roof of the tunnel, and sediment rained down on him. Not wanting to risk showering Andrea in sand, he waited for it to stop. Muscle spasms in his chest protested against the fine dust he'd inhaled, but he held his breath. When the dust settled, he squirmed his way through. Hand over hand, elbow over elbow, he forged ahead as the stretcher dragged behind him, working against gravity as he made his way up the sloping tunnel. The familiar rush of adrenaline and apprehension spurred him on. He twisted to check on Gillian and Andrea behind him, but all that got him was a mouthful of grit.

Seemingly suspended in time, Michael pressed his hands against the rocky walls and wriggled forward. Minutes turned into hours before the passageway opened. "Hold up." He turned and pulled Andrea through. He shoved her stretcher against the wall and bent to help Gillian.

Short rasping breaths came from the direction he'd come. He knew the sound of panic. "Gillian, can you hear me?"

Michael dropped to his stomach and reached through the gap. "Take my hand. I'll pull you through."

No sound of movement eased the tension in his shoulders. "Gillian! Listen to the sound of my voice. You can do this. The tunnel widens out after this little obstacle. Reach out and give me your hand. I'll pull you through." Would she respond?

As moments passed, Michael's mind raced to think of something else to say to break through the irrational barricade of fear paralyzing her. "Come on, Gillian. You can do this. Breathe and reach through."

Trembling fingers reached through the gap. He grasped her wrist and pulled. Gillian sat up and pressed her back against the tunnel wall. She looked at the widening passage ahead. Tears welled in her eyes.

"Oh, thank goodness." Gillian pressed her palm to her chest.

"Concentrate on slowing your breathing. Move aside so Johnnie-boy can get through."

"Aren't you going to give him a hand, too?"

"Nah, he can manage on his own." A quick check of the time showed it was just past 23:00 hours. "How's Andrea doing?"

Gillian scrambled over to where Andrea lay. "She's burning up."

Michael watched as Johnnie dragged the bundle of gear behind him. The beam from his headlamp swung and swayed as he shimmied through the hole.

"Michael, how much farther?" Gillian pressed her lips together and glared at him. "You don't know, do you?"

"I mean, I sort of know, based on the typography of the mountainside." A quick look ahead confirmed the passage turned downward, hopefully not for long enough to put Andrea's vitals in jeopardy. "It's safe. I promise." Michael forced a smile, but by the death stare she gave him, Gillian wasn't buying it.

Her high-pitched laugh, just in case he doubted she was spitting mad at him, emphasized her point. She poked him in the chest. "Michael McCann, when we get out of here, I will kill you."

Michael pointed toward their exit. "I think it's all downhill from here."

"Yeah, in more ways than one." Johnnie grinned and dusted the layer of dirt off Gillian's back. "Even I know not to tick Gillian off."

"Now, you tell me." He grinned in the dim light. "Come on."

They followed the downward curve and, with gravity on their side, picked up the pace. If any water found its way into this part of the tunnel, it would drain away quickly, leaving them damp but not drowned. When the tunnel once again narrowed, forcing them to crawl, Gillian pushed through like a trooper, too annoyed to care. She stopped only to check on Andrea every time there was room.

The fragrance of rain alerted his senses. They were getting close to the exit. He forced his tired muscles to move faster. The air was less stagnant, and he could hear the wind howling in the distance. "Almost there."

It was after midnight when Michael crawled out onto a narrow ledge and into the rain. His headlamp showed the mountainside dropping away, and below them, he could hear the stream that carved its way through the lush gorge.

He pulled the rope with both hands. Aside from a little dirt on her bandages, Andrea appeared unharmed. Gillian emerged and turned her face into the rain, her smile caught in the light of the half moon before it disappeared behind a cloud.

Johnnie dug into the bundle of gear and removed a plastic sheet. He wrapped Andrea in it to protect her from the downpour and moved the glow stick to illuminate the ledge. Michael caught his breath, then loaded his flare gun. He pointed it straight up and pulled the trigger. Gillian covered her ears at the *bang* and watched the flare sizzle. Orange smoke billowed into the night sky above them.

"You okay, Gillian?" Michael hoped she wasn't about to deck him for what she'd been through.

"I'm okay, but don't you ever make me do something like that again." The fiery look she directed his way was like a volcano spewing lava, ready to blow.

Johnnie couldn't hide his admiration. "You did great."

Gillian's glare morphed into a grin. "I did, didn't I?"

Johnnie whacked her on the back, sending her sprawling.

"Hey, watch it." The twinkle in her eyes contradicted her stern tone.

Andrea's strangled cry killed their premature celebration, and Gillian crouched to work on her patient.

Within twenty minutes, helicopter blades whipped through the air, bringing a wave of relief to Michael's heart. The helicopter hovered above them, and while blinded by their searchlight, Michael shaded his eyes, signaled there was insufficient space to land, and waved for them to lower the cable. He turned to the others. "Andrea goes first, with Gillian to stabilize her ascent."

Swaying and shuddering in the churning wind, the cable slithered toward them from the winch like an Amazonian tree snake.

Michael caught the end, and Johnnie helped him hook the stretcher up before he secured the lowered harness around Gillian. A look passed between Johnnie and Gillian, confirming his suspicions that the pair had far more history than they'd admit to him.

Gillian and Andrea bobbed in the wind like wind chimes in a storm, and he didn't relax until they were both safely on board and secured. The gorge only intensified the swirling air currents. It was their turn next, and he was looking forward to a long, hot soak in the tub when this was all over.

Except instead of lowering the cable again, the pilot signaled that the wind was too strong. That they'd have to hunker down and wait out the storm.

Michael shook his head, signaling that they needed to get out as soon as possible. While he'd been sitting on his rear in the dark, Johnnie had been swimming or wading out and back into the cave for eight hours straight. Had he gotten anything to eat? As weary and cold as Michael felt, Johnnie must be feeling even worse. From the way Johnnie swayed in the wind, he was not doing so well.

The pilot pointed to the ridge above them, obviously wanting them to get to higher ground. What choice did they have? It wasn't safe in the windy gorge, and there wasn't a place to land. He didn't want to put the helicopter crew at risk, especially with Gillian and Andrea on board.

Michael reluctantly gave the pilot a thumbs-up, then stood beside Johnnie as the helicopter swung around to leave. Michael bowed his head against the wind-driven rain and let relief sink in. Their mission was almost over.

He opened his eyes and turned to Johnnie. "Good job. You went above and beyond today, but how are you feeling? Should we hunker down or—"

"Are you kidding? That could be a while." Johnnie's shoulders sagged.

"Can't blame the pilot really. They expected us at the other entrance. We're already tired and cold, and sticking around in the gorge in this weather won't help matters." Michael reached out and steadied Johnnie against the wind. "They'll come back for us when the wind dies down, and when they do, we need to be ready."

He rummaged in their bundle of gear for a protein bar and a bottle of water and handed it to Johnnie. "It's not a burger, but..."

Johnnie accepted his offering as if it were.

Michael pulled the rock-climbing harness out of his backpack and kitted up. "I'm going to see if there's a sheltered spot for the chopper to land higher up out of the wind. You rest up awhile. I'll be back soon."

"Go ahead. I'm beat." Johnnie sat down out of the downpour and leaned against the rocky entrance, sipping his water. He unclipped his helmet and ran his hand through his matted hair. Michael was glad for his recent haircut; he'd have his hair mud free and dry before Johnnie had produced any suds on his first wash and rinse.

Climbing in dark, wet conditions wasn't ideal. Still, it beat waiting around for who knew how long when they were already exhausted. Aside from getting Johnnie warm and dry, he wanted to get back to base camp and then to Detroit. Time in the cave had given him plenty of time to think, and he had an important phone call to make.

Michael knotted his rope and fed it through his belay device. He clipped protection into the rock above him and climbed. Reaching for another piton, he blinked away the rain blurring his vision. He screwed the piton into the rock and clipped his rope in before he felt for a dimple in the damp rock and pushed up with his leg. His muscles cramped after being chilled for so long. He shook out his legs, jammed his hand into a crevice, and pulled himself up. The rock wall felt strange under his wet suit boots, but he was thankful not to have wet socks, boots, and a ton of blisters. Taking extra care with each foot placement, he was soon in his element, pulling his way up the rocks.

Michael heard Johnnie call from far below, but the wind drowned his words.

He looked down to see Johnnie standing with his helmet and backpack at his feet, the bundle of gear out of sight. His teammate cupped his hands and yelled again.

He needed to get to a place where he could have his hands free to signal Johnnie. Michael jammed his hand into another crevice and pulled up.

He climbed above the crevice and screwed another piton into the rock. "What did you say?" He cupped his ear in the hope he'd catch what Johnnie was yelling about.

Johnnie pointed to something above Michael's head that was hidden from his view. He'd have to clamber onto the ledge above him to see. His foot slipped off the wet rock. He focused on slowing his breathing, thankful for his rope and harness, and signaled that he was okay.

After changing his foothold, he pushed up onto the rock wall to see what Johnnie was gesturing at. A clump of mud hit his helmet. Maybe there was an animal up there? Above him, a steep incline with sparse vegetation rippled as rivulets of rainwater gushed down. Pebbles pelted his helmet. A cascade of sticks and mud surged his way.

He leaned back on his rope. "Mudslide!"

The force of the sludge and water washed his feet out from under him.

CHAPTER 26

SAVANNAH SET TEDDY'S BOWL ON THE ground and wrinkled her nose. "Goodness, but that stuff smells." She watched him lap up his wet food.

Teddy licked his lips as if to say, "Is there more?"

The opening bars of Handel's *Messiah* blared from the living room. Her ringtone. "What in the world?" Who would call her at six thirty in the morning? It couldn't be Mrs. D in trouble already? Her heart stopped for a moment while she pictured the dear woman, kidnapped by thieves demanding a ransom Savannah couldn't pay.

She skidded into the living room and lunged for her phone. The number on the screen was unfamiliar, so she disconnected the call and returned to the kitchen, tucking the phone into her back pocket.

"Now, Teddy, if I give you more, you'll put on weight, and Mrs. D will have something to say about that when she gets back."

He shoved his nose into the air and stalked out of the kitchen as if to say, "Fine. Be like that. See if I care."

Who knew cats were so quirky? Teddy had more personality than some of the men Evelyn had offered to set her up with after the ax-throwing instructor's flirting fiasco. Savannah had finally told the girls politely—but firmly—she was not interested in dating and she did not need a man to make her happy. Well, that was before—

Her ringtone interrupted her thoughts again. It was the same number. Perhaps she should answer it. "Hello."

"Is this Savannah Sanderson?" An unfamiliar voice on the other end sounded official.

"Yes, that's me. How can I help you?"

"This is Sheriff Tanner with the Teton County, Wyoming, police in charge of search and rescue. There's been an accident, and Michael McCann is unconscious." She clutched the countertop for support as her heart sank. Wyoming. Rescue. No wonder Michael hadn't texted her back. The room spun.

"How fast can you get to Jackson Hole?"

Savannah hung up the phone, her brain in a fog. Whom could she call for help? Donavan! She tapped a brief text to Donavan and slumped down onto the kitchen floor next to the empty cat food plate.

Five minutes later, Donavan burst through the front door. He saw her on the floor and gasped. "What's the matter?" His chest heaved. "Is it Teddy?"

"No. It's Michael. He needs me."

From that moment, Donavan took control of the situation in surprising ways. He called her in sick and then drove past her place, where she could pick up an overnight bag before driving to the airport. He was the answer to the prayer she hadn't even prayed yet. Talk about God knowing her needs before she did. Who'd have thought the aspiring biologist would be able to pilot a small, high-winged monoplane? Not only that; he owned one. Guess his days working in law had had their benefits after all.

The dear man did everything in his power to reassure her on their eight-and-a-half-hour flight to Wyoming that he was a competent pilot. His chitchat distracted her from her mind-numbing fear, especially with that quick landing and takeoff when they refueled in Iowa City. But she was still stuck hyperventilating in a four-seater plane, afraid of flying but even more afraid for Michael.

She begged God not to take Michael from her, and she pleaded for clear skies and no turbulence. Could she trust God to protect her heart, too, no matter what the outcome of Michael's accident? If she risked loving him, would it be worth it, even if their time together was not guaranteed? Would staying in her safety zone bring crippling regret?

The uptick in her prayer life was an added benefit, but after surviving the long flight, now she faced another of her fears. Hospitals. The smell alone caused a physical reaction in her, bringing with it memories of Nick's last months.

But it had been eleven hours since the phone call, and Michael needed her.

It wasn't supposed to end this way. With Michael close to death's door and no chance to tell him how she felt. Donavan stood against the wall while Savannah paced in front of the nurses' desk and signaled once again to the woman slumped in her chair, talking on the phone.

She'd forgotten her glasses in the rental car in their rush to get upstairs to the trauma ward, and everything looked blurry. The tears weren't helping matters. She couldn't even read the nurse's name tag.

The woman finally hung up the phone.

Savannah rushed to the counter and offered a nervous smile. "We're here to see Michael McCann."

The nurse sighed and peeled herself off the chair. "Are you family?"

"Well, no, but I'm on Michael's next-of-kin list. I'm Savannah Sanderson."

The nurse tapped a few keys on her keyboard. A sloth could have outmaneuvered her. She looked over Savannah's shoulder at Donavan. "And who is he?"

"I'm—"

"He's my husband." If they didn't let her in, Michael would suffer alone.

Donavan puffed out his chest. He stood steadfast, staring down the nurse, looking quite feisty. She'd struck gold when they'd become friends.

Savannah hugged the bundle in her arms tighter and shifted from foot to foot. Michael needed her. He must be badly hurt if he couldn't call her himself.

The nurse sniffed. "Turn off your phones." Miss Sloth-on-the-Job glowered at them until they turned off their phones. She rounded the desk. "Keep your voices down and come this way." She strolled down the hall, her white tennis shoes dragging with each step.

The sterilized semiprivate room brought unwelcome memories of Savannah's time spent in the hospital with Nick. Dread settled in her stomach like she'd swallowed a jug of wet concrete. The curtains were drawn around the first bed. In the other, hooked up to tubes and machines, lay the man she had come to see.

Savannah gasped and clamped her hand over her mouth as tears welled up. Michael was in a worse condition than she'd expected. One eye was swollen shut, and bandages covered his head and most of his face. An oxygen mask covered his mouth and nose, and what she could see of his face was bruised and discolored. He seemed to have shrunken, with his shoulders not as broad and strong as she remembered.

Donavan took the bundle from her and walked over to the window, giving her some privacy to be with the patient.

She inched toward the bed. "Oh, Michael." She sank onto a nearby chair before burying her face in the crisp sheets of the elevated hospital bed. She sobbed, her tears leaving a wet patch on the sheet. "I should have been here for you."

For the second time in her life, she cried at the bedside of the man she loved. Only, this man didn't know how she felt about him. She'd only recently realized it herself. She'd lost Nick in a hospital, and her heart wouldn't survive going through that again. Michael lay unconscious and battered. How could this happen?

Donavan put his hand on her shoulder. "The nurse is here. You need to give her some room to work."

Savannah followed Donavan back to his position by the window. People bustled about in the street below at day's end, oblivious to her world unraveling. The machines beeped, and Savannah turned in time to see the nurse noting the readings and leaning to adjust the oxygen mask.

"How bad is he?" Savannah hugged herself, steeling herself for the bad news to come.

"The doctor will tell you more, but we're glad to see him hanging on. He's a fighter." She scribbled something on the medical chart and left the room. Her footsteps echoed down the empty hallway.

Savannah returned to Michael's side and leaned in close. "You will be okay. I'm here now."

"Take your hands off my boyfriend."

Savannah whipped around to face someone who looked vaguely familiar. Where had she seen that face? No, it was the hair. She remembered a woman with bleached blond hair on the news report. Savannah had replayed the reports on her phone enough times all the way to Jackson Hole to be sure this was the same paramedic.

"Wait. Your boyfriend?" Savannah clutched her stomach like she'd been gut punched.

The blonde leveled an icy stare at Savannah. "It's complicated."

Complicated was right. The woman was pretty in an athletic, woman-in-uniform kind of way. Her platinum-blond hair was short but feminine. Michael really had moved on since their time in Niagara four weeks ago. Cold terror wrapped around Savannah's heart. Maybe this woman planned to take advantage of Michael's inability to defend himself. Men were such suckers for women falling over themselves to nurse them back to health. Savannah pursed her lips. And why did guys always go for the blondes?

"We went to high school together." Savannah crossed her arms but did not step away from the bed.

The blonde stepped up on the other side and narrowed her eyes. "So did we, but I don't remember you."

Savannah looked down her nose. The woman looked way too good to be the same age as her. Perhaps she'd gone overboard on the Botox. "I don't remember you, either." Savannah twirled a lock of her own butterscotch hair around her finger. Girls could be as territorial as tabby cats.

The curtains around the other bed rustled. Through the gap between the floor and the hem of the curtain, Savannah watched a pair of bare feet on hairy legs plant themselves on the cold tiles. They'd disturbed the other patient.

"Michael and I have known each other since high school." Savannah lowered her voice and tried again to stake her claim. "You can't have him!"

The woman frowned. "Michael?"

The curtain was pulled back, revealing the man they'd disturbed.

* * * *

Michael's heart had almost beaten out of his chest. He knew that voice, that accent. In his hurry to leap out of bed, he'd forgotten that hospital gowns left a man practically naked in the back until he'd felt a sudden draft. He had never been a fan of hospital gowns. Even less so now that he stood with his grazed knees hanging out and two women gawking at him. Awkward.

"Michael?"

"Savannah."

"What...happened to—your hair?"

He'd almost died on the mountainside, and that was the first question she asked him? "I got a haircut. Like it?"

Savannah pointed toward the other bed and squinted. "Then...who's that?" Her voice wobbled.

"The guy in the bed is Johnnie." He nodded a sheepish greeting to his favorite paramedic, all the while holding the back of his gown closed with his uninjured hand. "That's Gillian."

Michael noticed the fancy man by the window staring at him, sizing him up, making him feel uncomfortable while he stood in a flimsy hospital gown.

Savannah's face turned the same shade as the gray walls. "So, are you all right?"

"Aside from a fractured humerus, a few bruised ribs, and scrapes and bruises. Six weeks in a cast, I'm fine. When I heard your voice, I thought the bump to my head had done a number on me."

Sagging against Johnnie's bed, Savannah sighed. "Thank goodness."

Now probably wasn't the best time to bring up the fact that he'd heard her staking her claim on him—well,

Johnnie, who she'd thought was him. He took in her disheveled look, the tears, and the obvious fact she'd rushed across the country just for him. The realization was like a jolt from the defibrillator hanging on the wall. "Sheriff Tanner called you, huh?"

Baring her teeth, Savannah growled like a wolf guarding her den. "Michael McCann, do you know what you've put me through?"

"Don't blame me. The sheriff forced me to put a name on that call list."

"And did he force you to get caught in a landslide?"

"Er, technically, it was a mudslide."

"Are you saying if my name wasn't on that list, I'd be none the wiser?"

"I've been waiting for the doctors to leave me alone long enough to call you." Michael glanced over his shoulder. The hallway was clear. "I smuggled my phone into the waiting room at the X-ray department. These gowns don't have pockets, so it was quite a feat. Almost succeeded, too, but the technician spotted my phone. He confiscated it, returning it only after they'd x-rayed me from every angle. I got back here about ten minutes ago and dialed your number. You didn't answer."

"When the sheriff called, he didn't mention you were just fine." Her gaze swept over him, lingering on his bruised lips. "And if you think having a cast on your arm and some nasty bruises counts as being *fine*, then you have a weird sense of…well, fine."

"Compared to Johnnie, I really am fine."

"He's got a point." Gillian was backing him up? Good for her.

Savannah's eyes flashed. "Did you get my text?"

Michael nodded. "The one ending with 'If you get hurt, I'll kill you!'?"

"I meant every word."

"Get in line," Gillian muttered.

So much for her backing him up.

The man who had been lurking in the background came forward and stood beside Savannah. As he handed the bundle to her, it wriggled and yowled.

Michael wasn't comfortable with strangers in his room, especially ones who were better dressed than he was. "Who's he?"

Savannah shoved the bewildered man behind her with one hand. "Don't change the subject, Michael."

Michael's throat went dry. "Is he with you?"

"I told the nurse he's my husband so I could get him in, but Donavan's a friend." Savannah bobbed up and down. "Calm down." She rocked her bundle. "I know you don't like to be wrapped up."

Michael couldn't see the little one's face, but since they'd been together in Canada, Savannah had apparently gotten herself a baby. Somehow. "Is the baby his?"

"What? You mean Teddy? We couldn't leave him behind or in the car, so we smuggled him in."

"You smuggled a baby into the hospital?"

"Keep your voice down. He's not a baby. He's a cat."

This was getting to be too much to process. All he wanted was to take Savannah into his arms and kiss her senseless. Donavan wasn't a threat to his happiness, and Savannah didn't have a surprise baby.

"Do you guys mind if we have a moment?" Michael sat back on the bed before his weak knees gave out. "I need to talk to Savannah."

Gillian placed a gentle kiss on Johnnie's cheek before leaving the room.

Donavan hesitated. "I'll take Teddy, too. Are you sure you want to be alone with him?"

"It's okay. I think I can handle a guy in a cast." Savannah grinned and handed Teddy back to Donavan. The door closed behind him.

Michael rubbed his hand over his stubble-covered jaw and looked at Savannah. She was here—for him. She was mad at him for getting hurt, but still. At least, that meant she'd somewhat accepted who he was and what he did, didn't it? "Are you mad at me?"

"No. I'm mad at myself." Savannah paced.

Michael watched her like he was at a tennis match.

"Remember in Niagara, at dinner, you asked me what I'd like to accomplish in life?" Savannah swung around to face him. "I said I wanted to learn to give myself permission to live again."

Michael's heart skipped a beat. "And have you?"

Savannah stood inches from him, but he needed to hear what she had decided before he reached for her.

"I have." The emotion in her voice tore at his heart. There was nothing more he wanted to hear than those two words.

He stood, ignoring his gaping gown, and with his good hand, he cupped her face. She leaned into it, her skin warm. Brushing his lips on her forehead, he breathed in the scent of her. She smelled of lemons and honeysuckle, summer and laughter, intoxicating him with the fragrance of possibilities.

Savannah tipped her face to him, the sparkle very much back in her eyes. "If Nick hadn't made me promise to go to the reunion—"

Michael drew back. "Wait. When did he do that?"

"Hours before he died."

Michael released Savannah to run his fingers through his hair. He slumped back onto the bed as the truth of what she'd said slammed into him like a wall of water, stealing his breath. "Remember, I told you I always felt guilty about my feelings for you, like Nick was watching over my shoulder?"

Savannah nodded.

"But I just realized that Nick was setting us up all along."

Savannah frowned. "What do you mean?"

"You know I was shocked to learn Nick had died. What you don't know is that, almost a year ago—just after Labor Day—I got an email from him asking me to promise to go to the reunion. And he kept emailing every other day, until I gave him my word."

He'd face this last hurdle in putting the past to rest with as much dignity as he could in a hospital gown. Then, he'd sweep Savannah off her feet. "Don't you see?" He stumbled to his feet and reached for her hand. "It's like a sign of his approval."

Tears trailed down her cheeks.

"Don't cry." Michael brushed her tears from her cheeks. "We've got another chance. If you'll have me."

Savannah smiled through her tears. "I was so afraid I'd lost you. I stormed the gates of heaven, interceding for you so often today that poor Saint Peter must have a headache. I promised myself if you survived the accident, I'd give myself permission to live again. Someone once told me, it's harder to recognize an opportunity you're missing while you're in it. If what you say about Nick is true, he wanted us to meet up again."

Savannah wound her hands around his neck. "I'm still terrified of dangling off a cliff, McCann, but I'm not afraid to show you how I feel."

She tugged his lips to hers. She kissed him with no hesitation, little restraint, and a fire that showed she was all in. And then, she eased back.

"Savannah Du Toit–Sanderson, I love you. Always have. And I always will. I promise." He drew her closer, already counting the weeks until he could hold her in both his arms.

He wasn't about to drop to his knee in a hospital gown—he still had a shred of dignity—but he wouldn't let the opportunity pass him by. "There's this record-holding tiny chapel close to Niagara-on-the-Lake I want to show you."

Savannah winked. "Only if there is a minister and a marriage license to go with it. Hold the lilies."

Michael laughed and gazed into her eyes. "Did you just ask me to marry you, sunshine?"

"Not very smart, are you?" Savannah pulled him in close for another searing kiss. "I can't live without you."

Savannah inspired him to be a better man. They had so much more to discover together. Michael was ready for the challenge of showing Savannah how much he loved her in every moment of every day. And to show her how much God loved her just the way she was. "I guess I'll call Beverly and…"

"Stop thinking, McCann, and kiss me again."

Now, *that* he could do. He lowered his lips to hers, lost in a landslide of emotion only Savannah could evoke.

EPILOGUE

SAVANNAH MCCANN WATCHED THE SUN RISE over the mountains in Yosemite and snuggled closer to her husband. Her life now, with Michael, resembled nothing of the years prior. The crippling fear of living again had lifted like the morning mist on the dewy grasses waving in the valley below them. Savannah tilted her face to watch Michael. A hint of a smile played at the corner of his mouth.

"And the reason for the smile?" She ran her fingers through his short hair.

"Nothing. I'm just thinking of how much our lives have changed in the last year."

"I was thinking the same. I'm not the same, and neither are you. I mean, you still have the annoying habit of putting the toilet roll on the holder the wrong way, but other than that...you are the—"

"The perfect husband. I know." He pressed his lips to her forehead.

His gentle kiss sent warmth all the way through her, and gratitude blossomed within her. Discovering Michael's faithfulness and sincere desire to be a Godly husband had made her journey to courage all the sweeter. They'd promised to live and love—for always.

It had been her idea to come here to celebrate their first anniversary. A smile tugged at her lips as the memory of their tiny church wedding played through her mind in vivid color. The minister had barely got the words "You may kiss the bride" spoken before Michael swept her into his arms and kissed her senseless. And they'd spent their first night as a married couple at Bruno and Beverly's B & B. Then, Michael had whisked her off to an extended honeymoon in the Canadian Rockies.

Savannah knew he loved the mountains, but Yosemite held a special place in his heart, and now, it would in hers, too. This is where Michael was most at peace, where he seemed to breathe deepest and laugh loudest. And since their peaceful lives were about to be disrupted, it was the perfect spot. It was the perfect moment.

Michael pulled her close. "Do you think it will be a girl or a boy?"

"The vet said the litter was mostly boys, but there is one feisty little girl available."

"One feisty girl is enough for me." Michael tweaked her nose and kissed it.

He still sent shivers down her spine when he looked at her that way. Like she was his Mount Everest.

"Fine. You get to pick the cat, but I picked out the blanket already." She rummaged in the bag hung over her shoulder.

"I'm in charge." Michael read the words on the cat blanket. He kissed her lips, lingering before pulling away. "I like it, Mrs. McCann."

"He or she will only be in charge until the baby arrives." Savannah stifled a grin. "I'm partial to the names Nicola for a girl or Nicholas for a boy?"

"The—Are you—We're having a baby?"

Savannah had waited to tell him until she'd passed the twelve-week mark and her doctor assured her everything was fine. Savannah pressed her lips to his, stilling the questions of the man who had been so patient with her, who'd taught her to face fear with courage.

"You will be a wonderful dad, Michael McCann."

ABOUT THE AUTHOR

MELONY TEAGUE is a freelance writer who believes everyone has a story to tell. As co-author of *As the Ink Flows*, she loves to inspire and motivate others through her written words. She writes Contemporary Romance with a dash of humor. Member of ACFW. She has never met a Starbucks she didn't love and has been known to eat vegetables for breakfast—well, pumpkin pie—same thing. Melony was born in South Africa and now lives in Toronto with her husband, their two teenagers, and two cats.

WEBSITE: https://www.melonyteague.com/

FOLLOW ON TWITTER:
https://twitter.com/MelonyTeague
FOLLOW ON FACEBOOK:
https://www.facebook.com/melonyteague/
FOLLOW ON INSTAGRAM:
https://www.instagram.com/melonyteague/
FOLLOW ON GOODREADS:
https://www.goodreads.com/author/show/14249646.Mel
ony_Teague
FOLLOW ON BOOK BUB: @MelonyTeague
https://www.bookbub.com/authors/melony-teague
FOLLOW ON AMAZON:
https://www.amazon.com/Melony-
Teague/e/B07V57GN1K
A PROMISE TO KEEP BOOK CLUB:
https://www.facebook.com/groups/490991801725364/

9 781947 327726